gonzález and daughter Trucking Co.

Also by María Amparo Escandón

Esperanza's Box of Saints

María Amparo Escandón

gonzález and daughter Trucking Co.

a road novel
with literary license

THREE RIVERS PRESS • NEW YORK

Published in the United States by Three Rivers Press, an imprint of the Crown Publishing Group, a division of Random House, Inc., New York.
www.crownpublishing.com

Three Rivers Press and the Tugboat design are registered trademarks of Random House, Inc.

Library of Congress Cataloging-in-Publication Data

Escandón, María Amparo.
  González & Daughter Trucking Co. : a road novel
with literary license / by María Amparo Escandón.—1st ed.
  1. Women prisoners—Fiction. 2. Fathers and daughters—
Fiction. 3. Trucking—Fiction. 4. Mexico—Fiction.
I. Title: González and Daughter Trucking Co. II. Title

PS3555.S264G66 2005
813'.54—dc22
                                        2004061812

ISBN 1-4000-9735-5

Printed in the United States of America

DESIGN AND ILLUSTRATION BY ELINA D. NUDELMAN

10 9 8

First Edition

For Julio Escandón, my father

gonzález and
daughter *Trucking Co.*

bringing back to life all the people I killed is the one wish at the top of my list." Had she said those words aloud? Libertad sat up and looked around to check if anyone had heard her.

Maciza, dozing a few feet away, had trained her ears to listen for rats tiptoeing around their prison cell. She easily heard Libertad's impossible wish.

"So, who did you kill?"

"It's none of your business."

"Did you kill anyone?"

Libertad couldn't get herself to confess anything. She opened her journal and in the darkness searched for her pen between the folds of her blanket. A cellmate in the far corner snored. Someone in one of the upper bunks yelled, "Shut up!" With so many women sleeping in such a small cell, it was hard to tell where one body ended and another began, making it difficult to identify oneself as an individual.

"I don't think you killed anyone, Libertad. I think you want me to believe that just to impress me. Were you pushing chocolate in Tijuana?"

"Chocolate?"

"Mud, tootsie roll, heroin. Maybe you kidnapped some rich bastard. C'mon, Libertad, give me some trust. You've been in this shit hole for almost a year. It's time to share."

"I said it's none of your business."

"Were you hanging with one of those narcos, or was

it fraud? Or a scam? I bet it was one of those educated people's felonies."

"I'm not going to talk about it."

"At least tell me what the hell you're doing locked up in a Mexican prison. Your government should be trying to get you out of here. Isn't that what Americans do in their movies?"

"Just drop it, will you? I'm not digging around to find out why you're here."

"That's because you already know."

"All I know is that you killed your husband. It's no secret. You've told everyone."

"Yeah, that's right. But why I did it is what I don't discuss with just anyone. Only with someone I know will understand. That means you, and no one else in this goddamn hen pen."

"All right, why did you do it?"

"I did it for love."

Libertad wished she were as certain as Maciza was about why she had made her own mistakes. But her memories were in disarray. She needed to do some serious mental housekeeping.

In her first few days at the Mexicali Penal Institution for Women, Libertad had kept to herself, but the more she tried to avoid conversation with the other inmates, the more she was stalked with questions in the hallways, in the showers, in the toilet, in the kitchen. Every so often she tried to tell them why she was there, but she found it impossible to explain. Once, when she was asked directly, she uttered a fetus of a word, something like, "Iaaggrhh."

Since she was in the cafeteria, the woman next to her thought she was choking and proceeded to pound her on the back with all her might. Her tray fell off the table and her poor man's chilaquiles—with no chicken, that is— spilled on the floor.

Libertad was not complying with the unwritten rule that all new prisoners had to declare and make public the reason they had been incarcerated. Everyone had to know who had done what to whom and why the prisoner claimed to be innocent. Of course, extensive details of the crime were expected. Otherwise, what would they all talk about in those long desert days?

Because Libertad's strange behavior had brought out a chronic uneasiness and a desperate curiosity among her fellow inmates, she tried to belong in other ways. She taught Diva, one of her seven other cellmates and an authority on prison fashion, how to calculate the time by positioning her fingers in a certain angle against the palm of her other hand.

"It's a hand sundial."

"Very useful around here," said Diva as she tried it, nearly burning her eyes from staring at the sun in the middle of the exercise yard.

Libertad also helped Maciza train for a nonexistent marathon by timing her laps around the cellblock's hallways and shared her tamales with Culebra, the woman with the longest fingernails she had ever seen.

But even after curfew, after the lights were out and everyone had settled in to sleep, a question would shoot into the darkness of her cell.

"Are you in for murder?"

As the first couple of months went by, Libertad's cell-mates began to lose control of their curiosity and tried all kinds of techniques to squeeze the story out of her, even the hard-core ones they'd been exposed to firsthand during their encounters with the Mexican authorities. But just before they resorted to torture, Maciza put a stop to it. She knew Libertad would crack sooner or later. She had subtler, more effective psychological ways to work her over.

"It's okay, I can wait. You can blab your guts out when you're ready," Maciza would say. "That's all we do around here, anyway. We blab our guts out."

"It's not that I won't talk, Maciza. I just can't."

"Don't worry, it will come out. We'll make it come out."

A book changed everything. Which book, Libertad didn't remember. All she knew was that a few months after she arrived in the Mexicali Penal Institution for Women, she went to the library, picked up a dog-eared paperback, and began reading aloud, the way her father had taught her and the only way she knew. Sitting in that dark and sorry-looking room, she noticed that the words on the page were different from the words she said.

She wondered if her thoughts were getting tangled with the plot. It happened to her sometimes, when she was tired. She tried to read again, this time paying more attention to the story, but it didn't work. By the time she looked up, a small group of inmates had gathered around her and were listening attentively. From then on, she'd go to the library, pick any book, and read as loud as she could. Somehow, between the chapters in those tattered paperbacks and the stories in her mind, the words transformed themselves into her own account of the events that led to her incarceration.

When she read to her fellow inmates, she felt the pressure in her chest ease. She imagined her lungs backed up with words and her voice pushing them out, letting her breathe. Wiping her soul clean of remorse had turned out to be most difficult and slow, but she had more time than life. This was her only way of alleviating the pain.

We started the business together when I was born, my father and I. The sign on the door of our truck read GONZÁLEZ & DAUGHTER TRUCKING CO. I'd touch those words before I got in the cab. This ritual gave me a sense of comfort. It was part of my routine. To feel the subtle texture of the pink words and the purple border and with the same fingers make the sign of the cross. Then, to open the gate of the tiny plastic altar glued to the dashboard and kiss the Virgin of Guadalupe. All that had to happen before I put the key in the ignition.

Libertad made eye contact with the other women listening to her story in the prison library and wiped a drop of sweat off her forehead.

Soon after she realized that whenever she read aloud she drew an audience, and that the stories she told were not in the books but in her head, she decided to find a way to turn her time in the library into a prison activity. It would be her way of confessing her crime to her fellow inmates. So, in a long letter written on the back of an unused visitor permit, Libertad proposed to Warden Guzmán to set up and run a library club at no cost to the government. Her suggestion was immediately approved.

That hot and arid day she pretended to read from *The Three Musketeers*. The paper in the mangled book was so brittle and dry that it absorbed her saliva, desperately quenching its thirst every time she licked her finger to turn a page.

The air, too, was a prisoner here. No drafts. No fresh air. Only heat, the kind that injures the nostrils. This jail was the hottest place in Mexicali, a city known to be the hottest in the world. But the inmates' attention never wavered. Maciza, sitting in the second row, blew quick breaths down her shirt in an effort to dry the sweat that pooled between her ample breasts.

Like millions of other Mexicans, I was born in Los Angeles, California. But I never lived there. I was always on the road, traveling with my father. We took our truck across the country, from coast to coast, on interstate highways, back roads, even small dirt roads that would never make it to a map. But we didn't cross over to Mexico. Ever. That country, as much as I'd learned to love it, was off-limits for us and I never set foot in it until much later in my trucking life. Everywhere else, I was known as González's daughter, González's girl, González's kiddo.

And what about my education? What I know I learned from my father. We'd make a special stop in every city to browse for books, in English or Spanish, particularly in those small, cluttered bookstores almost always located in busy downtown streets where it was impossible to maneuver, let alone park, our rig. But the ordeal was part of the thrill. Wherever we went, no matter what type of road we traveled or how heavy a load we hauled, we read aloud to each other over the constant rumble of the engine. I never went to school. I was truck-schooled.

As a little girl, I read while my father drove. Later, when I finally took over the steering wheel, he did the reading. Then we'd trade places. Because we couldn't store the books we'd already finished in our truck's tiny sleeper, we'd throw them out the window, leaving the highways scattered with knowledge. *What We Talk About When We Talk About Love* is probably lying by the carcass of a skunk on the shoulder of Interstate 10 just past Indio. Loose pages of *Hamlet* tangled in tumbleweed must be rolling across Highway 86, over by Salton Sea. Sand dunes on the way to Palm Springs, right where the windmills catch the air from the desert and turn it into electricity, are digesting the deluxe edition of *Don Quixote*. If I could string together all the lines of text I've read aloud on the road, I'd be able to tie a bow of words around the world.

Libertad stopped to check the time on the clock hanging high on the wall across the library. Once again, as it had been since its inception a couple of months back, the hour allotted to their weekly Library Club had gone much too fast. She put *The Three Musketeers* on the shelf next to *Crime and Punishment* and announced to her audience, "That's it for today. We'll continue next Wednesday."

"Where's the mother?" asked Maciza on the way out. "Where the hell is the mother?"

"It's coming up in one of the next chapters."

"Why isn't she in the truck with her little girl?"

"You'll find out."

Break 5; put her up to 5, Chaquiras. Can you hear me? Copy.

Hey! Frito Burrito. Thought you were in Rosarito with that alley cat you picked up in Sacramento.

Are you kidding? The lot lizard. She dumped me faster than I can slam the brakes. I guess she missed her chicken ranch. Where are you?

I'm stuck on Interstate 5, going southbound just past Norwalk. I'm doin' ten miles per hour on the hammer lane.

What the hell are you doing on that freeway at this hour, Chaquiras? You're such a Gatlin' Jim, you should know better.

I was gonna leave earlier, but I lost my comic book in the fleet manager's office. Now I have to deal with all these four-wheelers trying to get home in time for dinner. Where are you heading?

I've got to take this shitty load down to Long Beach Harbor, but the 710 is not so bad right now. Hey, guess who I saw at the Mercury Café?

Spit it out.

González and his girl! It's true what they're saying about them.

You mean the book thing?

The whole thing. They had all these schoolbooks on the table. He was teaching her math or something. And then he took out a brush and braided her hair. She's a cutie. They live in their truck. I checked. That's their home twenty. Anyways, I'm moving on.

Careful with those seat covers. Better stick to your better half.

Roger.

While Libertad ran the tortilla machine in the kitchen on a Thursday afternoon, a group of inmates formed a circle at the center of the yard, screaming and pushing the others aside as if they were ants on a dead spider. One of them, Rarotonga, a hefty woman with nappy hair in a high bun like a bird's nest, swung a large stick, barely missing the heads of the inmates and guards. With her eyes blindfolded, she was giving a vicious beating to the piñata dangling from a rope.

When one of the guards herself smuggled it into the prison, the piñata had the shape of a star, but now it was trying to hold on to the contents of its guts. When Rarotonga finally broke it open, muggers, thieves, embezzlers, shoplifters, tormentors, drug dealers, kidnappers, dysfunctional mothers, scapegoats, murderers, and guards jumped on top of one another in a democratic pile to grab the candy and fruit that spilled from the piñata and rolled on the ground. Apples, bananas, guavas, lollipops, chewing gum, and half-empty cigarette packs were scooped up and stored in shirt pockets, bras, underwear, socks, panty hose, and the occasional paper bag. Someone lost a shoe. Another inmate scraped a knee. Rarotonga, the birthday girl, fell on her elbow and then smeared blood on Maciza's shirt. After a couple of minutes, all that was left was broken pieces of terra-cotta and snarled tissue paper of all colors. Most women hastily walked away with their loot, like stray dogs that had just stolen a bone from the trash bin of a restaurant. Some lingered to give Rarotonga a birthday hug; one even shared a squashed banana with her.

As was customary, the inmate whose birthday was being celebrated was the one who had to sweep the yard after the party. Maciza stayed with Rarotonga. She liked to help.

"It's not fair," said Maciza. "Libertad always leaves us hanging."

"She's supposed to. If she didn't leave us wondering what the hell's gonna happen next, maybe we wouldn't go to Library Club," said Rarotonga, chewing on a stick of sugar cane. "She's using the soap opera technique."

Maciza knew there was nothing else to do but wait until Libertad decided to reveal the mother's whereabouts. It could take entire chapters before she would even give them a hint. But unless they were paroled, no one was going anywhere. "We're a fucking captive audience," Maciza grumbled under her breath.

By ten o'clock at night the inmates were in their cells and the lights were out. Actually, the lights had been out since five. Blackouts were common in Mexicali, and although the prison was equipped with an emergency lighting system, Warden Guzmán had it shut down to avoid additional operating costs.

Libertad's cell was in the middle of the second tier. She had to count forty-two steps from the staircase to the door in order to identify it, since the numbers on the metal panel indicating which cell it was had faded long ago, and walking into other inmates' cells, even by mistake, could mean trouble. Nosy people were punished with silence, and silence in a women's prison hurt as bad as a blister on a day at the market. She occupied the upper bunk right next to the one and only window overlooking the hallway. It hadn't always been hers. Rata had slept there ever since she came back to the prison for the third time, now for shoplifting. But Libertad had convinced her to swap beds. In the difficult negotiation, Rata, who would gladly have given up that particular spot for nothing, sensed Libertad's interest and began making unreasonable demands. In the end, Libertad had to give Rata a bandanna, a set of barrettes, and a couple of faux-jewel-studded plastic combs, aside from her own bed with its newer mattress.

"I don't get it," said Maciza. "You give that bitch your bed in the back of the cell where it's more private and the ladder has all its steps, and on top of that, you let her have hair accessories in good shape."

"It's the moonlight," Libertad said. "It falls right on the pillow."

Precisely four nights of every month, when the moon happened to glide across the skylight above the hallway, Libertad could enjoy a couple of extra hours to write in her journal, lit by the beam that squeezed in through the bars.

This night, she opened her notebook but did not enter the date. She never did. There was no point in torturing herself. Time was just as capricious in prison as it was on the road. Early on she had learned not to ask her father "Are we there yet?" The more she anticipated their arrival at any destination, the longer it seemed to take to get there. Her patience, nurtured over many years of trucking all over the country, was now being tested in prison and she was surprised to be doing just fine. Eventually she would be paroled and set free, but keeping track of the days would only stretch the months and years. So instead of the date, she entered the behavior of the clouds:

Stubborn clouds hung over the prison for most of the morning. Finally after lunch, fed up with the urban landscape, they decided to head out to the desert.

I see the midget. I see his expression of shock. The little man is screaming and running around aimlessly, like a kid's top. I didn't kill him. Somewhere, he is telling his story. And I am here, knowing why he lived to tell it.

She wrote in minuscule handwriting across the entire page. Her notebook had cost a fortune, just like everything else sold at the prison canteen, and she wasn't about to waste an inch of it on margins.

Libertad had been incarcerated with no money on her. No one outside the prison protected her. No one sent her an allowance. She owned nothing she could sell. Matriarca, a rich lady who was serving time for burning her father's factory—with her father in it—to collect the insurance, employed her as a maid. The job consisted of cleaning the woman's private cell every day, making her bed, washing her sheets and clothes, ironing, cooking breakfast, lunch, and dinner, and running errands. It had taken Libertad seven months to save enough money to buy the notebook.

"Just feeling the pen sliding on the smooth paper is worth the extra work," she confessed to Maciza, who could not understand the things that made Libertad's heart thump.

Fifteen minutes after lockdown, all eight women in Libertad's cell had settled in and were in bed. The prison had been designed to fit two to a cell, but the drug wars had overpopulated it with the wives and girlfriends of dealers. Most of them had nothing to do with the crimes other than having fallen for the wrong men, but now, because of love, the prison was as crowded as a Mexico City subway train.

The women around Libertad fell asleep immediately. A couple of them snored side by side in bunk beds so close together that inmates could only access them by jumping over the footboards. Libertad, in the first upper bunk bed by the bars as you walked in, straightened her pillow to get a better angle and laid the notebook in front of her. That night she would write about her first day at the prison. But when she picked up the pen, the moon seemed to have sped off past the skylight. One minute it was there, beaming, the next, it had moved on, leaving her in darkness. How much time had she been listening to her cellmates snore? How long had she been staring at her blank page? Again, time was being a jester. She closed her eyes. There would be another moon, another night. She pulled the covers over her head.

Her first night seemed such a long time ago. She hadn't been able to sleep at all. The admissions guard had applied a delousing chemical to her hair and it had made her entire head itch. It was part of the initial processing and she had to go through it, even if she didn't have lice.

"Everyone's gotta get fogged, that's the rule, and you better start getting used to going by the rules," the guard had said.

Libertad had wondered why inmates were deloused when entering the prison as opposed to when they were released back to a cleaner environment. In any case, it had been a God-sent distraction for her. She was so busy scratching her head all night that she didn't think about the reason she was in prison.

On the second night she felt another kind of itch. The itch to write. She needed to put down her own account of what had happened, an explanation that made sense. She searched for something to scribble on, a few words even, but no one would give her a single piece of paper for free. Only toilet paper was available, two rolls per month per inmate. She decided to stretch the first one over four weeks and save her second roll for writing.

On Libertad's third day at the Mexicali Penal Institution for Women, Maciza gave her a ballpoint pen.

"A pen is considered a weapon around here," she said. "Don't show that to no one."

Libertad thanked Maciza and slid her new treasure inside the fold of her pillowcase's hem. She hadn't been jailed long enough to know that in prison nothing is a gift.

That night in her cell, she rolled out three squares of toilet paper, being careful not to tear them off, and pressing her pen delicately so as not to dig through the thin tissue, she wrote:

I have wasted paper thoughtlessly. Notebooks, pads, loose pages, pretty stationery. I doodled. I wrote in big handwriting. I skipped lines. I kept wide margins on both sides. Now this paper is my only option. I am in a place where constipation is a blessing.

She wasn't sure how long her toilet paper would have to last her, so she tried to use as few words as possible. She carefully rolled her journal around the empty cardboard cylinder of her first roll and stashed it under her mattress. Now, after months of having filled hundreds of yards of toilet paper with words, she finally had a notebook. The luxury of it thrilled her.

Libertad? Are you awake?

No. I'm sleeping. Who are you?

It's Rata. Could you wake up for a minute?

What do you want?

I can't sleep.

So, you need company?

I'm thinking about you. You said your dad never put you in school, is that right?

It's not me. It didn't happen to me. It's a fictional character.

What?

It's all made up.

Now you're telling me this. I've been thinking it was you all the time. You fooled me!

I'm not fooling you. I am entertaining you.

But then why do you say "I did this" and "I did that"?

Some stories are told in the first person, but that doesn't mean what's happening actually happened to me. It happened to the people in the story.

And I was feeling so sorry for you. I even let you have the good pillow, goddammit!

That's the least you could do. You have the good mattress.

he worn wooden benches in the library were lined up facing a table that served as a stage for Libertad to sit on when she read. It wasn't much of a library. As a hallway it would have been wide; as a room it was narrow. It had no windows. It was said to have been a dungeon where unruly prisoners died of various forms of torture years before Warden Guzmán turned it into a library. And now everyone was thankful that she supported Libertad's idea of creating a library club. But the extra popularity points were not the only reason the warden was pleased by Libertad's request. It was practical. It was sensible. In fact, she would have thought of it herself had Libertad not beat her to it. When she took the project to the Corrections Department's council meeting, it was approved on the spot and she received substantial praise from her boss for dreaming up such a notable improvement to the facility.

Ideas like Libertad's Library Club were the very reason the warden had stayed on the job for so long. It also helped that she purchased the inmates' clothes and sundries from a company owned by her boss's brother. She bought the prison's groceries and janitorial supplies from one of the largest distributors in the north, who was the first cousin of the Undersecretary of Labor. And all their medications came from a reseller who was the godfather of the President himself, as did the disposable diapers used at the day-care center in the prison. Even the guards' uniforms were manufactured at an assembly shop in Ciudad Juárez owned by one of the warden's uncles. She herself received a small percentage of the profits that all the companies involved had agreed to share with her.

Everyone in the chain of command, from the director of the Corrections Department to the last guard, made money. Everything the inmates needed to survive in prison generated a commission in clean, untraceable cash, even items legally sold at the canteen.

The warden was also open to trade with the inmates. She allowed perks that added comfort and security to those who could offer something in return. Cleanliness was costly. Privacy had a higher price tag. Protection ranked the most expensive. But since the warden needed to have her customers around in order to do business, freedom was not negotiable.

Since Libertad began reading aloud, the library had become her audience's favorite space, except for those inmates who had children living in the prison. For them, the ideal hangout was the day-care center. Inmates with children under six had an entire cellblock downstairs with a large room where their kids could play with old toys and take naps under guards' or volunteers' supervision while the moms did their chores. Once the children reached the age of seven, they had to go home to their relatives, usually the grandmother, almost never the father, but were welcome to visit every day. For all other inmates, the library was the number one spot. More than the rec room, the exercise yard, the visitors' hall, or the West Gate. Even more than the beach, a stretch of sand that ran along the South Wall, where inmates sunbathed on colorful lounge chairs or gathered under the shade of umbrellas and enjoyed fresh horchata drinks while they watched other inmates play volleyball. On Tuesdays the children from the day-care center could spend a couple of hours at the beach, and once a year the warden organized a sand castle contest, awarding a brand-new shovel and bucket to the winner.

To enjoy the beach, you had to wear a swimming suit, not underwear, and you had to pay a fee to Matriarca, the richest member of the exclusive White-Collar Clan, twenty or so wealthy women who had bought the right to be housed in private cells in the South Wing. They called them their "quarters" and decorated them with furniture and artwork brought in from their homes. These rooms were well lit, and had wall-to-wall carpeting and a beautiful view of the beach below.

This strip of sand had been quite different before it became the beach. When Libertad first began her job as Matriarca's maid, she looked out the cell window and saw only an abandoned vegetable garden. She imagined the lot as a beach and saw herself taking a nap on a lounge chair under a sturdy straw palapa. A few days later, she approached Matriarca with the idea.

"Why don't you do it, Libertad?"

"I don't have the money."

"What do you want in exchange, then?"

Libertad hadn't thought of her idea as having any value, so she took a few seconds to answer.

"I want to get in for free whenever I feel like it."

"I see. A lifetime membership."

"And a swimming suit and a large towel. New."

"You got a deal."

"And I want to be able to bring a guest every time if I want to, at no cost."

"But just one at a time."

"Fair enough."

After negotiating the details of the beach project with Warden Guzmán, Matriarca ordered eight truckloads of pure Rosarito sand brought in by one of the warden's acquaintances, a neighbor who owned a construction materials hauling company, and quickly turned the old vegetable garden into a prosperous business. Everyone knew that Matriarca made decent margins, even after paying a hefty commission to the warden for the concession.

"Only in this prison can you be hundreds of kilometers from an actual ocean and still have a beach. This has got to be worth something," said the warden, pleased to receive her first cut.

When Rata, who had served time in a Louisiana prison, first heard about the beach, she chuckled: "You could never pull that off over there. Mexico is the real Home of the Free."

Janisjoplin, an American inmate, was even more amused than Rata. She had spent a couple of years in an Oregon jail years back for possessing a few joints, and now she was doing time in Mexico for playing in a rock band at a Tijuana club without a work permit. She felt qualified to give her worldly opinion as well.

"It's the criminals in the States who are getting the raw deal," she said as she turned belly-down on her lounge chair to get an even tan.

heading north on Interstate 605 past the 5, you'll find some of the most beloved homes in the world. My father and I went there when I was eleven and a half.

Libertad looked at her audience, excited to be telling this particular story. She held the thick book tight in her hands. The cover of *The Three Musketeers* was ripped on one side and the pages were unbound and out of order, but it didn't matter. She wasn't reading.

We parked our rig on Telegraph Road and walked all the way to the far end of the city known as Pico Rivera, in California. Our mission that day was to find the woman who would get us in touch with my mother. We didn't know her but she had come highly recommended by Maestra, a prostitute friend of my father's who lived in a trailer park on the outskirts of Sacramento.

"She'll find your wife, all right. The question is, do you really want her found?" said Maestra.

Unfortunately, she couldn't give us an address, or precise directions, so we had to comb the entire area looking for a lavender house with rusty wrought-iron garden furniture on the front lawn and an old, hairy mutt napping on the doorstep.

"What if the mutt woke up and left?" I asked.

"It's always there," said Maestra.

Some of the homes were more loved than others, with

bright paint jobs and pots with pansies on their windowsills. Others seemed ready to crumble, at the mercy of termites and time. Because it was a Saturday, the streets were sprinkled with children riding their bikes and making chalk drawings on the sidewalk, their mothers hanging freshly washed sheets out to dry in the sun. I wanted to know what it felt like to be one of those girls playing in their backyards, with a set schedule, three homemade meals, and a pink bedroom to come home to after school with a wall full of pinups of their favorite stars and clippings with smart quotes from famous people. But my trucker life, as it was, wasn't all that bad. At least I didn't have to deal with mean teachers and bullies, as my father would point out every now and then.

We walked past hundreds of homes. Mexican music came out of every other one. I glanced into their living rooms if their doors were open, and if I was lucky, I could see all the way into the kitchen, where someone was always handling several pots and pans at the same time. I caught at least a dozen images of the Virgin of Guadalupe and immediately felt I was in a safe place. Some of the houses had the American flag on their front porches. Others had the Mexican flag. Others had both.

"In America, houses are built to last ten years and roads to last one hundred," my father would say sometimes when we glided on the smooth surface of one highway or another. "In Mexico, houses last one hundred years and roads last ten."

He explained that people in the United States are always moving, so they need good roads to come and go on and homes they can sell, remodel, or demolish without having to experience any emotional sacrifice. He'd say, "There are no words in Spanish for tear-down or fixer-upper. In Mexico, homes are left to age slowly with dignity and grace. And when their inhabitants leave for good, it's feet first and in a casket. But we're in the States and we're destined to be moving. Always."

I knew what our destiny was. My father had been clear about it since before I was born. But still, in secret, I wished to live in one of those houses. I'd keep the lawn mowed and very green, as green as a lawn in heaven must be, with hydrangeas and bougainvillea growing along the fence all the way to the sidewalk cracked by the roots of the jacaranda tree out front. I'd have a little herb garden but I wouldn't know what to do with it because I've never cooked, though it would add a quaint touch. My neighbors would invite me to their quinceañera parties in their backyards lit by Christmas lights in the middle of summer and I'd dance salsa and merengue and cumbia and Norteña with the boys. I'd marry one of them, the most hard-working one with eyes the color of molasses. Maybe there was a home in my future. I was hopeful at eleven and a half.

It was past two and we still hadn't found the woman we'd come to see, so we made a lunch stop at a taco stand with a line of customers that went out the door and around the corner.

"We could live in one of these houses," I said, almost to myself.

My father held the rolled tortilla between his fingers,

cupping it upward so as not to let the salsa drip on his shirt, and before he took a bite, tilting his head sideways, he said, "Drywall does not hold a family together."

I drank three large glasses of horchata in silence and we left to continue our search.

By 5:20 we found the lavender house with rusty wrought-iron garden furniture on the front lawn and the old, hairy mutt napping on the doorstep. Before we even rang the bell, the door opened. A short woman with a black braid down her back and all the way to her knees stared at us from inside.

"What took you so long?" she asked my father, and without waiting for his answer, she continued, "I already spoke with your wife."

We followed her inside. The mutt did not wake up. Did the woman mean I would not get to talk to my mother? Had I lost my one chance? Was I late to the only opportunity to ask her many questions, to tell her so many stories from the road that I knew she'd enjoy, to tell her how much I needed her?

"What did she have to say?" asked my father.

"She is fine. She wanted to know about you and the baby. I take it this is the baby," she said, pointing at me with her crooked finger, choked purple by a turquoise ring. "She wants you to come again, as soon as you can. I told her I'd get back to her after your visit. My name is Clara."

"I have some questions for her," I said to Clara, handing her a piece of paper where I'd written them down.

"I'll make sure I go through this list with her," she said,

folding the piece of paper without even glancing at it and setting it under a can of coffee in her kitchen.

We told Clara about our trucking life. She told us her conversation with my mother had been very brief, but that she'd have more information on our next visit. She gave me an apple. A game show in Spanish was on the television in the other room. The soap operas were coming on soon, right after the news. Or not really, because it was Saturday, it was the big variety show instead. A smell of beans drifted in through the window. The neighbors were preparing dinner. I wasn't hungry. At six we paid Clara and left. I wondered if I'd have another chance to talk to my mother. The mutt didn't wake up.

"I don't believe a word this woman said."

"Me neither," I said out of solidarity. "Are we coming back?"

"Of course."

Not many convicts had been to a library, but still they suspected theirs wasn't the best one around. Warden Guzmán had allocated a percentage of the prison budget to purchase used books, all of which came from her own home's shelves against her husband's wishes. A few had been underlined. Others were missing a cover. Most were dog-eared and mistreated paperbacks. Libertad had already gone through all of them at least twice.

More inmates than Libertad expected had signed up for Library Club. About ninety women could fit in the space if they all sat close together. They met every Wednesday at four o'clock. Since Libertad had to be there to read, the club had given her an excuse to permanently drop out of Garment Assembly Workshop, which happened to be held at the same time.

By the way she read *The Three Musketeers*, the inmates surmised that she'd had a good education. She didn't look as if she should be locked up in jail. Her long curly hair was the color of Oaxacan chocolate and hung loose most of the time, each curl with a mind of its own, sometimes covering half her face, as if hiding that regretful past that everyone in prison wanted to know about. On extremely hot days, she tied her hair up in a bun. Her narrow hips and her skinny thighs earned her the temporary nickname of Gorrión until she convinced the other inmates that Libertad was already a nickname in its own right and that it was even more ironic than being named after a sparrow now that she was imprisoned.

"Why would anyone use that nickname in a prison, Libertad?" Maciza asked.

"I'm doing it for my dad," she said as a long sigh lingered in her chest. "He was into freedom when he was young."

"That's more than I'd do for mine."

Libertad seemed to be at peace with her breasts, always compared by men to some tropical fruit, the kind that weighs down tree branches, but because of their size, she was sorry to have to turn in her underwire bra for security reasons when she was admitted into the facility.

"These wires can take out someone's jugular," the guard had said, handing Libertad another bra one size too small.

"This one's a little uncomfortable."

"You'll grow into it," said the guard.

"I've already grown out of it."

"There's no one you would want to seduce here, so take it and shut up."

A few days later, the same guard took off her sweaty shirt to cool off in the middle of a volleyball game. Libertad, on the other side of the court, looked over. Was that her nice underwire bra?

"She just liked it because it's a Maidenform," said Diva.

In her readings, she revealed bits of her life, insignificant events as well as milestones, all coming to her memory in spurts, disobeying chronology, defying her desire to alter them in favor of what she wished the truth to have been. But since no one could tell for sure if what she read was fact or fiction, she had managed to replace the inmates' burning curiosity about her crime with an aura of mystery that surrounded her everywhere she went.

"She must be some wealthy bastard's mistress," said Rarotonga.

"A political prisoner," said Rata.

"A secret agent," said Rarotonga.

"Will someone translate for me?" asked Janisjoplin in her poor Spanish.

"Isn't she a trucker?" asked Maciza.

"She looks too young to handle a truck," said Matriarca.

One day, during lunch, Libertad overheard Maciza talking with Rata as they chewed with their mouths open.

"You won't believe this, Maciza. You know the stories Libertad is reading to us at the library?"

"Yeah, what about them?"

"None of that happened to her. She's made up all that shit."

Maciza stopped chewing, stared at Rata with profound certainty in her eyes, and answered with the full weight of her wisdom.

"I know."

Then again, did she? Maciza's stare turned into a squint and a sense of uneasiness settled in her seldom-visited realm of self-doubt.

As she quietly chewed her rice, Maciza reached into the far corner of her mind where certain thoughts benefited from shrouds of denial, and pulled one out. After all those months of knowing her, no one really knew for sure anything about Libertad. She could be a trucker. She could be the trucker she was reading about at Library Club, but then, maybe she was too young to handle a truck, as Matriarca had pointed out. Available to them was either theory or fiction and it was up to each one to take it as fact or not. The only sure thing was her name: Filomena Hernández. That's what her California driver's license said. Jerfu, the warden's secretary, had revealed this information to Maciza once, in exchange for a deep-tissue back rub. Maciza was determined to find out the truth about Libertad, but patience was her friend and she knew it. So she decided to play along with the rest of the inmates and let Libertad do the job herself.

Libertad was indeed mysterious. Oftentimes the other inmates heard her singing in the shower in perfect English. She never swore or picked a fight. She cried to the point of wailing every now and then, for no apparent reason. She volunteered to baby-sit at the day-care center whenever everyone else wanted to watch a big special on TV, like Miss Universe, and taught the children songs and rhymes in English. And she had no money. Everything about her was odd. Was she twenty? Twenty-three? Nineteen? It was hard to say. She could pass as a Mexican, but officially she was a U.S. citizen. And those green eyes, how could one explain them? As the weeks and months went by, they all lost track of how long she had been doing time. A few years give or take, would be any prisoner's guess. To Maciza, it could have been an eternity.

Most inmates who knew her agreed that she probably didn't belong at the Mexicali Penal Institution for Women at all, but they appreciated the fact that she was around to entertain them. Her audience had grown larger since Warden Guzmán had taken the television out of the rec room as punishment for a commotion that had left two inmates bleeding, one from a scratch on her cheek, the other from a bite on her neck. They had been fighting over which soap opera to watch.

The crowd that gathered at the library to listen to Libertad's stories had become too large for the room. Even a few of the White-Collar Clan members, most of whom had their own TV sets and their own collection of books, put up with the close quarters so they could listen to Libertad read. They pushed and shoved, tricking one another out of their seats, like when they played musical chairs in the cafeteria. Some brought their own pillows to avoid sitting on the bare floor. Janisjoplin sat through the entire readings just to practice her Spanish. "You can give me the Cliffs Notes later if I don't understand something," she said to Libertad.

"Where were we?" asked Libertad to test her audience's memory as she opened the book.

"The mother," said Maciza. "What kind of a bitch is she? Or why did Maestra ask if they really wanted her found?"

Libertad was impressed to hear that Maciza remembered not only characters' names, but also bits of dialogue. She'd have to be more careful with her choice of words.

"Oh, the mother. There's so much to tell about the mother. But before we get to her, and for everything to make sense, you must hear a crucial story about Joaquín González, the father."

Hey, Pata de Perro, do you copy?

Ten-four, Pito Loco, loud and clear.

Careful out there. A wiggle wagon just hit a crotch rocket. The biker's smeared all over the pavement. It's a bloody mess. Traffic's backed up three miles.

Should I get off the big road?

You betcha. The meat wagon just got there and the paramedics are scooping up the pieces. It's gonna be a while before they clear up the hammer lane.

I have to drop this load in Sin City before they close the warehouse.

Hang in there. You'll catch up. Pull over in Winnemucca and get some shut-eye.

That shouldn't be so bad. They've got the best birria tacos. I haven't been to that truck stop since González's wedding. Was he already going by Holden González, or did that come later?

Much later, I think.

Remember that wedding?

Who doesn't? The priest almost fell off the flatbed with so many of us pushing and shoving.

I was too wasted to remember that.

He had to climb on the sleeper's roof to bless the couple. Got his cassock stuck on the fifth wheel. I was standing way in the back, on the very edge.

They should've gotten a sixty-ton Expando low-bed trailer to accommodate all the guests.

I'd say an eighty-five-ton Triple Twelve model for oversized loads.

I just wanted to steal the bride.

I hear ya. She was a dream.

Too bad it all ended the way it did.

Hey, nothing's guaranteed.

I'm here. I'm bugging out.

See you in Shaky-Town next week? I promised Edna I'd take her to a Dodgers game and I have an extra ticket.

Roger.

Of all the inmates in the prison, Libertad felt most comfortable around Maciza and another woman who called herself Chapopota. That wasn't her real name, everyone knew that. Neither was Verónica, the name she'd been given when she was incarcerated. Libertad knew Chapopota didn't want people to know that her mother had baptized her Snow White to compensate for her dark skin. As if anyone cared.

Chapopota was responsible for the prison wedding. She had organized it all, from getting permission from Warden Guzmán to coordinating all the grooms and making sure they'd bring white dresses and fresh flower bouquets for their brides. Seventy-three brides. The chaplain broke his own record and he made sure everyone knew it by bragging about it for ten minutes during the homily. People brought in cameras, gifts, and bags full of rice to throw at the happy couples as they walked down the makeshift aisle to the end of the yard, and pots with tamales, mole, and homemade beans. No one checked for smuggled drugs or weapons. No one thought of escaping. Not even for a quick honeymoon at the local brothel.

The image of the yard so overcrowded with inmates, family members, and children brought Libertad memories of her father's account of his wedding on top of a truck's flatbed trailer. She wished she'd been one of the guests, balancing on one of the wheels to get a better view of her parents, just to make sure it had really happened and her mother was not her father's invention.

The last mass wedding in the prison had taken place three years before, and since then, Chapopota had seen relationships begin and end without a trace, other than the emotional damage that they left behind. By experience, she knew that these ceremonies, as structured and serious as they were, even in the prison, did not guarantee permanence or fidelity, happiness or stability. It wasn't really that she cared to make it right for her fellow inmates. She just wanted to party. In a couple of days she would be released from prison and wanted to give her friends a good time before she left. So she had enlisted Libertad to help her get permission for the event from the warden and ask her to allow the newlyweds three conjugal visits in a row. Libertad had also helped draft the invitation without spelling mistakes, since Chapopota could hardly write. She was permitted to use the phone in the Administrative Office to convince the mariachi band to donate their time. She also talked the neighborhood bakery into sending a seven-tier wedding cake for free. Even the inmates with bad cases of diabetes could not pass up the opportunity to have a slice. As far as the alcohol, she had managed to refill dozens of bottles of soda with cheap rum that was brought in by one of the guards whose brother owned a liquor store.

After dancing all afternoon with Maciza, Chapopota, covered in sweat, stood by the West Gate and said goodbye to all the guests, like a seasoned hostess.

"I wonder how many of these marriages will last more than six months," said Chapopota.

Maciza looked down to the ground and didn't answer.

Her own estimate of the success of those marriages was too sad to say aloud.

The cellblock was quiet, except for the sound of Nora's footsteps. Because Nora was a guard, she felt she had the right to stomp her feet as she walked. It was a habit she acquired when she started her job at the Mexicali Penal Institution for Women twenty-three years ago. She marched down the hallway followed by Chapopota, still affected by the hangover she'd gotten from so much drinking during the wedding the day before.

Nora's experienced hands could turn keys in all kinds of locks, more so while under the influence. In fact, only after her morning shot of tequila could she pick the right key for each lock, aim it at the keyhole without missing, and turn it in the appropriate direction the correct number of times. It was a point of pride for her and she bragged about it with the slightest encouragement.

With Chapopota trailing behind, she walked in silence through rusty gates and squeaky doors, down urine-smelling corridors, and up the narrow stairs of the prison. The last hallway led to Warden Guzmán's office. She knocked on the door. A mere formality. She opened it before hearing any answer.

Warden Guzmán was checking for food on her teeth in a makeup mirror when Nora and Chapopota came in, sweaty from their brisk walk, and stood straight and stiff in front of the desk as a sign of respect.

"So, you're being paroled but you don't want to leave," said Warden Guzmán to Chapopota.

"That's right."

"Is it your husband? Are you afraid he might do something to you again?"

"No. I don't have to worry about him anymore. His father shanked him last month."

"I didn't know. I'm sorry to hear that."

Warden Guzmán didn't seem to be sorry at all. Neither did Chapopota.

"So, what is it, then?"

Chapopota didn't dare answer. Warden Guzmán turned to Nora for an explanation.

"She wants to stay until Thursday."

"I should be in the hotel business," Warden Guzmán said to Chapopota. "You've been locked up for nine years and now you want to extend your stay. Are you comfortable with the all-inclusive package?"

"I don't want to cut loose just yet," said Chapopota, a bit embarrassed. "I'm in Library Club on Wednesdays. I can't leave without knowing how the book ends."

Warden Guzmán thought she'd heard everything, but every so often Chapopota surprised her. This time would surely be the last. She was leaving and taking her wits with her. And she wasn't coming back to visit. No one ever did.

"Just this one time," Warden Guzmán said.

The clouds have bunched up on the northeast corner of the sky. Are they planning an ambush? Who is their victim this morning? The sun again?

Togetherness. Too many women surround me. I am afraid we might become one. Is there anyone left out there, on the streets? I know my fellow inmates' secrets. I am familiar with their desires. At night I have nightmares about their fears. Too many bruised childhoods delivered to me in a whisper. Vanishing fathers written off as bad rubbish. Unfaithful husbands tolerated out of self-pity. Children unwillingly abandoned, now only images on photographs that have been kissed too many times. These are the women who mistake me for a handkerchief. They weep on my shoulder. We sleep together, we shower with the same water, and we bleed in synchrony. I am not yet used to such intense intimacy. But I must admit that it has its comforts. I should not resist sliding my tired foot inside the sheepskin slipper, but I do. Why can't I hand out crumbs of my guilt, share it, give it away, make the weight lighter?

My father became a trucker, met my mother, and I came to exist, because he killed a man. It was in his destiny and there was no way to avoid it," Libertad said to her audience even before she opened *The Three Musketeers* to page 254.

Chapopota savored every word. She sat among the other inmates, happy to have gotten permission to stay until Thursday, just to hear these passages. She'd heard they were crucial to understanding the whys and hows of the entire story.

"My father, Professor Joaquín González, taught literature at the University of Mexico, but his academic career only lasted one year," Libertad continued, pretending to look for the paragraph where she had left off.

In spite of his young age, he quickly earned the respect of his students. Oftentimes, during breaks, they would gather around his desk to listen to his advice.

"Don't let the government get scared. If they think you're powerful, this whole thing can become dangerous. Remember, you're a spider, they're a shoe," he said.

He was among the faculty supporting the 1968 student movement in Mexico City. Witnesses claim to have watched on the night of September 18, when the campus was besieged by the military. Over nine thousand soldiers armed with assault weapons arrived at ten sharp in buses, Jeeps, and artillery tanks, and ordered everyone to lie belly-down out on the esplanade. Teachers preparing their lessons for the following class. Parents attending an orientation meeting. Janitors washing chalkboards. Students rehearsing for a play. Plumbers fixing the sewer. Radio University's deejays. Three hundred unarmed people startled by the sudden storming stood surrounded by an army of soldiers, most of whom had been spanked too much as children, and therefore were incapable of making their own decisions. What else could these students, parents, teachers, plumbers do but sing the national anthem? They sang and sang the same stanzas, since no one had ever memorized past stanza two, as they were taken in buses to Military Camp Number One. Many were never seen again. It has been said, and as years go by more stories on the subject go from rumors to testimonies, and from facts to legends, that the students were taken in helicopters to the Gulf of Mexico and thrown into the water, hundreds of miles from the shore. Those who survived the fall were eaten by sharks.

That night, my father's class had been dress-rehearsing a scene from *The Merchant of Venice*, which they had planned to perform in conjunction with the Drama Club. The student who played Bassanio was absent, so my father filled in.

And just as Antonio and Bassanio agreed with Shylock on the three thousand ducats' bond, the soldiers entered the theater and chased everyone out.

"Come out or I'll shoot, you bunch of queers," shouted a commander at the sight of the men in tights.

The Prince of Morocco, who had not been able to remember his lines a few minutes before, pushed my father behind a set decoration depicting the Palazzo Ducale in the Piazza San Marco and pleaded with him to hide.

"They're after you," he whispered.

The rest of the students ran in every direction, like prairie dogs escaping a flooding burrow, but were quickly rounded up by the soldiers and taken at gunpoint to the esplanade.

Libertad put the book down to unbutton her shirt. Most inmates were too immersed in the story to think about refreshing themselves, their faces covered with drops of sweat that swelled as they slid down their cheeks to the wet collars of their blouses.

"Excuse me, Libertad, what was the Prince of Morocco doing at the university?" Chapopota asked. "Wasn't he supposed to be in his country exploiting his people?"

"It wasn't the actual Prince of Morocco. It was a student dressed like him for the play."

"An impostor? Is he gonna do a number on that Shylock motherfucker?"

"That's not important right now," said Maciza, looking for a sign of approval from Libertad. "The ones in deep shit are the actors in the play."

"That's right," said Libertad.

Considering the questions being asked, Libertad thought that she might have to simplify her story just a bit. She picked up the book again and turned the page.

Pink tights, velvet pants, and a feathered hat would not have been my father's choice of clothing to be running from the soldiers in, but destiny is the ultimate prankster. He grabbed his book bag and hid in a classroom, but when bullets shattered the window, he ran into a hallway.

It's amazing how in one moment a person's entire life can change in the most unpredictable way. This particular second, the one that changed my father from literature professor to truck driver, hit him head on. Literally. The collision was inevitable. As he turned a corner, he crashed into a captain who was running in the other direction. Neither man saw who was coming at him. There was just the full weight of their bodies smashing against each other and the sound of a gunshot. The captain had accidentally shot himself in the neck. He collapsed to the floor, bleeding. No one saw the accident. It was just the two of them, wondering how their destinies had conspired to reach that very moment.

When the captain's eyes turned glassy and fixed, my father knew he would not be the same man again. Someone had died because of him, because instead of walking, he ran, because instead of being an engineer as his mother wanted, he was a teacher. But at the same time, had he not killed the captain (for though it was an accident, my father felt entirely responsible for this stranger's death), he would have stayed in Mexico instead of going to the United States. He wouldn't have met my mother and I wouldn't have been born.

Alone in that hallway, my father wished that the captain would get up, dust himself off, and leave. He sat next to the body until he heard footsteps. He barely had time to run into the women's restroom. People yelled outside. He balanced himself on the toilet seat and looked in his bag for a bandanna to wipe the sweat off his face when he realized a book was missing. *In Cold Blood*. He wondered if it had slid out of his bag next to the captain's body, and in his most fatalistic mode, he believed it had. Written in his own hand with a marker, right on the cover, it read: "This book is the property of Professor Joaquín González. Thou shall not steal!" He might as well have left his picture and address, too.

After a couple of hours, my father climbed on the sink to reach the small window above the mirror, high up, just below the ceiling. He could barely make out silhouettes outside in the darkness. Some had flashlights. Suddenly he saw two soldiers carrying the captain's body away on a gurney. A general—he seemed to be a general—was supervising the operation. He heard him say something. He thought he'd said, "Not a word of this." At least he wished the general had said that.

By then the entire campus had been vacated and the soldiers stood guard at every entrance. It would be impossible to escape. He looked in the mirror and saw his image: a scared man, still wearing a feathered hat. He noticed blood on his costume and it was not his. He took the vest off quickly to wash the stain, rub it off, erase the incident once and for all, but the faucet spat out a brownish, rusty liquid. He remembered seeing the plumbers fixing the sewer. The water on campus had been shut off.

My father spent twelve days in the restroom while the soldiers camped outside. He lapped water from the toilets. He ate the leaves of a vine that crawled through the window into the restroom. He nibbled them slowly, savoring each tiny bite. He read every book in his book bag four times without paying attention. He pulled out his students' papers—ones he'd collected the day before the siege—and tried to grade them, but all he could manage to do was stare at them over and over again. On what turned out to be the last night of the occupation, when the soldiers had had too much marijuana and beer, he managed to get away.

Thinner, his hair snarled, his beard overgrown, he walked downstairs quietly and climbed out of a side window and onto the esplanade, running in the darkness to the bushes behind the building and hiding in the brushwood until he reached the boulevard.

Libertad closed the book, looked at the clock on the wall, and slowly scanned the room in silence. She understood the value of suspense, having learned this storytelling skill by watching Mexican soap operas at truck stops with big TV sets in their cafeterias and lounges. Regardless of what room it was, they all smelled of overcooked lard and underestimated loneliness. Most of the time Libertad had to turn up the volume so she could hear the dialogues over the truckers' snoring on the vinyl couch next to her, their eyelids shut tight with yellow gunk.

"We'll have to stop here," she said.

Chapopota raised her arms, aghast. "You can't. You've got to finish today!"

Libertad shrugged.

Chapopota turned to Nora, the guard, devastated. "Tell her. Please."

"Time's up. Sorry," said Nora, who had come there to supervise the line of inmates on their way back to the yard.

This was a job that she could do single-handedly. She was the most respected badge, the number one shield, the ultimate turnkey. No guard was more esteemed in the prison, because she was consistent in her policies. She never bent the rules unless there was money involved, and a lot of it.

"You're going to price yourself out of the market," Patrona had once advised Nora. Patrona was Matriarca's best friend, financial adviser, and an honorable White-Collar Clan member. "Other guards have let me keep groceries in my fridge for less." But Nora was not concerned about her competition. Her fees were high, but she never backed out of her deals. When she agreed on a favor with a prisoner, she came through. And since Chapopota had no money, the rules could not be bent for her. Library Club time was up, and she would have to obey as she always had.

Chapopota knew that where Libertad had stopped reading couldn't be the end of the story. There was so much more to find out. She had stayed to hear the whole thing and was going to hear it one way or another. So, before anyone could stop her, she leapt to the front and grabbed *The Three Musketeers* from Libertad's hands.

"At least let me take it to my cell tonight. I can't go home like this."

Nora nodded, amused. How much could she get in exchange for such a small favor? Not enough. And Chapopota was leaving, anyway. She let her take it as a farewell gift.

"I'm gonna be checking your bags when you get out and I don't want to see that book in there. It's federal property."

She watched Chapopota leave with the rest of the inmates, holding the book tightly under her sweaty armpit and smiling like a child who had been given a new kitten to hold. When Libertad walked out of the library, Nora grabbed the back of her shirt.

"What's she gonna do with the damn book, anyway? She can't read."

"I guess her guardian angel will have to read her a bedtime story tonight," said Libertad.

Chapopota and Libertad lived in adjoining cells. As they had agreed, once the inmates were quiet and the guard had made her usual rounds, they each sat by their cell's door, located side by side. Chapopota squeezed *The Three Musketeers* through the bars, set it on the hallway floor, and pushed it far enough for Libertad to reach.

"Go on now, finish it off," said Chapopota.

Libertad stretched her arm, grabbed the book, and pulled it into her cell.

"We're going to have to talk on the pipe. I heard the night guard's going to make a surprise walk tonight and I don't want trouble for reading to you over the grill. I'd have to speak too loud."

"Give me a few minutes, then," said Chapopota.

Chapopota went to the toilet in the back of her cell and forced the water out by bouncing up and down on a folded blanket that she had placed on the bowl to use as a plunger. Libertad did the same in her own cell. Once the connecting pipes were clear of water, Libertad could speak into the toilet and Chapopota could hear her through her own toilet next door. Of course, everyone around Libertad's cell found out about the unscheduled reading and forced the water out of their own toilets so they could eavesdrop.

"Listen, stories don't really have an ending. Everything continues. I'll try to wrap it up somehow, but I just want you to know that there will always be more."

Libertad picked up the book and pretended to read in the semidarkness, barely whispering into the bowl, just loud enough so that Chapopota could hear her.

After being trapped in the restroom, my father knew that he had officially become a man on the run. He could never again present himself as Joaquín González, the professor. He would have to become another person, change identities, and worst of all, throw away his precious faculty badge.

He thought of warning his mother and his sister, but he couldn't go to them. The soldiers would find their house and turn it upside down looking for evidence, something, whatever, and along the way, they'd loot it without mercy, taking everything of value. Then they'd want to know his whereabouts. He knew the horrors his mother and sister could go through in the interrogation process. The only way to protect them was not to tell them where he was.

He walked the streets without direction. People afraid to know why such an oddly dressed man would have bloodstains on his shirt looked the other way. Those days the air was infected with fear. It was safer not to know. A little girl standing on a corner stared at him. He looked like a homeless man with no future. And he was. When the girl's mother saw him, she turned away and dragged the girl across the street. He may have been disgraced, but he wasn't about to go around scaring children, so he went straight to a thrift shop and spent the little money he had left in his wallet on a used pair of pants, a shirt, socks, and shoes. Then he burned the Bassanio costume in an empty lot on the way to a public shower, where he let the hot water run down his body for a long time. He scrubbed with enough strength to peel off his skin. With a toothbrush he'd bought at the shower's gift shop, he brushed his teeth, good and hard, until his gums bled.

He walked around the streets for a few days. He slept under parked cars, ate from trash bins outside hotels, and wondered what to do next. An eerie sense of normalcy had settled in the city, but he knew it was fictitious. There was no point in checking what the newspapers had to print about the university siege. They knew very well what not to publish if they cared to stay in business. The government had its own interpretation of the meaning of freedom of the press. Yes, you could buy the newspaper of your choice. He suspected there was more repression coming.

Then one morning he overheard two men who were having breakfast at a sidewalk café. It was hearsay, but that was the only trustworthy kind of news those days. They were talking about a massacre that had taken place the day before. Hundreds of students had been murdered in the Tlatelolco Square. He could have gone there to confirm the events. He'd probably have found the area cordoned off and the soldiers washing down the blood. But if he went, he might be recognized.

Scared as a deer in open season, he headed for the highway. He saw the colorful banners announcing the 1968 Olympic games that were opening in Mexico City in a few days. The entire metropolitan area had been tidied up the way a housewife cleans her home when she is expecting company. The living room and the dining room look nice and sharp, but the closets and drawers are a disaster. My father kept walking, thinking about the games, about the world watching his country, a country so hurt inside, so broken, and yet doing all it could to pretend it was in good health.

When he finally reached the edge of the city, where the poor settled on land that wasn't theirs, without sewerage, water, electricity, where the landfills wished they were landscapes and the road widened and lost itself in the foggy distance, he tried to hitch a ride. He was now a fugitive and fugitives cannot stay in one place.

After a while, a huge truck hauling a bulldozer slammed its brakes just past him. It was so heavy it took a while for it to stop. The pavement rippled to the friction of the tires and my father smelled the burning rubber as he chased the truck a couple hundred meters. When he finally caught up with it, he opened the door and jumped into the passenger seat. And that's how he became a trucker. The end.

"**The end, my** foot," said Chapopota into the toilet.

"All right, it's not *the* end, it's *one* end. I told you. Stories go on and on. They all have many endings. Not even death puts the final period on a story. It can drag on for ages. Just ask Abraham."

"Who?"

"Forget it. He's not a character in this story. For your peace of mind, just imagine that Professor Joaquín González became a trucker and lived happily ever after. Then you can put this story to rest."

"I really don't think any professor-turned-trucker could live happily ever after. I just don't fucking believe it."

Libertad was beginning to lose patience. It was three-thirty in the morning. The wake-up bell would ring in two hours, and she'd have to go to the South Wing to heat up the water for Matriarca's morning shower and prepare her coffee and she hadn't slept one minute.

"Okay, he had his ups and downs, but basically he did pretty good as a trucker. Is that a better ending?"

Chapopota pursed her hairy upper lip in disappointment, but her time had run out, and she had to settle for it.

"I guess so."

She and her seven other cellmates, who had wakened and gathered around the toilet to hear Libertad's story, went back to their cots.

Chapopota sat on her bed trying to imagine other endings to the story, but none came to mind. She looked around and saw her cellmates in the semidarkness squirming under the sheets, trying to find a comfortable position in which to sleep, for the little time they had left before wake-up. She would miss these women, except for Culebra. She farted all night, and the smell always lingered until daybreak. But even putting up with that was far better than trying to find a job and then not getting fired. She promised herself never to overreact again and to count to one hundred before losing her temper. She panicked suddenly at the idea and her nervous tic came back. It was as if her right eyebrow were a separate entity from her, twitching repeatedly until it became numb. She wished she had done something worse than beat that taxi driver nearly to death when he tried to rape her. She wished she'd killed him instead of leaving him paralyzed, and stealing his cab. Then she wouldn't be worrying about getting out of prison. Second-degree murder would have qualified her for a much longer term and she would have been able to hear the real ending to Libertad's story.

By noon the next day, Chapopota had said good-bye to all her friends and packed her bag with a change of clothes, her old toothbrush, which was clearly in need of replacement, and a brand-new bottle of shampoo that Maciza gave her as a farewell gift. She walked down the hallway accompanied by the counselor in charge of parolees, crossed the exercise yard, and made a quick stop at the beach, where some inmates drew hearts in which they wrote names of people in relationships long dead in the freshly hosed-down sand. They discussed in great detail who had betrayed whom, how many years this or that marriage had lasted, when did so-and-so walk out, who had been a platonic love, who had been a real nightmare. The morning sun was beginning to heat the wet sand and the hearts gave off steam, as if those relationships were finally vaporizing into nothingness.

"This is for you," said Chapopota to Libertad, who was sunbathing with Janisjoplin on a lounge chair nearby.

Libertad took the paper bag that Chapopota was handing her and opened it. Inside were four sanitary napkins. Unused. She pulled them out to inspect them.

"Why are you giving me these?"

"Because."

"But you'll need them."

"They're far cheaper to buy out there."

"Thanks, you really shouldn't have."

"The way I figure it, I owe you."

"You owe me nothing."

"Oh, yes, I do. And I'm good at paying back. Maciza knows where to find me."

"You be good, okay?"

"If I come across a book, I'll send it to you."

"Just don't put someone in a wheelchair to get it."

Chapopota smiled enough to show she was missing a front tooth, gave Libertad a long hug, and walked toward the West Gate escorted by the counselor.

From her office window, Warden Guzmán saw Chapopota say good-bye to Libertad. She saw her give her the bag with the sanitary napkins. And she knew, by that single act, that Chapopota had been completely rehabilitated. No one gives away a black-market item of such high value except to a true friend. She wiped a little tear off her cheek and hated herself. Chapopota was not coming back.

I agree with Chapopota. There's no way a teacher could become a trucker and be happy about it. I dated a trucker once; I should know. He had the worst temper and even worse teeth. And he wasn't a teacher, like Professor González. He was a lowlife scum, if you ask me.

Why did you date him, then?

Truckers are deceiving. I didn't realize he was such an asshole until after he left me.

I see.

What?

Nothing. I mean, you could have guessed.

Sometimes you only get to know someone long after they're gone.

Yeah, once the damage is done.

That's what I mean. I don't think the professor was a happy trucker. No way.

I bet the authorities are going to track him down and lock him up in the stone dump. No one gets away.

What do you mean? A lot of people get away.

Oh, yeah? Then what the hell are we doing in this goddamn slammer?

Volleyball was the favored outdoor activity among the inmates. That morning the wind blew from the north, cooling the temperature a couple of degrees, so they were playing harder than ever.

Maciza sat on the bench waiting for her turn. She had never liked sports, but the doctor who gave her rabies shots when the rat bit her while she was organizing the kitchen pantry told her she had to exercise and get rid of her fat or she'd die behind bars.

"I'm not getting no pine box release," she said.

And she meant it. She was determined to stay alive until she could walk on the streets again. For the past three years she'd been volunteering to unload potato crates, flour sacks, and hundreds of bags of groceries from the supply truck and carry them all the way to the kitchen. She lifted the steel cots in her cell while the other women swept the floors underneath them. She climbed up and down her cell's grill, sticking her fingers and toes through the holes in the steel mesh, hanging on like a scorpion. She ran along her tier's hallway until she could move no more. Once a week, she sparred with her friend Rarotonga. On the side, she dug ditches and scrubbed bathroom floors. She also dragged the lounge chairs to the shade at the beach and relocated the umbrellas for some of the rich inmates, a service she provided for a small fee. She had buffed up her muscles to the point that even the two male guards were afraid of her. Had there been a gym on the premises, she would have bench-pressed 155 pounds without breaking a sweat. Once she was wolf-packed by four inmates and within two minutes she had sent them all to the infirmary.

"Nobody's gonna be breathin' my air," she threatened through the Judas slit on the door of the segregation unit where she spent an entire week. Better than having her head shaved like the punishment given to the women who attacked her. According to her, it had all been well worth it. Her reputation was now established and no one dared to touch her. Besides, she couldn't complain much. Her time in solitary confinement hadn't been all that bad thanks to Libertad, who had convinced the guard to let her bring Maciza dessert every day.

Libertad had suggested that Warden Guzmán include sweets with their meals when she found out that Pinche Bruja, imprisoned for stabbing a customer with a kitchen knife, had been a pastry chef at a fancy restaurant in Tecate. The warden figured the addition to the menu could only improve her relationship with the inmates, and she did know someone in the governor's cabinet who could supply the ingredients.

During all of Maciza's stay in the segregation unit, Libertad pushed Jell-O and flan and rice pudding through the narrow slit, leaving whipped cream smeared around the steel edges. Of course, as payment for the favor, Libertad had to give the guard her own dessert, and that was that.

Maciza was busy rearranging her breasts under her shirt when the coach sent Libertad to sit next to her. Libertad didn't complain at all. She was tired of playing volleyball.

She'd do better the next time around. Using her sleeve as a handkerchief, she wiped the sweat off her forehead. Maciza pulled a letter out of her shirt pocket and offered it to Libertad to use as a fan. It was addressed to Maciza. Libertad smiled, surprised.

"You've got a letter. Now, that's unusual."

"The fucking bitch," said Maciza, holding a bobby pin between her teeth. "I haven't heard from my mom in four years and now she wants to come and visit."

Maciza unbuttoned her shirt and pulled it down to show Libertad a burn scar in the shape of a dinghy across most of her back. Libertad had seen it before, every time she showered next to her or during heat waves when the women were forced to walk around naked to endure the insulting weather. She had wondered how Maciza had gotten such a wound, but didn't mention it out of respect. Now that she had it so close, she barely touched it with her middle finger, careful not to cause pain, as if it were a recent injury.

"She pushed me to the floor and put the hot iron on my back so I would learn a lesson."

"What lesson was that?"

"Not to tell my dad when she had visitors. How was I supposed to know? I was eleven. She said the guy was an uncle."

Maciza buttoned her shirt and stared at the volleyball game as if she were interested. There was an unspoken understanding between the two women. Libertad knew that Maciza had withstood much more pain than the scar could show.

"Nobody visits you either, kid. Don't think I haven't noticed," said Maciza, grabbing the letter from Libertad's hands and stuffing it into her pocket.

Libertad looked in the direction of the game, too. She looked beyond the inmates playing, beyond the prison wall, beyond the city, beyond the border and into the United States.

"Yeah. Nobody."

"C'mon, Libertad, why don't you unload your garbage once and for all? The counselor says it's healthy. Why are you here?" asked Maciza, offering Libertad yet another chance to talk about her crime.

Libertad needed to tell her story, to let out everything she had been holding in since she first arrived at the prison, her life in the shape of the truth, a confession, not a narration, but again her voice did not listen to her command, and she did not answer.

"I thought we were getting cozy here. I even showed you my scar," said Maciza.

Maciza had to know the reason Libertad was imprisoned and she had to know immediately. A bet was on with Rarotonga and she needed the money.

"I have my little secrets, too, you know," she said, trying to pique Libertad's curiosity.

"Look, Maciza, I can't hear your private stuff. I'd only do it if I wanted to tell you mine. Otherwise it's not fair to you."

"It's okay. I don't believe in fairness anyway—I don't even know what that is. You'll spill it all someday one way or another."

"Maybe, maybe not."

"Why don't you tell me now? Just say it. If I win the bet I'll give you a cut."

"What? A bet?" The news of the bet disturbed Libertad.

"It's your fault. You've got everyone wondering. Some say you're in for murder and others say you committed fraud. I'm betting you're here by accident," said Maciza, checking for a reaction that she could read in Libertad's expression.

Libertad had plenty to reveal about her past and much of it was still blurry and distant. That was the disturbing part. On the other hand, she felt amused about the fact that her unintentional mystery was stirring the inmates' curiosity so deeply.

"I don't need a cut. It's not about money, Maciza."

The referee blew her whistle to signal for the women on the bench to take their places on the court. Libertad and Maciza got up and took their spots side by side next to the net.

"Is it about friendship, then?"

"It's about suspense," said Libertad, although the word on her mind was *fear*.

The clouds have been gone for three weeks. Do they think the other side of the border is a better deal? Perhaps they decided to cross over and stay for good. I should have warned them about the Salton Sea. The dead fish. The stench. The mistake.

This morning I woke up thinking about the nine children, the ones I didn't kill. Where are they now? How old are they? How much do they miss their mothers? And their fathers? Would they remember me? I am afraid to see their faces. The horror. The loss.

the story I'm telling you is so long that it doesn't fit in a single book. It continues through several books, so we're going to continue with this other one," said Libertad in a matter-of-fact way to the group of inmates sitting in the library, so close together that their sweaty shoulders crowded against one another, like big teeth in a small mouth. She put *The Three Musketeers* aside and opened the first page of Fodor's *Caribbean Ports of Call*. Not giving Libertad's literary license a second thought, the inmates leaned forward in rapt attention.

Ever since the accident where the captain lost his life at the university, my father became paranoid and lived in hiding, on the road, working as a trucker. He was so scared of being tracked down by the authorities that he changed his name whenever he could: Pantaleón González, Juvenal González, Pascual González, Severo González, José Arcadio González, Aureliano González.

"Did he ever change his name to Speedy González?" asked Rarotonga, sending the entire group into laughter, except for Maciza, who was concentrating on the story.

"Stop interrupting, dammit! Where did you learn your manners? Jeez!" said Maciza, pushing Rarotonga off the bench.

Rarotonga got up, dusted off her dress, and went back to her seat, still with a grin on her face.

"Yes, other truckers called him Speedy González for a

while," said Libertad. "But that wasn't until he got ahold of a lot of cash and was able to buy his own truck. It's coming up in the next chapter."

"Was the cash just laying there, on the sidewalk?" asked Maciza with a smirk.

"You'll find out."

It was a brand-new Kenworth Seminole W900B. A beauty. Top of the line. And to make it all complete, it had a fifty-ton detachable three-axle lowboy, one of the strongest flatbeds in the market, ideal to load bulldozers, cranes, and hydraulic excavators. My father even ordered the Optional Sleeper Extender so we'd be more comfortable. After all, it was our new home, our one and only place of residence. And we owned it. I was about two months old. He fastened the bassinet on the floor behind the seats with a tie-down right next to the bed so he could watch me at night.

From the dealership yard we went straight to see Cholito, in Santa Ana, California. He was short, fat, and had a beard that resembled a soccer match: eleven hairs on each cheek. When it came to producing counterfeit documents, he was the man. Green cards, Social Security cards, birth certificates, driver's licenses, all kinds of IDs. He made the best ones my father ever had. Every time he changed his name, he had Cholito make him a new driver's license. That's when he baptized himself as Speedy González.

From Cholito's place, we headed to the sign shop. My father was very picky. He had the lettering guy touch up the sign on the door over and over until it was perfect.

"You forgot the accent on *González*," my father finally said.

He was holding me with his right arm, football style as he liked to call it, and at the same time he was trying to point at the misspelled word with the pacifier he had in the other hand.

"Say what?"

"The accent, the little slanted line on top of the letter *a*."

"But we don't use those things here. This is the States, man."

"I don't care. González is spelled with an accent on the letter *a*. It's proper Spanish and we're not going to argue with the Royal Academy of the Spanish Language, are we?"

"You're the boss. But I'm not responsible if the sign gets all messed up."

The lettering guy took a brush, wet it with paint, and traced the accent over the letter *a*, from left to right.

My father put me on the passenger seat and took the brush and paint.

"Get me some thinner. The line goes from right to left."

Once my father had redone the accent, he gazed satisfied at the sign that would define us from that day on. Big, shiny pink letters surrounded by a purple border: GONZÁLEZ & DAUGHTER TRUCKING CO.

"We're in business, baby."

With this truck, my father discovered an entrepreneurial streak he didn't know he had. After all those years driving other people's trucks in Mexico and then in the

United States, he had become a savvy trucker. Now he had his very own rig.

Our business was to haul heavy-duty construction and farming equipment. Bulldozers, cranes, wheel-loaders, mass excavators, compactors, combines. But what set us apart from the rest of our competitors was not the fact that we were a father-daughter trucking team and that one of the two partners—me, that is—was two months old; it was that we had a niche in the market that no one had ever catered to. We would find old and useless machines that nobody wanted anymore, buy them for next to nothing, haul them to the border, and sell them to Mexicans who could refurbish them to look like new and operate for another twenty years. Nothing goes to waste in Mexico.

"You mean he drove the truck, bought machines and sold them, *and* took care of the baby?" asked Maciza. "I've never seen a man juggle like that without dropping the oranges."

"Sometimes he did. Just listen to what comes next and you'll know what I mean."

As my father told me many years later, on a cloudless day we were driving on Highway 2 on our way to Broken Bow to pick up an old Cat Pipelayer that needed a new fly-wheel and a definite makeover. Once we were loaded, we'd head down to the Mexican border. Our buyer would be waiting for us with his own truck and trailer on the other side of the bridge. We were ahead of schedule by a day, so we had time to spare. I was barely twelve months old. I sat in the passenger seat chewing on the little rubber tire of a toy truck when my father spotted a stream right between Cairo and Hazard.

"Ready to stretch those legs?" he said to me as he pulled over and parked the truck.

After we caught some sun while lying on the tall grass, he washed my diapers in the creek, scrubbing hard on a slanted rock that stuck out at the edge of the water. I picked up a bug and put it in my mouth. He later found half of it on my tongue and, without much worry, stuck his dirty finger behind my two front baby teeth and pulled it out.

He said, "Well, I guess that's your protein for the day."

I was learning to walk. I wouldn't sit still. I crawled, stood on my feet, wobbled a bit, and fell on my butt after every other step.

"Now, don't you fall in the water, you hear me, little lady? I don't have any dry diapers for you. Everything's wet," he warned.

When he was done, he hung dozens of diapers on a tree branch behind him. Then it was playtime. He liked to chase me around pretending to be a monster just like his mother did with him when he was little. He raised his arms and curled his fingers as if they were claws. He stomped his feet, always three steps behind me.

"Here comes El Santo Demonio!" he'd say.

I screamed in excitement and ran until I lost my balance. Then he caught me and tickled me.

"My dad didn't have to pretend to be a monster when he chased me around," said Rarotonga.

"Mine neither," said Culebra.

Libertad realized that the passage had created a fierce need among the inmates to vent their own feelings. They had begun comparing their fathers' behaviors, clearly competing against one another for the Most Abused Award.

"Why don't you all go tell this stuff to the counselor and let Libertad finish the goddamn story?" said Maciza.

Libertad was envious at the ease with which the other inmates admitted their ordeals. The room was soon silent again, and as she was about to start, Rata interrupted.

"Excuse me, Libertad, just one more thing. How do you remember all this shit, if you were a baby?"

"There you go again," said Maciza. "It's just a story. We've already gone through this."

Maciza looked at Libertad quickly in search of some sign, any gesture or involuntary twitch of her nose or movement of her eyes, that would reveal the truth about her stories, but Libertad was just eager to continue.

After a while, when the temperature began to drop, he picked me up, sat me in the passenger seat, naked as I was, and drove off toward the border. Then he remembered that he had left the diapers behind. From the road, they must have looked like a flock of whooping cranes resting on the tree branches by the creek.

"Damn! Not again!" he said as he slammed his fist on the steering wheel.

We didn't return to get the diapers. As my father drove unsteadily, he searched desperately in the diaper bag next to him. Relieved, he found one.

"This better last you until tomorrow, sweetie, so no pooping tonight," he said.

Even years later, whenever my father spotted any kind of white fabric rotting along the highways, he'd say, "Look, somebody forgot their diapers."

"And the mother? What happened to the mother?" asked Maciza, anxious to get an answer.

Libertad turned the page and took a long, slow sip of water from a plastic cup.

"I'll get to it. Take it easy."

She picked up the book again, but just as she was about to start, Warden Guzmán opened the door. The inmates stood up immediately, as the warden had taught them.

"You may sit down, girls," she said. "Libertad, I need you to come by right after Library Club, please." Then she turned and left.

Libertad slammed the book shut. "That's all for today. We're going to have to leave the mother for next week."

"I hate it when you do that. Can't you just give us a clue?" said Maciza.

"Sorry. No can do."

Maciza got up and walked out, banging her fist on the wall. Libertad could hear the other inmates speculating about the mother as they left the library. She would have to be careful not to give anything away that evening during dinner.

On her way out of the library, Libertad came across Culebra, who pulled her aside. Culebra had made up a couple of spoilers before, but after they turned out to be false, the inmates had stopped believing her.

"I know why you got called in to the warden's office," Culebra said. "Deny everything."

"What are you talking about?"

"It's for your own good. Just say you don't know anything. That's all I can say."

Break 19. Break 19.

Go ahead, breaker.

What's it look like over your shoulder?

You got a picture taker at the 105 westbound and he's got the radar going.

Thanks. I'll keep my eyes peeled. Is that you, Ghost?

Yeah. Who's this?

Tourniquet. I thought I recognized your voice.

What's up, my man?

Nothing much. Just dropping a load in Blythe. Hey, did you hear what happened with González?

Speedy?

He got a huge settlement from the thing with the wife. Bought a brand-new Kenworth Seminole and a lowboy. Owns them free and clear. Twister says he's got enough dough left over to buy himself a whole fleet if he wanted.

Some people got all the luck.

I don't want that kind of luck. I'd rather keep hiring on, driving someone else's trucks, than go through what he went through.

What did he do with the baby?

He's driving with her.

The crazy Mexican.

I saw him at the Fiesta Inn and Dance Club the other day. He had all the waitresses lined up by his table. They all wanted to give him tips on how to raise the kid.

Like what?

Like how to make her burp, how to change her diapers. They even bathed the baby for him.

He's so damn lucky, I'm telling you. He's got women falling all over him.

You said it. Hey, you're breaking up. Don't vanish on me, Ghost.

Catch you on the flip-flop.

I had to fire Jerfu," Warden Guzmán said to Libertad. "I believe she was distributing cocaine to some of the girls and it wasn't brought in through the appropriate channels. She's being taken to the women's facility in Hermosillo as we speak. I'd give her three years, at least."

"I'm so sorry. Now you'll need a new secretary, someone you can trust."

"I don't trust anyone. I've lived too long to make that mistake. The reason why you are here is because I know you spell flawlessly, but most of all, you are not into the drug market." Warden Guzmán looked straight into Libertad's eyes. "Or are you?"

Libertad understood Culebra's warning. She was not selling drugs, but she knew who was, and Culebra was among the guilty. The warden would try to get this information out of her. She had to think fast.

"Do I need to give you an answer you already know?"

Warden Guzmán smiled. Of course she knew everything that went on in her prison.

"Then tell me, who is involved?"

"You'll find the smugglers, you don't need my help."

Other women are easier to manipulate, to coerce into telling it all, the warden thought. Libertad was too smart to jeopardize her integrity. In a way, she was pleased to realize that Libertad was loyal to her cellmates.

"I know. But you can be helpful in other ways."

Until the warden hired a new secretary, Libertad would be doing Jerfu's job, only better and for a fraction of Jerfu's wage, which, luckily for her, was much higher than what Matriarca paid her. She would have to organize the prison files, answer the phones, prepare Warden Guzmán's coffee, type letters and memos, and make the warden's appointments with the hairdresser and the Avon lady. Thanks to the warden's entrepreneurial vision, these women ran their businesses inside the prison while they served time. But with their busy schedules, they could not take walk-ins, even if it was the warden herself, so she had agreed to make appointments just like any prisoner. It was a small effort, but it allowed her to act like she was just one of the girls.

The warden instructed Libertad not to discuss with the other inmates anything she did, heard, or learned at her new job. She would keep regular full-time office hours but would be allowed to leave at four in the afternoon on Wednesdays to continue with her duty at Library Club.

"As for your little gig with Matriarca, I've already made arrangements to get her a temp maid. Don't worry. She'll be taken care of. I only need you until I find a reliable secretary."

"Thank you."

Libertad should have felt happy. This move could be considered a promotion. But she knew she'd miss making Matriarca's bed, dusting her dresser, vacuuming her carpet. She never got to do these chores while she lived on the road and now she'd lost that chance again.

"Remember that I'll be keeping a close eye on you."

Libertad didn't need the warning. She had no reason to do anything the warden would qualify as illegal. So she was escorted to the office every day and worked the full shift, doing everything she was expected to do.

Until she came upon Maciza's file. It was so thick it filled three folders. Her job was to store it in the right cabinet, but instead she sat by the window, hefting the file in her hands, knowing that Warden Guzmán was at a Tupperware party in the South Wing and would not be back that afternoon. And without wasting another second, she began reading every letter, every document, and every report. Some were in English, others in Spanish. At the time of her incarceration, Maciza had been employed as an undocumented worker at a flower shop in Calexico, California, where she lived within walking distance of the Friendship Wall, a rickety, colorful, and futile barrier that divided the United States and Mexico. Everyone knew that she had killed her husband while on a grocery shopping trip to Mexicali, Mexico.

"I did it because I loved him," she had testified.

She couldn't take the double betrayal. The other woman had been her friend, or so she had made Maciza believe.

"I would have killed her, too, but there's no point in killing someone whose soul is dead already."

According to the prosecution's accusations, the judge, a female judge, was biased. In one of the transcripts that Libertad read, the attorney maintained that because the judge's husband had betrayed her as well, she had been sympathetic to Maciza and had put her in a lower sentencing bracket than her crime deserved. Maciza's sentencing structure allowed her to earn one day of freedom for every day served in prison. This meant that her sentence of twenty years would be reduced to ten if she displayed good behavior. And, perhaps unwillingly, she had. Carrying all those food crates from the produce truck to the kitchen would surely count as good behavior in Warden Guzmán's eyes. Maciza had saved the government a lot of money in tips to the delivery guys.

In the third folder, Libertad found some paperwork in English indicating that Maciza had a son, Pollito, and that he had been placed in foster care at age five. Given that Maciza had been imprisoned for seven years already, her son should be around twelve years old. The report was missing pages. Maciza had never mentioned this boy. Why had she kept this fundamental part of her life from everyone in the prison?

Adding up the dates she found in the report, Libertad figured that Maciza would be free in three more years. She could go to Children Services, get her boy back, and start over.

Libertad wondered how much time she had left until her own release. All she had to do to know was to look up her own rap sheet. A file cabinet here. A drawer there. Then, a folder with her name on it, the name on her fake driver's license at the time of her incarceration. Filomena Hernández. There it was. She pulled it out. She held it in her hands. She could have opened it. She could have checked the dates. But she didn't.

A small suicidal cloud lingered in the deserted sky this morning. Hesitant, indefinite. Wondering what to do, she let herself drift, and by the afternoon the wind had taken care of her.

Before, I could look ahead. Now I can look up. Even behind these bars, there is a view. The sky has become a horizontal windshield framed by the prison walls. Suspended above the glass is a premonition thick with implications. I read the skyscape every day. I want to look ahead to the horizon again. But by looking up I feel protected.

My cell is much larger than the truck's sleeper. In the beginning I expected it to go somewhere, anywhere, but it didn't grow wheels. The first month I lay on my bed and tried to anticipate the sound of the air being pushed by a passing truck. Then I waited for the vacuum behind it to sway me a little, leaving a void. But the noises in my cell were erratic and restrained. They were metallic and had no rhythm. With time, I've learned to understand them. They mean that Fridays will be just like Saturdays, and Sundays, and Mondays. I am safe here. It may have to do with the horizon. It is always so close.

running from the authorities all over Mexico turned my father into a paranoid wreck. He developed a pursuit delirium, believing that someone was after him at all times. Roadblocks were impossible obstacles. People in uniform were murderers. He was sure that his head had a price tag. At first he rode along with truck drivers, helped drop loads, change tires, make repairs," Libertad read from a copy of *Kiss of the Spider Woman*.

"**Don't you want** to know where we're going?" the truckers would ask.

"Anywhere is fine," he'd say, scared to stay in one place.

He got by on whatever the truckers were willing to share with him.

"Where there's food for one, there's food for two," they'd say.

He became known as El Hippie. He changed his look frequently, always emulating John Lennon. He let his hair grow, styled his beard. Eventually he started driving a truck, under the false name of Valentín González. A transportation company hired him. He hauled loads from the tropics to the desert and from the mountains to the ocean, always looking back, trying to identify those who stared ahead in the vehicle behind him.

Right around the time when the first John Lennon solo album came out, he had had enough. He suffered insomnia, he could not tolerate beer, a rash flared up around his belly button every so often, and he developed a dry mouth. So he headed for the U.S. border—listening to Lennon and the Plastic Ono Band on the radio—but instead of delivering his cargo of American jeans manufactured in Mexico to the transfer rig that would haul it across the bridge and into the United States, he parked the truck on a dusty Matamoros street, walked to the border line, jumped in a container filled with cotton packs when no one was watching, and waited to cross over. He wasn't worried about the truck he'd abandoned. The transportation company would find it in a couple of days, looted, of course.

The ride in the container was long and dark. He could not get his bearings, but he knew he was in the United States, because as he sat on the floor between the cotton packs, he noticed how smooth the road felt. He figured that shock absorbers would last forever under those conditions. How often would springs and shackles need to be replaced? And what about the wheels? Forget cracks, bent rims, or broken spacers. He imagined the highway, wide and silky and eternal. He wondered what kind of landscape lay outside. He realized he was four hours into the United States and still he had seen more of it in movies. By midafternoon, cotton fibers that had gotten loose and were floating around in the air had crept up his nostrils and were making him sneeze.

When he finally felt the jerk of the first stop, all his fears came back. But he convinced himself that a fellow trucker, regardless of his nationality, would certainly not turn him over to the authorities as the illegal alien he now was. He'd probably help him by sharing advice as to what to do and where to go during his first visit to the United States. But what he saw when the door opened was not the rugged American truck driver that he had imagined. It was the startled face of Virginia Ryder. She let out a little yelp followed by broad laughter.

"You scared me!" she said. "Come on out, guapo."

She had a tattoo of a butterfly on her buffed-up biceps. She was blond, her skin was tanned, her eyes were inexplicably green, a smile the size of the Mexican border adorned her face, and she wore hoop earrings that dangled all the way to her shoulders. This was the first female trucker my father had ever seen. In his mediocre English, he asked her for a ride. Neither of them could stop staring at each other in surprise and awe.

"Where to?" she asked.

"Anywhere is fine," he said.

And that's how my parents met. Not even Cupid could have pulled off a faster maneuver.

On their first day together my father told my mother that he was a fugitive. His English would have to improve substantially and his trust in my mother would have to grow to a full scale before he could explain why. But she didn't mind not knowing then. Just the fact that he was on the run—for whatever reason—along with his deep brown eyes framed by shadowy eyelids, awakened in her a desire so powerful, it almost got her fired from her job. Hauling a load across the country would take them weeks instead of days. Every couple of hundred miles they'd park at a rest area and make love in the sleeper, oblivious to the thousands of cars passing by on the interstate highway. The truck would rock and sway for a while to the rhythm of their lovemaking. Then, sweaty and satisfied, they'd resume their journey, my mother logging far fewer miles than her usual average and missing important delivery dates.

"I got a final warning from the fleet manager, the stupid prick," my mother said one morning on their way to Omaha. "I need to go back to my average or he'll fire me."

"I'm so sorry I got you in trouble, baby. I promise not to distract you again," said my father, stretching to kiss her neck as she drove.

"Could you ride inside the container, hon? I can't afford to lose this job, and if I keep on looking into your eyes while I drive, I'm going to get us into an accident. You know I can't resist undressing you before I even pull over."

And since my father pleased my mother in any way he could, and because he believed containers to be a safer place to travel without being seen by the authorities, he agreed to be locked inside, with no view of the road.

Two months after they met, they were married in a ceremony on top of a flatbed trailer parked at the truck stop outside Winnemucca, famous for its birria tacos. From then on, theirs was a well-paved marriage.

But there was a pothole ahead: my mother's barren womb. After eleven years of marriage marked by countless attempts to get pregnant, she became desperate. Nothing else was on her mind. Once my father started riding in the sleeper instead of in the container (he was still afraid of being found, but my mother made him feel more at ease), she hung a baby shoe from the rearview mirror of their truck. She knitted a sweater so tiny that not even a doll could wear it. Their latest attempt centered around a fertility clinic in Tulsa recommended to them by a trucker friend whose wife had triplets after the intensive treatments.

"The doctor must have used Drano to unclog my wife's plumbing," the husband had said, laughing loud and alone at his own joke.

My parents went every month for a year or so with no results. They kept a thorough log of my mother's vaginal temperature, had sex at the right times, received fertility shots made out of Italian nuns' urine. A few times my father even locked himself in a tiny restroom and masturbated, with no naked women's magazines to look at, delivering his sperm into a specimen cup for the lab.

The waiting room at the fertility clinic smelled of new carpeting and disappointment and made my mother feel nauseated. But it wasn't the kind of nausea she so yearned to feel, the one that sends expectant women to spit out their anxiety in the toilet every morning for the first three months of their pregnancy. Posted on the wall was a medical illustration of a naked mother-to-be, her womb showing a fetus in situ. She stared back at my mother and it seemed to her that the woman was mocking her. She felt the urge to take down the poster and rip it up.

My father watched my mother pacing back and forth. At times, he leafed through a magazine, not really paying attention to its contents. He was getting desperate himself. Having a child of his own had become a need impossible to suppress. He wanted to begin a new family. Perhaps then the hurt he felt from having left his mother and his sister back in Mexico would diminish.

Some of the other women sitting in the waiting room were already expecting babies. Their full bellies and fulfilled smiles poisoned my mother with envy and made her want to run out into the hall and scream. Why was she being denied the privilege of motherhood?

When they finally were called in, the doctor asked my parents to sit across the desk. He was a skinny, tall white man with a long nose and a big dewlap. If he were an animal, he'd be a stork.

"I'm sorry. I know how badly you want a baby," he said in a dull voice, the kind my mother imagined some doctors used when they'd rather be golfing. "But there's not much more we can do," he said even more slowly. "If you'd like, we could extend the treatments another month and see what happens."

My mother's patience had run out by then and the doctor's seeming indifference to their ordeal was becoming intolerable.

"Listen, Doctor, if I get my period one more time, I'm gonna bring the Kotex and smear it on your face!"

"Please, Mrs. González, you don't have to get so worked up. If you're ready, I could give you the numbers of a couple of adoption agencies."

"Yeah, let's give this healthy baby to these truckers to raise in a sleeper. Is that what you think the adoption agency will say?"

She turned to my father and pulled him up from the chair.

"C'mon, honey, we've hit a dead end."

As they walked out, they realized that they had exhausted every possibility that conventional medicine had to offer. Their only alternative was to find experts outside the medical field. My father knew exactly where to go, but it meant that they had to cross the border into Mexico, and just the thought of it made his rash flare up again. He gathered whatever courage he had left and bought a curly-haired toupee to avoid being recognized by the Mexican military. Then, because they didn't have a car and my father believed that in a passenger bus they were nothing but sitting ducks for the Mexican authorities to find them at any given checkpoint, he hitchhiked with my mother all the way to Catemaco in seven different trucks. This small town in the middle of the Veracruz jungle was known to be the favorite haunt of curanderos, shamans, and witches. People came from as far as Patagonia to cure ailments and rid themselves of curses.

As soon as my parents got off the last truck, on the outskirts of town, they caught a whiff of optimism in the air. When they arrived at a windowless adobe shack, a hundred-year-old shaman, a thousand wrinkles on his face, met them at the door, as if he knew they were coming.

"I've seen you before," he said, pointing at my father with a long, skinny middle finger. "You came with your papa some years ago. He suffered from consumption."

"Yes. You cured him. I was sixteen."

"I know," he said. "Call me Don Silvino."

"He died the next year, Don Silvino."

"I can't prevent car accidents."

My father stared at the dirt floor for a few seconds, surprised by the shaman's knowledge of his father's fate, and thought about his mother and his sister. They learned to accept his father's tragic death, but his own disappearance was different. He hoped they believed he was dead, eaten by sharks in the Gulf of Mexico. It was their only way to find closure.

"We're Joaquín and Virginia."

"I know," Don Silvino said again. "Take your shoes off before you go inside."

My mother wondered how the place could be so dark when so many votive candles were burning. She could barely make out the shape of the furniture. A table. Two chairs. Maybe there was a sofa in the back, or was it a person? She thought she saw the bundle move slightly. Don Silvino had them sit on a coir rug on the floor and immediately began conjuring a prayer in his native dialect. He removed a dead rabbit from a basket on the table. He cut it open and pulled its liver out. He hastily put the warm, slimy organ in a molcajete and ground it along with oils and herbs.

"Joaquín and Virginia, your disbelief will turn into hope, your desperation into joy. You will follow these steps and I will see you again in twenty-two days."

Don Silvino gave them a piece of paper with instructions, then spooned the paste-like substance into a baby-food jar and gave it to my mother, along with a votive candle that had a decal of Saint Jude on it.

"Now go and do what I ask," he said.

Libertad stopped reading to swat a fly with the book. It had been buzzing around her head the entire time and was getting on her nerves.

"I've been to Catemaco. That was when my husband

was still fucking me over. Any of you guys ever been there?" said Maciza, taking advantage of the pause.

"One of those shamans cured my cousin of dementia," said Rarotonga. "He works at the post office now."

"My sister had a job done on her husband's lover. She mixed a potion in the woman's drink and it made her teeth rot," said Rata.

"Is she still with your sister's husband?"

"Yeah, but he won't kiss her now."

"Let's get back to the story, Libertad," said Maciza. "We don't have much time left."

My parents were ecstatic. They read their instructions several times and traveled the area until they found the cornfield by the side of the road. Then they picked a flat section and made a large circle out of hundreds of corn husks. In Step Three, they were to lie at the center of the circle and make passionate love. They did as instructed.

"Okay, that's five times now, what next?" my father said, exhausted.

Following Step Four, my mother took the jar out of her purse and gave it to my father. He opened the lid and smeared the paste on my mother, painting circles with his fingers around her belly button and breasts. Then she lit the Saint Jude votive candle and set it by her side. They spent the night there, staring at the moon as if it would give them assurance. And after twenty-two days of rampant anxiety, they headed back to Catemaco.

Don Silvino, still alive and lit by candles, asked my mother for a urine sample. He held up the glass as my parents watched the yellow liquid develop opacities that floated to the surface. Don Silvino stirred the urine with a rooster's feather and then, when it was saturated, let the urine drip from the feather onto a piece of handmade paper that sat on the table. He then held the paper up to the candlelight, looked at the formations the drops made, and proclaimed, "You have a girl in your womb."

My parents walked out of Don Silvino's shack in silence, keeping their composure. But after a few seconds, my mother couldn't hold her excitement in and screamed, scaring off the chickens and roosters and rabbits that were milling around the shaman's yard.

They hugged and danced, laughing and yelling little words with big meanings, like, "I love you, goddammit!"

The animals in the yard took shelter behind buckets and piles of hay. They were used to these displays of joy by their master's happy clients, but if they didn't run for their lives, the next ingredient in the shaman's potion could be their own livers, brains, or beaks.

My mother twirled my father around until she lost her balance, ending on the dusty ground. My father, concerned about the baby's health, caressed her still-flat womb. They kissed. Don Silvino looked at them from the door and smiled like the wise do, with a hint of sadness.

So, after many attempts and thanks to the shaman's expertise, my mother was finally pregnant with me. But her destiny was set from the beginning, and the very thing she most yearned for was the cause of her downfall.

bet she's gonna die from childbirth. Am I right, Diva?

No way. This is no soap. It's a book, a bestseller.

So?

It's gotta be a more dramatic death. She gets poisoned or something.

Then I'd have an angry trucker stab her.

But why? You need a motive, Maciza. Haven't you learned anything from Matriarca's mouthpiece, Mr. Whatshisname Attorney? He yells her entire defense statements all over the cafeteria, as if we cared.

Okay. She took his parking space, how's that?

That sounds reasonable, but they have to be in a big metropolis, like El Paso.

Yeah.

Or, you know what? How about if she gets hit by a truck or dies from a terrible terminal disease with a scary name, like lupus?

First you say it's gotta be dramatic and then you give me shit that happens all the time. She gets killed by someone who tries to kidnap the baby—now, there's a whole book right there. Hell, it's a Hollywood movie!

We're just making stuff up. Maybe she doesn't even die. Maybe she just takes off with another man.

And leaves the baby after all she's gone through? A mother never abandons her kids on purpose. She's gotta die, I'm telling you. She's history. Period.

What's the matter with you, Maciza? You have something against Virginia?

You're the one who wants her dead whatever it takes.

Get the hell out of here. I like Virginia. You just want to get rid of anyone who pushes your key.

Listen, Diva, if you're getting drove at me for what happened with Culebra at Library Club last week, you're stone crazy. Your acey-deucey friend had it coming. Virginia's not even real, dammit! She's a fucking character! I can't break her pinky even if I wanted to!

Culebra's pinky—sandwiched between two pieces of worn-out emery board and three Band-Aids—was still swollen and a bit twisted to the side when Library Club resumed two weeks after the brawl. Warden Guzmán had canceled it temporarily and had sent Maciza to the segregation unit for three days before listening to any explanation. Had she heard it, she would have sent Culebra instead. Now Maciza's hard work to reduce her prison term with good behavior was in jeopardy. A dark stain on her parole package could mean months, even years, added to her sentence. Unless Libertad spoke up.

"It's too late to change Maciza's punishment. I already gave the order. It's final."

"Would you at least let me tell you what happened?"

"I'm listening."

"Culebra said that no one in this prison should've had kids at all. We're a bad example to them, and they end up being raised by someone else anyway. Of course, all the mothers in the room wanted to kill her. Maciza jumped up and grabbed Culebra's hand and twisted her finger. She yelled, 'Take it back. Take it back.' But Culebra wouldn't take it back, so her pinky snapped. The way I see it, Maciza really stopped a riot."

"That's not her responsibility. She should have called the guards."

"Well, I guess she took it personal."

"But she doesn't have children. What's her problem?"

Libertad realized that either the warden hadn't read

Maciza's file or she had forgotten about Pollito. In any case, she would not bring it up. What if there was some obscure agreement between Maciza and the warden to keep it a secret?

"I guess she can relate. Don't you? I mean, you don't have children, either, we all know that, but I bet you can understand what these women must feel to have to leave their kids behind."

Warden Guzmán's throat swelled with words she could not speak. The concept of motherhood, an abstraction she had long ago given up trying to grasp, came back to her in the form of a rush that went up along her spine and made her quiver. She did understand.

"I am a mother, Libertad. Or should I say a grieving mother? There really is no word to define what I am. I've looked for it in every dictionary and I haven't found it. A woman who has lost a parent is an orphan. A woman who has lost a husband is a widow. But is there a name for a woman who has lost a child?"

Libertad felt an unfamiliar sadness, the kind that comes with a little pinch to the heart.

"There isn't, not in our language."

"See? The pain of losing a child is so unfathomable that we don't even have a word for people who go through that."

Libertad thought about it for a couple of seconds.

"Was it a girl?"

Warden Guzmán nodded but her mind was not there. Her memory had taken her to the tiny pink coffin where her baby's remains rested in her family's mausoleum, and for the first time she felt a quiet peace, new and sorrowful, but a relief all the same.

"I can see why Maciza defended the mothers. But I can't back down on her punishment. All I can do is not record the incident."

"That'll do. Thanks."

Libertad shook Warden Guzmán's hand in gratitude and walked to the door, but Warden Guzmán stopped her.

"Wait."

"Yes?"

"Thank you."

"You're welcome. I guess you don't talk about these things at your Tupperware parties."

"You got it," said Warden Guzmán, offering Libertad a grateful smile. "Now beat it."

That afternoon at Library Club, Libertad decided it was time to reveal what had happened to her mother. Maciza was back from her three days of solitary confinement and she would enjoy this chapter of the story. She pulled out a dusty copy of *The Fountainhead* and opened it randomly to page 32.

Back on Interstate 35 between Owatonna and Faribault, the hills seem to roll forward and then regret that they did. They are like waves of soil, indecisive and apologetic, unwillingly covered, if not by snow, by thick manes of wheat and barley and corn that the wind tosses and combs every which way. The Midwestern wind, capricious and irresponsible, smelling of cow dung and pig sheds, is known for pushing cars and trucks off the roads and into ditches. I know those roads. I was just a few days old the first time I traveled them. My mother had given birth to me two weeks before in Los Angeles. As soon as she felt better, we left the hospital and, with my father at the wheel, headed toward Minneapolis to pick up a cylinder/walker combine. Had I not been born, my mother would have been driving and she would be alive. Most of the way, we lay in the sleeper doing what a brand-new mother and her daughter were supposed to do. I slept, cried, soiled my diapers, and ate. My mother nursed me and watched me in amazement.

A short distance from our destination, right before the Northfield off-ramp, a station wagon approached in the left lane, and for a mile or two it rode parallel to our truck, perhaps to use us as a shield from the autumn winds, which were more rambunctious than usual. As my father drove, he glanced at the man sitting in the passenger seat. He had a black tote bag on his lap with a National Rifle Association logo on it. My father saw the man pull a gun out of the tote bag. He handled it carefully, as any seasoned gun owner would, and showed it to the driver, explaining things my father could not hear. The investigation would later disclose that it was a .357 Magnum. The man in the passenger seat cocked it and pointed at a couple of targets. A tree, a cow, a distant barn. Then it happened. According to the defendant's declarations, the glowing ash at the tip of the driver's cigarette blew off and fell down the edge of the tote bag, finding its way between the gunman's legs. As he squirmed in the seat trying to keep the ash from burning a hole in his pants, his finger pulled the trigger. The ballistics expert would later explain that the bullet didn't get deflected when it shattered the station wagon's front passenger window, went straight through the metal of our sleeper's wall, made its way across our pillow, and came to a stop inside my mother's head.

When my father saw the bullet hole in the station wagon's window and behind it the expression of surprise on the man's face, he called to my mother, but she didn't answer. Then he yelled, "Virginia! Are you all right?" No answer again. So he slammed on the brakes, pulled over, and jumped into the truck's sleeper. He found me still attached to my mother's warm nipple, sucking her milk, my tiny body snug in her arms.

The men in the station wagon pulled over a couple of hundred feet ahead and ran to our truck. The wind was so strong that their hats blew off into the fields. Neither of them returned to pick them up.

"Is everyone okay in there?" asked the gunman as he opened the door and climbed into the cab.

"Get an ambulance, please!" yelled my father.

The man looked behind the seats, into the sleeper, and saw my mother, the pillow soaked with blood, her exposed breast, and me, a newborn baby wiggling in her limp arms. He knew right then and there that there was no hurry to call the paramedics.

"C'mon! Libertad, that's so hard to believe. What are the odds," interrupted Venadita, a blind woman who had just been transferred to Libertad's cell. She had lost her vision when her husband threw car battery acid at her face during a fight.

"A freak accident. That's all I can say. They happen all the time, as unbelievable as they may seem."

"But why not kill the father? Why did it have to be the mother?"

"There's a dead or an absent mother in every Disney movie. Why shouldn't there be one in this story?"

Venadita didn't quite understand Libertad's reasoning, her way of giving the protagonist a handicap, a victim's burden she would have to endure and overcome.

"Disney?"

"Yes. Did you see *Bambi*? I mean, when you were little, before your accident?"

"Don't give me that shit now, Libertad. Mine wasn't an accident and you know it. It's just that the poor little girl is so helpless all of a sudden."

"See? Now you're feeling pity. I told you. It never fails."

"I just can't imagine growing up without your mother."

When Rata heard Venadita say this, she just had to remind her, "I don't know where you're coming from with this, Venadita. Didn't your mother sleep with your husband for three years right under your nose?"

Venadita hated when the subject of her mother and their atrocious relationship was brought up.

"How could I see them? I was already blind."

"At least you could have heard them moaning."

For a second the room was silent.

"You're scum," said Maciza, grabbing Rata's throat with both hands and squeezing tight. "And I'm going to treat you like the scum you are."

"Stop it!" said Libertad, fearing another three days in the segregation unit in Maciza's future.

"You better apologize to Venadita, asshole," yelled Maciza, an inch from Rata's face.

"I'm sorry," said Rata, barely able to speak.

The room was silent again. Libertad looked around, picked up the book, and continued as if nothing had happened.

My father buried my mother in San Diego. No one except us attended the funeral. He tried to locate her foster parents to notify them, but they had moved away years back, and Children's Services doesn't keep such records after ward-of-the-court children become independent adults. At least that's what we were told over the phone. My father was on hold for so long he had time to heat up my bottle and feed me. And since my mother never looked up her biological mother for fear of finding someone she didn't like, we decided to respect her decision and said our good-byes on our own.

The headstone read "Virginia Ryder. The Road Ends Here." Hunched over from so much grief, my father stood for hours in front of her grave.

"What am I supposed to do now?"

He needed an answer but my mother, wherever she was, would not give it to him.

He leaned against the headstone and stared at the fleet truck parked on the curb under the shade of a tree. Even without a trailer, the tractor barely fit in the narrow street that ran along the well-groomed cemetery, populated by dead people with unfulfilled plans. The greener-than-green grass gave no sign of what was left undone and unsaid by those buried underneath. The jacarandas, splattering the main road with purple flowers, housed a dozen different kinds of birds, all oblivious to the souls that now and then passed by them on their journey to heaven.

My cries of hunger made my father dig in the diaper bag for a bottle. Still hoping for an answer from my mother, he fed me, rocking me with a gentle rhythm and humming a lullaby that he retrieved from the most remote hollow of his mind: "Sleep, my child, sleep now, 'cause if the bogeyman catches you awake, he'll eat you like a piece of cake."

It must have been the monotonous melody that he sang over and over that put him in a trance. He was nearly dreaming awake when the answer came to him as a fragment of a conversation he'd had with my mother long before I was born, and he repeated it to me once and again through the years: "Someday we're gonna stop hiring on, you'll see," she'd said. "We'll get our very own truck. Forget the fleet. Nothing like being an owner-operator."

With those words, his future had been clearly spelled out. He would become an owner-operator now, and I'd be his partner. By the time he reached that conclusion, the bottle was empty and I was fussing and wiggling in his arms.

"Come on. No time to cry. We've gotta get going. I need to buy a truck, a brand-new one."

All of a sudden, he was in a hurry to become an entrepreneur. He looked in the diaper bag for the pacifier, and when he pulled it out, it fell in a mud puddle. Without giving it much thought, he licked the pacifier clean and put in my mouth. The concept of germs was foreign to him. Perhaps that is why I've always enjoyed good health.

We left the cemetery chased by the shadows of that dying afternoon and never returned. My father would sometimes say that there was no point in going back.

"What for? In that place my wife lies dead. Where she is alive is in my head. Fortunately I carry it around everywhere I go."

Libertad stopped reading and left the library without wrapping up the session and thanking her audience as she always did. The inmates glanced at one another and did not make any of their usual remarks, nor did they demand that she continue with the story, though they were curious as hell to know what would happen next. They saw her walk to the kitchen where the tortilla machine waited. Maciza thought she was drained from the intensity of the episode. Diva wondered if the lack of good nutrition was getting to her. Pinche Bruja concluded that Libertad had been reading for so long that she was suffering from eyestrain. She estimated about six months of bureaucratic wrangling before reading glasses rested on her nose. Even Venadita, concerned about Libertad, forgot about Rata's nasty comments, at least until she had a chance to poke her eye. She was blind but she was not a wimp. And Maciza was on her side.

No one suspected that Libertad's head was brimming with memories of the mother she didn't grow up with. Some were borrowed from her father's stories and anecdotes, little incidents that went back to the time before Libertad was born. Others were made up. Or were they?

Always at the brink of disappearing into the blue of the sky. Destined to become nothing from the moment they are something. The clouds.

I think about my mother and all the mothering she did not do. She is nothing but unfinished business. If only the speed of the bullet . . . If only the NRA . . . All I'm left with is a flow of words that stop midsentence. A family suddenly depopulated by the presence of absence. Unanswered questions left for dead on the side of the road. A thought, sliced by the sword of fate. A sack full of undelivered kisses, caresses, and little nothings. Another day, another hour, another minute that cannot be negotiated. What is a ghost but loose ends?

I'm back out, Guajolote.

No, wait, Double-O-Seven. I forgot to ask you about Virginia, the Gratin' Jane that was killed last week, what was her pron?

Butterfly. But she was no Gratin' Jane. She had more experience than you and me together.

Whatever. What the hell happened?

It was awful. Didn't you hear about it? It was all over the news. The husband refused to be interviewed. Avoided the cameras like they were gonna suck out his soul. I guess he was too upset. He just hid inside his truck with the baby while the meat wagon took the wife away. Big mess.

I keep telling Celia that guns can kill you, but she won't listen. She's got three around the house, with the excuse that I'm always away. It's like we live in the Old West or something.

I keep one in the truck, but only I know where it's hidden.

See? What did I tell ya? It's like the Old West. By the way, how about that northbound container? You hauling it?

Nah, I'm driving deadhead to Bull City.

Fuck.

Of our thirteen visits to Clara, the woman from Pico Rivera who lived in a lavender house with rusty wrought-iron garden furniture on the front lawn and an old, hairy mutt napping on the doorstep, one, just one, paid for all our efforts and money.

"She loves you," Clara said to me. "That's what Virginia told me."

In a notebook where Clara logged her conversations with my mother, she showed me a single line right around the middle of the page, where it said, clearly, "I love my daughter."

Clara's notes were actual words that those who'd gone to the other world dictated to her in certain moments of inspiration. Whenever she was being dictated to, the handwriting was quite different, as she pointed out by showing us a grocery list she'd just jotted down that same morning. Definitely the person who wrote "tomatoes" could not have written the word *love*. The list of mangoes, avocados, chicken thighs, poblano peppers, tortillas, and laundry soap was written in chubby letters, the *a*'s and the *o*'s bigger and rounder than the rest, as if they'd just had a hearty meal. The writing in my mother's dictation was rushed and small and seemed to go on past the margins and off of the paper.

Clara explained that the souls that contacted her did the actual writing, moving her hand on the page as they pleased, giving her specific messages for their loved ones. And she dutifully delivered them for a fee.

My father was far more skeptical than I was about the whole operation, but he kept coming back for more: "Just in case it's for real. I don't want your mother to think I'm not willing to fork out the money."

Through Clara, we learned that my mother didn't know she'd died until nine days after the accident. She witnessed how the paramedics lifted her body and took it away on a gurney. She attended her own funeral in San Diego. She wandered around for days in a dark place, cold and uncertain, trying to understand why my father was so sad and why he couldn't see her. But she felt proud of herself when she managed to convince him, while he was dreaming awake at the cemetery, to buy his own truck and become an owner-operator. Then, on the ninth day, she saw a bright light and a woman she'd never seen before glided toward her, claiming to be her biological mother and asking her to follow her into the light. From then on, everything was happiness.

"Like I buy that," my father said on the way out. "Do you?"

The old, hairy mutt napping on the doorstep didn't even raise its head to watch us leave. It seemed to have aged.

"I wish Clara would tell us something we haven't told her before. Of course my mother loved me."

"But she said it in the present tense. That's different."

"Yes, I guess it's all in the way she says things."

We hopped on our truck and elaborated on my mother's

messages, interpreting them this way or that, all the way to the Continental Divide. I realized then, after two years' worth of visits, that far more important than Clara's powers to communicate with the dead was my power to believe. So I believed.

he morning that Janisjoplin was released, Libertad went to Warden Guzmán's office to work as usual, but her anxiety drifted along her skin like an illegal alien's bloated body in the Rio Grande. From the window, she watched Janisjoplin cross the West Gate, where a man in a U.S. Navy uniform waited for her. They kissed with the passion of lovers starving for each other's embrace and rode off on a brand-new motorcycle. Libertad shivered. Desire and fear fought against each other in her memory, a battlefield of contradictions when it came to the subject of men. She wished to be kissed again, but at what cost?

"Are you worried because you're the only American citizen left in the prison?" asked the warden.

"I'm fine here, really. In fact, I've been meaning to ask you to please help me stay for as long as possible."

"And may I know why that is, Libertad?"

"It's just that we have a great thing going with Library Club. I wouldn't want to leave that."

Warden Guzmán felt flattered. I do run a wonderful prison, she thought.

But Libertad had lied. She craved the security that the prison walls provided. And she was doing fine without men.

"Your release date is coming up soon. You could join a book club when you get out, if that's what you like. Is there any other reason why you would want to stay here?"

"I never went to school, so I wouldn't exactly know

what it's like, but somehow you make me feel as if this is my alma mater."

"Thank you, Libertad. Very few recognize my efforts. I believe that creating a sense of community, an atmosphere of belonging, is a positive strategy for rehabilitation," she said as if standing behind a podium. "I've even thought about establishing some sort of alumnae association so ex-inmates could get together at yearly reunions here at the prison. I could even publish a newsletter with a classified-ad section for job opportunities. It's in the future, you'll see. In the meantime, I'll help you stay awhile."

"What are you going to do?"

"Nothing."

"Nothing?"

"Yes. Nothing. To start off, we're going to 'lose' your file. I'll tell your attorney that it's been misplaced."

"Won't he have his own file?"

"Not at all. He never keeps copies of anything. Good thing you got the worst state-appointed attorney you could possibly have gotten."

"I understand what you're trying to do, but how long can you prolong my stay?"

"Procrastination can be a tremendous strategy, Libertad. Don't you worry. I've bought centuries' worth of time with it."

"Thank you."

"You don't have to thank me. All you have to do is put the money you receive as payment for working in the Administrative Office in this envelope every two weeks."

The warden took a regular number-ten envelope and put it in the bottom drawer of her desk.

"Let me know when you've placed your salary in the envelope by sticking a paper clip under my desktop glass. Money left around tends to disappear quickly."

Libertad nodded.

"This arrangement will secure your job at the office, and we're getting air conditioning next month," the warden said. "Isn't this a good deal?"

Libertad nodded again. For a second she worried that she wouldn't have any money. She couldn't be Matriarca's maid anymore and she had to turn her entire wages over to the warden. She would be back to where she started when she first entered the prison. But then she thought, God will provide. He always has. Well, maybe he won't.

hat's the problem with the help. You train them and when they finally get it right, they leave. I can't even keep one around in prison, for God's sake!

Can't you get over it? It's been months since the warden stole Libertad from you, Matriarca.

The whole thing makes me sick. Why am I still so upset? She's just a stupid little maid.

You're being unfair with Libertad. She would have stayed if it hadn't been for the warden.

I'm not too sure about that, Patrona. I've had dozens and they're all the same. They have no loyalty. That's why my mother always said, "They're like part of the furniture and you should treat them that way."

At least the furniture stays where you put it.

And it doesn't need deodorant.

And it doesn't talk behind your back.

And it doesn't steal your expensive moisturizers.

And it doesn't invite a boyfriend over when you're on vacation.

You know, Patrona, for a while there I thought that Libertad was different. She even speaks English.

And a much better English than my ex-husband's bilingual secretary. I don't know why he never fired her.

Don't you?

Oh, stop it, Matriarca. If you're implying that he was sleeping with her, it's old news. I say business is business. Fuck the woman, but hire a good secretary.

Too bad men think with the little head that hangs between their legs.

They wouldn't get in trouble if they didn't. So what are you going to do for a maid? Have you put the word out? I'm sure there are hundreds who would kill for this job.

The warden sent me a new girl. I'll just have to try her out.

They're all so basic.

I once had one from Oaxaca, a tiny little dark thing with long braids, your typical Zúñiga sculpture. I wrote her a detailed list of chores for her to do during her first week. I even typed it. For a few days she kept doing everything wrong, skipping chores, just ignoring my instructions. It was hell. After I finally fired her, the butler confessed to me that she couldn't read. Can you believe it?

And on top of it all, they lie to you in the interview.

Now I'm back where I started. My room is a mess. I have a pile of clothes waiting to be ironed. And see this pimple on my cheek? I've always had to sleep on a clean pillowcase or I break out. Libertad changed my sheets every day. She was good at everything. We even talked about art and literature and philosophy.

Maybe she comes from one of those old money-but-without-the-money families. I know some people like that in Puebla. They usually manage to keep their status for one or two generations.

Who knows? She never talked to me about her background, but it's clear she went to school. I haven't seen that level of sophistication in any maid before.

At least you still see her at the beach.

That's the problem with making that kind of deal with your employees. Now I have to honor it. It's only fair. And I am a fair player, unlike the warden.

Of course. She's a warden. A government employee. Who did you think you were dealing with, the Queen Mother of England?

have I ever told you how I ended up with this tattoo? Don't laugh, honey, this is serious. Your mom and I had been living together a few months. She was attempting to make me a trucker, a real one, which was like trying to load a hundred-and-fifty-ton locomotive onto a twenty-five-ton semitrailer. But I must say that in time she succeeded because here I am sitting in this truck stop drinking reheated coffee at three in the morning to prove it. I had just gotten my driver's license after flunking the exam twice. Imagine that. A literature professor going through such an embarrassment. It was enough for me to have to endure the career change, and to top it off, it was harder than achieving tenure. Good thing I met Cholito around that time, my fake driver's license expert. He quickly took care of the problem, and in trucker-like fashion, I decided to celebrate my official new status by having your mom's name tattooed across my chest. So we called the fleet manager and told him we were taking a couple of days off work. Personal time, no explanations. He could have another trucker pick up the load in Amarillo.

The tattoo artist was a big hairy man and all three hundred pounds of him were sweaty. He went by the name of El Shakespeare and had no friends. Offering a shot of tequila to his customers before he worked on them was his trademark. He was famous among bikers for his detailed spread eagles, his exotic mermaids, and most of all, his heart-shaped Mom designs. I asked him to write "Virginia" from nipple to nipple, a blanket of ink over my chest. I picked a nice lettering from a laminated cardboard sampler and prepared myself for the procedure.

The session lasted much longer than I anticipated. El Shakespeare was a perfectionist. He rolled the tip of his tongue from one corner of his lips to the other in deep concentration. I kept my eyes shut tight, as if that would diminish my pain, but from time to time I would glance at your mom, who could not stand to see the needle piercing my skin and had to drag a chair to the window and watch the people on the street passing by outside the parlor. Gritting my teeth, I asked El Shakespeare how he'd gotten his nickname.

"My aunt Maude says I look like that guy. You know the famous painter from the Middle Ages? But I've never seen his photo. Ever heard of him?"

"Not the one you're talking about," was my polite answer.

When he finally finished his creation, I stood up and was able to read, in big fancy blue and red letters, "Birginia." The illiterate son of a bitch tattooed your mom's name wrong. Do you understand the implications of this mistake? I was marked with a typo forever, in your mom's name, may she rest in peace.

She tried to calm me, to pull me away from the perplexed artist. He could not understand why I didn't like his beautiful tattoo.

"It's okay, honey," she told me. "My first foster dad used to write my name like that, too. I don't mind, really."

But I was ready to beat the guy.

"I do mind, goddammit! I can't go around with a misspelled name on my skin. I'm a professor."

Your mom, who had a keen sense of observation, said to me bluntly, "I hate to break the news to you, dear, but you're not a professor anymore. You're a trucker."

And she was right. For the first time I acknowledged I had become a trucker. I couldn't deny that I was no longer a professor. I was a trucker and I was beginning to like it. Thanks to your mom's love for the road.

Later that week, we stopped at the Three T's to fuel up, and while I browsed in the cafeteria store, I tried on a pair of Ray-Ban knock-off sunglasses that I grabbed from a rack. I looked at myself in the display mirror and just had to chuckle. I combed my hair back with a plastic comb that I had begun to carry in my back pocket and tied it in a ponytail with a rubber band. We left the Three T's with our oversized mugs full of fresh coffee, and just as I was reaching sixty miles per hour, I threw my John Lennon glasses out the window. In truth, my prescription was so low that they had really been little more than a statement, a look, the symbol of an era. I didn't need them to see and this was the time to admit it. So I assumed my new persona head-on. My colleagues from the university, my students, even my own mother would never have recognized me, clad in cowboy boots, tight jeans, a yellow *CAT* cap, and a leather belt with a big ol' longhorn buckle.

"Good-bye, El Hippie, hello, Troquero," said your mom when we pulled over at a rest area to stretch our legs. She gave me one long and tight hug. "Now they'll really never find you," she whispered in my ear.

That part I didn't believe. Your mom didn't know how

relentless the Mexican authorities are when they want to be. They will find me, eventually. By hiding on the roads in the United States I'm just stretching my luck. What if they cross over looking for me? What if the American authorities help them track me down? All I hope for is that they find me after I've raised you and you can live on your own. If I get captured before you grow up, you'll go straight to foster care, like your mom. I know she wouldn't want that for you, baby. And even if you went back to Mexico to look for my mother, she'd never believe you're her granddaughter. She must be certain that the soldiers killed me in '68. She may even be dead by now, for all I know, with her diabetes so out of control. She put three spoonfuls of sugar in her coffee. She drank eight Cokes a day. She must have died one limb at a time. All you and I have is each other and we must stay together as long as we can.

 Hey, Chisguete, you got your ears on? Can you read me there?

Who's this?

Cabezón! Going eastbound on I-10 over by the 216 yardstick.

What's up! I thought you were on a mission in Motor City.

That was last week. Picked up a rolling parking lot full of SUVs.

Did you drop it in Shaky-town?

Yeah. And get this. I stopped in Long Beach on the way to check out Speedy González's new rig. It's a beaut!

Wish I were pulling a skateboard like his instead of this drybox.

What do you have to say about this reefer I'm pulling? It's leaking.

I'm sure everything inside is thawing by now. I gotta drop it in Phoenix tomorrow morning and I don't have time to go horizontal.

Just gouge on it. You can get there tonight.

Nah. There are too many Harvey Wallbangers on the road. I better run the double nickel, sixty max. By the way, if you talk to Speedy, make sure to use his new handle.

And what's that?

He wants to go by Melquiades now. Melquiades González.

If he keeps changing his handle on us, we're gonna lose track of him.

You know what his real name is?

No. Nobody knows anything about him except he's got this girl tagging along everywhere he goes.

Is she his girl?

Hard to say. She kinda looks Mexican, too, but then how do you explain those green eyes?

Mexicans come in all shapes, sizes, and colors, you know that.

Yeah, but I bet she's got some gringo blood in her.

The mom must be a gringa.

I wonder if it's Birginia. Have you seen the tattoo on Speedy's chest? It says Birginia, with a *B*.

Who can't spell Virginia? Did he ever go to school at all?

Who knows? It's all mystery around Speedy.

Melquiades.

Yeah, Melquiades.

ibertad's bunk mate, Diva, well-known among the inmates as a dedicated fashion consultant, had learned the Polynesian technique of tattoo art while serving time in Chowchilla for stealing an entire selection of size-eighteen dresses from a garment manufacturer's warehouse in Sacramento. She was especially good at designing tattoos of tombstones, spiderwebs, and clock faces without hands. And now that she was at the Mexicali Penal Institution for Women—this time for stealing a truck full of shoes in Tecate—she began bartering tattoos for a variety of goods and services. Initially she had hoped to get hold of a needle at Embroidery Workshop, but these days security was tight, especially after Warden Guzmán discovered that an inmate was running an underground market of sewing supplies. Drugs? That was expected. But smuggled sewing supplies was an insult to her benevolence. And since she took pride in the fact that the Mexicali Penal Institution for Women was a harmonious place where a minimum of misconduct, contraband, obscenity, theft, and gambling occurred, her discovery angered her even more. To teach the inmates a lesson, she revoked every privilege and concession, even permanent deals. No more food in the cells. No hairdressing services. No tattoos, tats, or ink, or whatever they called the nasty practice. No birthday cakes. No piñatas. No possession of anything that could serve as a weapon, destructive device, or poison. That meant drugs, pens, pencils, matches, scissors, needles (for sewing, needlepoint, or knitting), laminated cards (including prayer cards of all saints and virgins), votive candles and altars, hair dryers, irons and ironing boards, nail polish remover, eyebrow tweezers, utensils, and tools. Only a small cardboard box of personal belongings was allowed under each inmate's bed, and guards constantly checked its contents. Family photos were fine. Grooming sundries, like combs, scrunchies, plastic hair accessories, and toothbrushes (except the battery-operated kind), were acceptable. But all those little things that had once made life at the Mexicali Penal Institution for Women a comfortable place to live were taken away and stored in a secluded vault. It sparked all kinds of protests.

"This is not the States. We're used to our freedom here." Matriarca had screamed all night when Warden Guzmán made her shut down the beach and give up the toaster oven, coffeemaker, TV, and electric fan she had in her private cell. She accused the warden of treating her unfairly and went on a hunger strike that lasted until chipotle tamales were served for dinner two days later.

So Diva had to resort to another method to create Libertad's tattoo. Anticipating a lack of access to the right tools, she had extracted a nail from the heel of her right shoe and hidden it in a crack that ran across the back wall of her cell.

"A butterfly on my upper arm," Libertad requested. "And the name Virginia right below it. Just make sure you spell it with a *V.*"

She tried to remember the description her father had given her of her mother's tattoo. Each wing had orange and black concentric circles, like bull's-eyes asking for trouble. She imagined her mother holding the truck's steering wheel with such a tight grip that it made the butterfly on her biceps come alive and take flight. She drew it with her ballpoint pen on her cot's headboard as she imagined it.

That night, Diva pierced Libertad's arm with the tip of her shoe's nail. She created a line of dots, following the butterfly design drawn on the headboard. It was barely lit by the moonlight but she could still make out the shape. Diva had volunteered to clean the kitchen for the past week, and had scraped the soot from the stove's burners and collected it in a shampoo bottle cap to get the black dye she needed for the outline.

"I'll have to owe you the orange in the circles. I can't get any dyes here. You can always get it finished when you get out. I know a guy in Hollywood who can do it for you, if you're thinking of crossing over."

"That's where my dad got his tattoo."

"What design did he get?"

"It's a long story."

"We're not going anywhere, girl."

Libertad told Diva about her father's tattoo experience. Both women laughed silently so as not to wake up the other inmates. After the moon finally swept by the skylight and left the cell in darkness, and after Diva went back to her bunk to sleep, Libertad began to feel a sharp pain on her arm. It was her mother's tattoo seeping into her own skin. A welcome pain it was, then. She turned on her side to avoid touching her wound with the blanket and closed her eyes, wondering if she should have negotiated with Diva beforehand what she was going to ask for in return.

The next morning, Libertad was called to the library to check out the new shipment of donated books. It had arrived the day before, a gift from a descendant of the man who claimed he had owned the rights to *La Cucaracha* against people's belief that it had always been public domain.

"I bet there's a lot of good stuff," said Nora, who escorted Libertad to the library.

"Nothing I haven't already read, maybe," said Libertad, emphasizing the word *maybe* to diminish her excitement. She didn't want to be disappointed.

She opened the box carefully and started sorting the books. Most of them were in good shape. Many she had read. Novels for the most part, some by American authors, others Latin American. A couple of collections of short stories in English highlighted by some student at Arizona State University. And at the bottom of the box, a few self-help books like *Seven Steps to Successful Retirement, Fine Living: Keeping Your Home Sparkling to the Last Drawer,* and *Feng-Shui for the Western Mind.* Libertad smiled at those titles, wondering if the joker who donated those books to the prison library had also donated other books that by now she had read hundreds of times, like *Flower Arranging: Twelve Months of Color in Your Home, Complete Guide to Five-Star Resorts,* and *Party Planning for Dummies.*

As she cleaned the shelves and cleared space for the

new books, she found one hidden under the how-tos that caught her attention: *Phobias and Delusional Disorders.* She sat on the table and began leafing through it. She checked the table of contents and started reading right on the spot, but Nora was in a hurry and made her stop to put the new books on the shelf.

"But I need to check which book I'm going to read tomorrow," Libertad said.

"I'll let you come in early before Library Club and you can decide then."

"Can I just borrow this one? I promise I won't let anyone see it. I'll return it in the morning."

"Only if you write me that poem you promised."

To earn some income, Libertad had started to write poems for the inmates who wanted to impress their men. She customized the stanzas according to each specific situation. What she got as payment wasn't much, but she figured she was making more money than most poets in the free world.

"You have to get in line. This is a first-come, first-served situation, and I have to write quite a few poems before yours."

"Then you can't borrow the book."

"What's the name of the guy again?"

"Severo, but I may send it to someone else, too."

"That's okay. I'll write it so that you can change the name. It'll be a one-poem-fits-all."

"I need it soon."

"Sure. I'll just put you ahead of the waiting list. Being a guard has got to have certain privileges. By the way, can I borrow your flashlight, too?" Libertad knew she was asking for more than Nora could agree to. "It's just so I can read this book tonight. There's no moon."

"I don't know about that." Nora was fond of Libertad, but not enough to make her bend the new security rules imposed by Warden Guzmán.

"C'mon, Nora. Why do you think we're not allowed to have flashlights?"

"I'm not here to question the rules."

"All right, let's say I intended to dig a tunnel to escape and I needed the flashlight. Don't you think I'd want to borrow it for more than one night?"

"I know how long digging a tunnel would take. I'm not stupid."

"I don't mean to offend you. I'm just trying to reason here."

"Besides, the only direction you can dig from your cell is west. You'd hit the New River bank and drown in the hole."

"So a tunnel is out of the question, right? Maybe you think I need the little piece of glass to slit my veins or to cut someone's throat."

"I hadn't thought of that, but it's quite possible. You people are very creative."

"All right, so keep the glass and let me use the flashlight. It's a harmless favor."

Nora agreed with Libertad against her best interests. She unscrewed the cap, took out the piece of glass, which was really a little circle of plastic, and put it in her shirt pocket.

"It's not that I don't trust you, but just in case."

"Thanks, really."

The night didn't come fast enough for Libertad. Consumed by her eagerness, she had to endure listening to the prison accountant's bad jokes, filing rap sheets, photocopying a hundred receipts for the warden, and then putting in her three hours of duty at the tortilla machine in the kitchen. Finally, when the last bell rang, the inmates were locked up for the night, the lights were out, everyone in her cell was asleep, and silence took over the prison, Libertad settled in her cot and pulled out *Phobias and Delusional Disorders* from under her mattress, along with the flashlight. Tucked under her thin blanket, she read about many and varied phobias. Monophobia: fear of being alone. We don't have to worry about that one here, Libertad thought. Or ablutophobia: fear of washing or bathing. Given the drought conditions, this is a non-issue, she figured. What about arachibutyrophobia? Fear of peanut butter sticking to the roof of the mouth. Now, that was very real and possible, considering that this food item was among the most frequently smuggled into the prison, especially the kind brought in from the United States, the crunchy more than the creamy type. She knew one or two who would kill (again) for one of those precious plastic jars. She particularly liked hippopotomonstrosesquippedaliophobia. How could anyone be afraid of long words? But there it was: fear of long words. She was sure she was on the right track to finding the information she was looking for, so she kept on reading, her book lit only by Nora's flashlight's beam, a beam so faint it could well be a soul estranged from God. When she was about to reach the chapters she wanted so desperately to read, she felt someone approach her cot in the darkness. It was Diva.

"I want your hair, Libertad."

"Are you dreaming?"

"No. In fact, I've been watching you read."

"Does the light bother you?"

"It's okay. I was just thinking, I know you don't have money, but you do have really nice hair and I want it in exchange for the tattoo."

"Why would you want my hair?"

"I want to make a wig out of it. We'll cut it up to the neck."

Libertad had never worn her hair short. She trimmed the ends every now and then to keep it above the waist, but that was it. Even when she was a little girl her father had always let her hair grow long, leaving her curls to the will of the wind.

Tonsurophobia is the fear of haircuts, she had just read. She tried to feel afraid. She imagined big, gleaming scissors coming right up to her defenseless earlobes, slashing closely around the nape of her neck. No. It didn't do it. It was definitely not haircuts that she was afraid of. Was she afraid of anything at all? Fear. She was afraid of fear. Phobophobia.

"You can have my hair."

Getting hold of a pair of scissors was a real challenge. Diva went around the prison for days trying to borrow, barter, or steal some, but no one seemed to have any. The last resort was the warden's office. There would be at least one pair in some drawer. But since Libertad refused to take them out without permission, Diva had to wait for the warden to go to an off-site meeting and sneak into the Administrative Office, dodging a couple of guards along the way, to cut Libertad's hair right at Warden Guzmán's desk.

She clipped away, carefully catching each lock in a paper bag. Libertad pulled a little makeup mirror out of the warden's top drawer and checked her new look. When they were done, she said what everyone says right after a mediocre haircut: "It'll grow back."

The most time-consuming phase of the wig-making technique, according to Diva, who had trained herself back in Guadalajara, was building the wig one hair at a time. Of course, she would have to save the hair for when she had the tools necessary to make the wig: a net, combs, needles, pins, duckbill clips, and tape. Everything that was now forbidden. She figured she'd probably be released before she could buy or steal any of those items, the way things were going at the prison.

But the most immediate problem was only a few feet away, and they only realized it when the door opened abruptly and the warden walked into her office to find them sitting at her desk. A punishment, a tough one, was coming.

by pursuing my mother's dream, my father chose my destiny. Just like some people are born with a rare genetic disorder, I was born a trucker. There was never an option for me, nor did I ever think of the possibility of being anything else. My profession was written all over my DNA, and there was nothing I could do about it.

"**Excuse me, what's** DNA?" asked Culebra, who raised her hand as if she were in school.

"It's kind of like your rap sheet," volunteered Maciza, one hundred percent sure of her answer.

"Yes, in a way," said Libertad, in her new short hairstyle.

Diva was serving ten days in the segregation unit for entering the warden's office without permission and for using her scissors. Libertad served only twenty-four hours before the warden decided to change her punishment. Locking up her secretary obviously worked against her interests. Instead, Libertad had to stay at the office from seven in the morning till nine in the evening for one week. There was enough to do to keep her busy for two shifts. With this schedule, it was difficult for her to write in her journal. By the time she made it to her bed, she was too exhausted to think. Prisons are, by nature, fertile places to reflect, Libertad believed. But unless imprisonment offers plenty of spare time, all those thoughts become a blur, a mist impossible to hold. She cataloged her punishment as a setback in her quest for answers, but still, on Wednesday during her reading, she found a way to face the events she had been so successful at denying.

Every three months, my father would measure my height by making me stand straight up next to the truck. He'd set a book on my head to make a right angle against one or another part of the truck. He kept a log.

"Seven years old: Top of the rim," he'd enter in a small pad. "Her hair has grown down to her elbows."

I knew that log by heart. I still can go back to the very day that my father wrote each entry. On my seventh birthday, he wrote my height and put the pad in the pouch behind his seat. That afternoon we had parked at a rest area to brush our teeth and wash up. The sun was setting. The mountains were purple like in a postcard. The air was orange. The cacti were in full bloom. We were on our way to pick up a backhoe loader in Albuquerque. I pulled my long curls away from my face. It was a game that my hair and the wind had. They played around together. In early summer, it is a welcome feeling.

I walked by one of the enormous tires. It was taller than I was. I looked up at our monster of a truck and wondered if I could reach the window. So I climbed to the step of the cab on the passenger's side and made my way up with a great deal of difficulty, hanging on to one of the rearview mirrors. My father came out from the restroom zipping up his fly when he spotted me dangling from the mirror post.

"Don't move!" he yelled, and ran toward the truck just in time to catch me.

Safe in his arms, I kissed him all over his face and he

couldn't help but hug me, but then, all of a sudden, his hug became a tight grasp and his mood turned angry.

"Don't you do that again! Can't you see that I need to take care of you not just like a daddy, but like a mommy, too? I've got double duty," he hollered.

He stared at me for a good, long minute and then his eyes got watery and sad. Since children do not expect apologies, I looked at him in disbelief. Without saying anything, he lifted me up in the air and shoved me through the open window, went around the truck, and climbed into the driver's seat. I took the keys from his shirt pocket and slid them into the ignition, as had been my job for the past few months. We traveled for a while without talking.

"It's getting dark. We have to shut down for the night," he said.

"Can we stay at the Jolly Trucker?"

"That's in Las Cruces." My father showed me the compass on the dashboard. "We're going in the other direction, see? This little arrow is pointing up."

"Can't we just loop back? Sonia said I could have a whole bag of buñuelos if we stopped by."

"Yes, I know. We need to go through Las Cruces soon. I promise you that when we do, we'll stay with Sonia and you can have your buñuelos."

I didn't know it then, but just naming Sonia made my father's guts rumble. She owned the Jolly Trucker and seemed to like me a lot, perhaps because she liked my father even more. Whenever we went to her truck stop, she'd invite him to sleep over and I'd stay in the guest room. But if they went out to a bar, I'd stay with Doris, one of the waitresses, in a trailer park down the road. Doris went from being single to getting married, having a baby, divorcing her husband, and then becoming a widow when he was hit by a taxi as he left the courthouse. All this in a single year. Going through five stages of womanhood in such a short period of time made her lose her balance altogether, and she was always spilling drinks on the cafeteria patrons and tripping over the linoleum floors where there was no apparent obstacle. But she was Sonia's favorite waitress and confidante, so her job was secure. Besides, she baby-sat me for free.

That night we headed north on Interstate 25 in our truck, a transcontinental ship snorting smoke through the tailpipes, while I answered a Social Studies pop quiz.

"What's the capital of Chile?"

"Santiago."

"Give me three major cities with that name."

"Santiago de Chile, Santiago de Compostela, Santiago de Querétaro."

"That's my girl."

Just before we got to the outskirts of Truth or Consequences, the traffic got slower than usual until we had to stop. There was a roadblock up ahead.

"Oh, my God!" my father mumbled and stepped on the brakes.

He changed lanes quickly and got off the highway, turning in the other direction.

I noticed the flashing lights from the roadblock in the rearview mirror but I couldn't understand why we were turning around.

"No reason. I missed the exit. Go to sleep now, it's getting late."

"Are we going to the Jolly Trucker?"

"No, we're not."

I checked the compass, still not understanding. "But we're going south now."

"I said go to sleep."

He wiped the sweat from his hands on his jeans and kept on driving in silence. I realized that my father suffered from some sort of malady, a constant anxiety that made him jittery and irritable. It took me years to realize what fear could do to a man.

I curled up on the bed and covered myself with the blankets. I knew I should be worried because my father was, but I didn't know the reason why, so I just stayed awake waiting for something awful to happen. To distract myself, I looked around and began making an inventory of our belongings. Our sleeper was small. Everything we owned was there: a few clothes hanging from hooks on the walls, a couple of pairs of shoes, pots and pans, a cooler, a medicine cabinet, a body shop calendar with the photo of a nearly nude woman sitting on the hood of a Ferrari, a portable stove, toilet paper. Stuff of all sorts was stashed away in the minuscule compartments.

While I tried unsuccessfully to fall asleep, my father parked the truck just outside Deming.

"I know what you need," he said.

He snuggled under the blankets and began reading to me from *Little Women*: "'So the spring days came and went, the sky grew clearer, the earth greener, the flowers were up fair and early, and the birds came back in time to say good-bye to Beth, who, like a tired but trustful child, clung to the hands that had led her all her life, as father and mother guided her tenderly through the Valley of Shadow, and gave her up to God.'

"And that's it for tonight. Don't you worry now, everything's all right. We have a long day ahead of us, little woman," he said, putting the book on the shelf above our bed.

He gave me a kiss and turned the light out.

"Daddy?" I said in the dark after a few seconds.

"Yes?"

"Did you guide my mom through the Valley of Shadow before you gave her up to God?"

"Yes."

"Can you show me that valley on the map tomorrow?"

"It's not on the map. It's not on any map. Go to sleep now."

I can't get used to seeing you in your new haircut," said Maciza to Libertad. "Why did you cut it, anyway?"

"I owed Diva a favor and she needed my hair to make a wig."

"Now we're into trading hair. Next thing we know, we're gonna start a fingernail clippings black market. What the hell are you doing in the library? We were looking for you."

Libertad put the book *Phobias and Delusional Disorders* back on the shelf. She had been studying it on and off, as her duties permitted.

"I can't stand needlepoint. How did you manage to ditch the workshop?"

"Nora let me. And you?"

"Nora."

"She likes you."

"She must like you, too. She's not about to let everyone do whatever they want around here."

"She's cutting us a little more slack lately, haven't you noticed?"

"She must be in love."

"Oh, that I'm betting on. By the way, she says she needs her poem now."

"I was planning on giving it to her tonight, after Library Club."

"Is she paying you for it?"

"It's more of a favor. She's letting me do a few things."

"Just because you went to school and all, that's why you can get away with this."

"You got it wrong. I didn't go to school and all."

"Oh, no? So where did you pick up all that shit you know?"

"The road."

the hardest part of my education was having to get rid of my books. But my father made me. As I read those novels in the truck, they became a part of me. Losing them felt like an amputation. Not being able to read a character's words again was like losing a relative to a terminal disease.

Once, when I was around thirteen, we had picked up a track-loader in Jacksonville and were driving down Highway 94 to Valdosta. Our load was heavy and we were missing a couple of reflectors in the front of the cab, so we avoided the big roads, particularly Interstate 10. We had to get to Laredo in two days, and to make things more complicated, a tropical storm would be hitting us in the morning, according to a fellow trucker.

"Expect a window wash in New Orleans," he'd warned.

We were cruising sluggishly along the wetlands, which were covered with cypress and black gum and had water lilies floating at the water's edge. Our truck was a tugboat gliding through a flooded prairie where pitcher plants and bladderworts feasted on deerflies, and then decayed silently at the bottom of the bog.

A line of cars patiently trailed behind us waiting for their chance to pass us. My father drove while I sat in the passenger seat reading the last paragraph from *One Hundred Years of Solitude*.

"'. . . because races condemned to one hundred years of solitude did not have a second opportunity on earth.'"

I closed the book slowly, in ceremony.

"Do you want me to read it again?" I asked him.

"No. Three times is enough. If down the line we want to read it once more, we can always buy it again. They sell it everywhere."

"I wish I could keep this one. I made notes all over it."

"Let's not go through that again, will you?"

"Come on, Dad. Look, I've got the entire family tree on just this page alone."

"There's no more room in the sleeper. Think about it. What should we get rid of instead, the toilet paper?"

My father grabbed a roll of toilet paper stashed under his seat as evidence of our space problem.

"We can always wipe ourselves with the epigraph," I said. "It's not that important. And it's easy to tear off, right at the beginning."

"No, baby. Book paper is rough on your butt. Believe me, I've tried it."

There was no point in insisting. I leafed through the book quickly, kissed the cover, rolled down the window, and tossed it.

I stuck my head out to see where the book had landed and realized that it was only a couple of feet away from an alligator. And I don't mean a tire recap left behind by another truck. This was a real alligator, a fourteen-footer that had probably crept up from the Okefenokee Swamp. He didn't seem to take any interest in my book, its pages shuffling with the wind. He just lay there, quietly observing his surroundings, as if he were deciding whether to venture across the road or not. I had to act quickly.

"Stop!" I said.

"Now what?"

My father pulled over, unaware of my rescue plan, and I

jumped out of the truck holding a pair of shorts as my only defense. I was determined not to let the creature get run over. What if it was an endangered species? I got as close as fear allowed me to and started waving the shorts. The alligator slowly crept away, back toward the marsh. I saw it disappear behind the shrubs and wondered if I had saved its life or if it was road-savvy enough to know not to cross. Maybe it was just sunbathing and I had scared it. I wondered if it was a female and was now heading to its nest to watch its baby alligators hatch.

My father jumped out of the truck and grabbed my wrist tight, dragging me back in. I lost a shoe.

"Are you crazy?" he screamed. "Do you have a death wish?" He was fuming. "That thing can gobble you up in a second. You die and it's over for me, too. Do you understand?"

I did not. Why would it be over for him? My mother had died and there he was. I could die, too, eaten by an alligator, and he would carry on. Or not? I settled in my seat and wiped a tear off my cheek.

I gave my book one last look, quickly contemplating and then discarding the possibility of jumping out of the truck again to pick it up, then looked ahead, to the horizon.

We did make it to Laredo in time, drenched from the storm that hit us around Baton Rouge. We even had time to stop at the Swamp's Park Visitor Center to pick up a brochure about the wildlife there. My father believed that a well-rounded education consisted of satisfying curiosity; he would even make special stops, detours if needed, to seize any learning opportunities. But the incident with the alligator definitely drew a solid line between learning by reference and learning by experience.

Our client waited on the other side of the border with his own truck, and once we transferred the equipment onto his lowboy and collected our payment, we headed north, toward Muskogee, this time to check out a Cat tractor. My father was eager to use his new wear indicator to measure the thickness of dozer blades and bucket edges to determine the remaining wear life on any given piece of equipment. I complained to him about it. The gadget was about the same size as a paperback book, so why couldn't I keep *One Hundred Years of Solitude* in the truck if he kept that machine under his seat?

"You're blessed with an outstanding memory," he'd say. "Use it."

So I did. I read the passages I most enjoyed in a book until they were imprinted and secure in my mental library. That, my father's teachings, and whatever lessons the road had for me, was my school.

Libertad closed the book, thanked her audience, and looked for Maciza in the crowd. She was sitting in the front. When their eyes met, they both made a silent gesture of understanding.

Nora was there, too. She waited for everyone to leave before approaching Libertad.

"Where's my poem?"

Libertad pulled a crumpled page out of her pocket and handed it to Nora. She unfolded it as if she were plucking petals off a daisy and read it all the way through.

Libertad stood watching her quietly. When Nora finished, she sighed.

"He'll never believe I wrote it."

"Of course he will. I've written a lot of poems so far, and from what I hear, all the men have believed they were written by their women."

"I guess that's how men are. Very basic."

"They must figure that we're just sitting around with nothing to do, so we bring out our talents out of boredom."

"Maybe I should give it a shot myself next time."

"I don't see why not. You might have a knack for it and not even know it."

Nora's expression lightened. Her eyes gave off a little sparkle. Nora, the poet. Nora, the ultimate turnkey to every man's heart.

 Can I get a break one-oh?

Who's the breaker out there?

It's Sorry-eyes, you got a copy on me?

Hey, my man, it's Wiseguy from Syracuse.

God almighty! Where have you been?

I passed another stone two weeks ago. It was hellish. Ended up in the hospital.

You okay now?

Oh, yeah. I'm not that easy to get rid of.

So, what's it look like eastbound on I-90?

Better not be running a fat load, 'cause the chicken coops are open and checking ground pressure.

I got a load of garbage going to Dirty Town.

Again? Holy shit! Aren't you getting sick of hauling so many bananas?

It's the third time this week that my dispatcher sends me to New York.

He's gotta love you.

He's an asshole. I'm going solo next year, I swear. I talked to Melquiades González last month and he's doing dandy. Remember Melquiades? Now he's going by Abundio.

Abundio González?

Yeah.

He's still with the girl?

Yeah. He makes thousands hauling them Cats to the Mexican border. He's got his reputation with the heavy-haulers.

That so?

The girl, too. She checks the load's tarp, makes sure it's lashed down right, climbs all over the damn trailer. . . . She's as tough as a fifth wheel. You know Sonia?

Who doesn't?

She's taken it upon herself to watch the girl, but Abundio doesn't let her get too close. He's real fussy about that kid.

What about the Four-Wheeler Wreckage Museum? Does she have new cars in there? She keeps updating it all the time.

You betcha. That's how she makes most of her dough. All the tourists stop to take a look.

I'll be damned. So, hey, listen, I gotta bug out. Can I get a bear report?

You got a clean shot all the way to the state line, Wiseguy. See you around. And save those stones. They'd make a great ring for your better half.

You're funny, I gotta say, you're a real foglifter, Sorry-eyes.

When I met Sonia for the first time I had a nightmare in which she threatened to kill herself by jumping in front of a passing truck. I woke up, scared and disoriented, not knowing for a second where I was, and I heard her in her bedroom talking and giggling with my father. The faint light coming out of the half-open door flooded the hallway, but I didn't dare to knock, let alone go in. This was her house and, as little as I was, I knew it was bad manners to interrupt. I curled up on the floor outside their room waiting for my father to come to bed with me, but eventually I fell asleep.

When I opened my eyes, I found myself back in my bed. My father came in to tell me that Sonia was in the kitchen and that she had made us tomatillo salsa chilaquiles and freshly squeezed orange juice. We could have had breakfast at the Jolly Trucker, just down the street. She owned it. She could have sent us there to spend our money, but she wanted to take care of us. She said we were special. I thought that maybe she wasn't so fearsome after all. But then again, she looked scary to me. She was a thin, pale, and ethereal woman with long strands of gray hair. She dressed in black and never took one step without her cane. She was thirty-eight.

For a while I was hesitant to go near her. I was a little girl with meager affection skills. I wouldn't shake her hand or allow her to hug me. She tried different ways to make me feel comfortable around her. Gifts. Tricks. Bribes.

Nothing worked. Then one day she caught me standing on a stool, trying to reach the buñuelo basket on the top shelf behind the counter, and she knew what to offer me in exchange for my affection. Her famous homemade buñuelos were the first thing that ever motivated me to let anyone other than my father embrace me.

"One buñuelo for one hug."

"Two buñuelos for one hug," I said. I was a tough negotiator for a five-year-old.

"All right. Two. Nice and crispy."

She gave me the buñuelos in a paper napkin and hugged me. I stood stiffly, my eyes wide open, not really knowing what to do while the oil of the sweet fried bread seeped through the napkin and into my hand. I let her wrap her long arms around my skinny body for a few seconds and then managed to wiggle myself away from her embrace.

"You'll be okay," she said. She caressed my hair.

Did she mean I was not okay then, but that I would be in the future? What was wrong with me?

It wasn't easy to understand Sonia, but in time, I learned to like her. She was good to us. She made my father laugh and she didn't even have to tickle him. My father stayed with her and I had my own room. She even bought me a stuffed bear to place on the pillow so it would save my spot while I was on the road. And then there were the buñuelos.

After she built the museum, we just had to stop by every time and see what new additions were on display. She had come up with the concept after almost getting killed by an inexperienced driver, a tourist taking his family to the White Sands Monument. Sonia spent two months in the hospital and that's where she thought of the idea. The first exhibit would include both cars involved in the wreck. Since no one in the other car survived, she had to negotiate with the insurance company to purchase the totaled vehicle. Her own car was hardly recognizable. It had once been a green Corolla and now was a wrinkled metal twist of a thing.

She had renovated the big warehouse she owned behind the truck stop, adjacent to the cafeteria. A huge luminescent sign on top of the door read FOUR-WHEELER WRECKAGE MUSEUM, and below, a slogan: IF ONLY . . .

Thanks to Sonia's hard work and spunk, the museum grew quickly in size and popularity. Soon there were sixty or so exhibits of car wrecks, with the actual crushed vehicles involved in the accidents, photos of the sites, bios of the people who were killed, copies of the newspaper coverage, and a short text explaining how the accidents happened and how they could have been avoided. For the most part, they were cars she bought for next to nothing from insurance companies, as she had done with her own car. And as years went by, she started to accept cars as donations from victims' relatives. They even volunteered early photographs of the deceased, the funerals, and the family members left behind. Some supplied a write-up about the dead people's dreams and goals that had been cut short by the accident.

Visitors pulled over, used the restrooms, paid for their tickets to get in, and rushed to the most popular exhibits.

Some travelers saw the museum as one big cautionary tale. Others were just morbidly attracted to it. They all wanted to see blood, but usually they'd find more. On one car's shattered windshield there was a piece of flesh with hair and all. Another one still had the driver's shoe and bloody sock stuck between its crushed metal. A fireman on the rescue team had sawed off the foot at the ankle; his testimony of how he finally got the dead victim out of the crumpled car was posted on the exhibit wall, right next to his photo. One exhibit displayed the car of a man who had signed the museum's guest book a few months before he was killed in a crash down the road.

After walking along the winding path that took visitors through all the exhibits, they'd stop by the museum gift shop and purchase postcards and souvenirs, like toy cars, fire engines, tow trucks, and ambulances. For a small fee, the cashier would smash the little vehicles with a hammer, creating a mini-wreck before carefully packing the mangled pieces in a shopping bag. On their way out, everyone had to exit through the cafeteria, where they would inevitably stock up on snacks and soda for the road. Sonia had thought of it all.

I grew up into my preteen years knowing little about Sonia's past. She had been married before. Her ex-husband was killed on his way to Cabo San Lucas. He had intended to throw their wedding bands into the ocean on the beach where they had been married as a symbol of their breakup, but as he approached a treacherous section of the Baja highway, he failed to negotiate a sharp curve and ended up in a ravine. Years later, Sonia traveled to the car cemetery where she was told that the car had been towed. She went looking for the rings to fulfill his last wish. And even though she didn't know the car's make, model, year, or color, because her ex-husband had taken a rental on his final mission, and even though there were nearly two hundred totaled cars rusting away in that lot, she found the rings in their original jewelry box—after an excruciating, intensive, methodic three-week search— still lodged in the map pouch of a blue Galaxy.

"But I didn't throw the rings into the ocean. I left them in the car cemetery. They didn't deserve any better," she said.

After that, she moved to Las Cruces, where she suffered her own accident, and opened up the Jolly Trucker—with her husband's life insurance money.

Years later, while I was doing some math problems, my father and Sonia talked at a nearby table.

"There's something important I want to discuss with you, Abundio."

"It's Romeo now."

"Since when?"

"Since three seconds ago," he said as he took her hand and kissed each of her fingers.

"I wish you'd quit doing this. I can't keep up with your handles, Romeo. I've been thinking about our little talk from the other day."

"There you go again."

"I'm serious. You've got to do something about that girl of yours. You have to settle her down. She's already thir-teen."

"So what?"

"She needs to go to a proper school, have friends, a boyfriend."

"What do you mean a boyfriend? She's not ready for that."

"What do you know? She reads college-level books, why can't she have a boyfriend? Have you asked her?"

"No, I haven't and I'm not going to. The next thing you know, she'll be married and gone. I'm not in a hurry for that, Sonia."

"She can stay with me. She can go to school in Las Cruces. You can visit her anytime. How's that for a plan?"

Sonia fixed my father's shirt collar delicately, barely touching his neck, and looked him in the eye. Had I been more experienced then in the art of seduction, I would have guessed that aside from their friendship there had been passionate moments between them, many perhaps, but I was certainly way below grade level in that area of my education. All I knew was that he really liked to sleep over at Sonia's.

"Did you hear what I said, Joaquín?"

"It's Romeo."

"Okay, Romeo. Can't you see the advantages of what I'm suggesting here?"

"I won't let her stay with you, Sonia, and it's not because I don't trust you to raise her. She's not just my daughter. She's my business partner. I need her with me. What makes you think waiting tables is a better life for her?"

My father was beginning to get angry, as he did whenever he felt threatened or scared. I could tell by the way he bit his lips between sentences.

"I just think it's time she had a normal life."

"What are you talking about? We have a normal life. I know my girl better than anybody. We're fine the way we are."

Sonia had said something he could not tolerate and I didn't understand what it was. What was not normal about our life?

"Think about it, Romeo."

"Think about what?" he yelled. "Think about what?"

By then he had lost his composure, feeling cornered, and in a fit of rage shoved every plate and glass and mug off the table. Everything broke and spilled on the floor. My math notebook got ruined with gravy and smeared peas and everyone turned around to see us.

"What are you looking at?" he screamed.

Furious, he threw the chairs toward the customers, who ducked quickly behind the booths. Sonia limped to the counter and hid behind a showcase filled with all kinds of air fresheners and windshield decals. Finally, he slipped on the mashed potatoes and fell on a shard of glass that cut a gash along his left hand.

"Now, if you'll excuse us."

My father got up and grabbed me. I barely had time to pick up my notebook, which was dripping with gravy. Maybe some pages were still salvageable. We left in a hurry. He didn't say anything for about ten miles.

"Are we coming back to the Jolly Trucker?" I asked, afraid of hearing an answer I didn't want to hear.

My father bit his lips.

Clouds. An ill-fitting blanket for the earth. Too high to comfort it. Better off in the form of water. Yet I long to see them traveling slowly above my prison, like an innocent herd of sheep on its way to the slaughterhouse.

How long has it been since I kissed anyone? I'd rather not remember. At night, most of all, I slide my fingers over my skin, first with bashful strokes, then with the full weight of my palms. My arms, my legs, my breasts. Up and around my neck and my shoulders. Out there, someone would want to caress me. But only I know it and it is my punishment.

ibertad sat across the warden's desk, enjoying the cool air that blew out of the new air-conditioning unit installed in the window. She watched her boss pace back and forth across her office, going through her mental list of chores.

"I also want you to organize the accounting files. They're a mess and we're being audited next month. Thank God the auditor is my husband's cousin."

Libertad nodded and wrote her assignment on a pad. She was comfortable working for the warden even without making any money. Matriarca had been asking her to return. The temp maid was too lazy and the ceiling in her room was beginning to fill with spiderwebs. Her blouses were so wrinkled she wouldn't wear them. Her toilet had developed a revolting dark ring along the edge of the water. She missed the way Libertad fluffed her pillows and folded out her bed covers in a triangle just like a five-star hotel chambermaid would. But in spite of Matriarca's pleas, Libertad had honored the deal with the warden and went to work every day at the Administrative Office. Besides, there were certain advantages. She had access to paper. Pens. Pencils. Erasers. For free, if no one missed them. Life was good.

"See you tomorrow."

"Yes, ma'am."

Libertad headed toward the door.

"Wait."

"Yes?"

"Those books you're reading to the other girls at the

library, they're not really, I mean, what you're really doing is, well, you know."

"Yes?"

The warden checked behind the door to see if anyone was listening. She didn't want the truth about Libertad's literary license to leak.

"They're good. They're good stories."

"Thank you."

Libertad gave Warden Guzmán an I-know-you-know look. Oftentimes she had seen the warden outside the library listening to her read. She'd open the door slightly to catch the story without being noticed.

"Tomorrow's Wednesday. Would you like to join us?"

"Well, I don't know. Library Club is an inmate activity. I don't want to create any disruption with my presence." She said this in a school principal kind of way.

"Hey, why not give it a try?"

Libertad knew that Warden Guzmán couldn't resist the offer, and the next afternoon, she was pleased to see her come in with the inmates and sit in the front row, between Maciza and Culebra, who had been previously warned by Libertad and knew to behave like straight-A students.

Libertad opened *The Old Man and the Sea* to page 46.

I must have been fourteen when I finally got my first bras. We were driving in heavy rain. A once-powerful Category 4 hurricane named Florencia had come ashore the day before on the Texas Gulf Coast, but by that morning it had weakened over land as it swerved west, and was downgraded to a tropical storm. Another trucker had warned us about a flash-flood watch that had been in effect for parts of the county. But we kept on going. We were hauling a knuckleboom loader from Corpus Christi to McAllen. Our client waited for us on the Reynosa border and we had to be there on time to transfer the machinery onto his rig or we'd have to pay late-delivery penalties. We drove south on Highway 281, and as we passed Falfurrias, with its water tower bearing a rusty billboard advertising the best butter in the world, my father said, "This town's future is long gone."

Then, a few miles down the road, we spotted a stalled car not quite on the shoulder. Despite the fact that we were behind schedule and that my father believed all stranded motorists were plainclothes cops looking for him to avenge the captain's death, I pleaded with him to stop and help out. It was the right thing to do, and I figured it was a good and safe opportunity to push my father into facing his fear. He gritted his teeth but managed to pull over in front of the car, and we jumped out of our truck without minding the rain.

A man got out of the car. He tried to protect himself from getting wet with a newspaper, but it was no use. He was soaked already.

"It must be the battery."

"Do you have emergency lights?" asked my father.

"No."

"How about a red rag? You need some sort of caution signal or you're gonna get hit."

A station wagon filled with children sped by, almost scraping the stalled car and honking its horn.

"Damn four-wheelers!" said my father, insulted at the lack of experience some occasional drivers had, and gave the disappearing car his middle finger.

"Let me get something red," said the man.

We followed him to the trunk of his car. It was filled with hundreds of bras in all colors, shapes, and sizes, neatly spread out in a clever pop-out display operated by some sort of springs that made it jump out at us in the middle of the pouring rain.

I couldn't help but stare at all that wonderful merchandise. For months I'd had a dream in which I tried on a green bra in front of a mirror. I cupped my hands and placed them carefully over my breasts as if sizing them, and suddenly, when I looked at my reflection again, my face had become my mother's.

My father pushed me aside in the rain and quickly grabbed a size-44DDD red nursing bra with bustier, tied it to a stick that he picked up from the side of the road, and ordered me to caution the passing traffic.

For a while I stood in the rain waving the bra like a flag. A couple of cars skidded on the soaked pavement. Others tooted their horns. Someone even had time to roll down his window and curse at us. My father ran back to the truck to get some jumper cables and a battery. He worked under the hood while the bra salesman tried to start his car. Finally, we heard the engine running. My father shut the hood. I returned the stick with the bra. The car was fixed.

"How can I pay you?" asked the salesman.

"It's all right. No big deal," said my father.

"At least let me sell you some bras at half-price."

"What the hell do I want bras for?"

The salesman turned his eyes in the direction of my growing breasts, my nipples sticking to my drenched T-shirt.

"What are you staring at?" my father said to the salesman, furious.

"I think I have her size."

The salesman hastily pulled out six size-34C bras, each a different color, put them in a plastic bag, and gave them to me.

"Hey, no charge, sweetie," he said to me.

"Thanks."

"You two have a nice day."

The man left in a hurry. My father and I stood in the rain for a while. All I wanted was to open the bag and touch those bras. I wanted to feel the fabric, run my fingers across the curve that the seams made around the cups. I was becoming a woman and a stranger had acknowledged it. My father looked at me, confused, angry.

"Don't even think about wearing those things until you grow up," he said.

Weeds started to swallow up the beach. The hair salon was now filled with storage boxes overflowing with pipes and faucets from the director of the Corrections Department's plumbing business. Desserts were no longer served after dinner. Because of the warden's prohibitions, the inmates' spirits were lower than the National Reserve.

Vedette, the mistress of a notorious drug lord and a close friend of Diva's, contacted her man's associates—the few who were still at large—and broached the subject of kidnapping Warden Guzmán's husband. They'd ask as ransom for things to return to the way they were before the warden uncovered the black market in sewing supplies.

"Tit for tat," said Vedette, expressing her uncompromising sense of justice.

Even the members of the White-Collar Clan, who normally stayed away from the drug lords' women, supported the plan. The decisions had all been made. Everything was set up. Warden Guzmán's husband would be ambushed as he left a seafood restaurant where he had dined every Tuesday night for the past eighteen years with his friends from the Dominoes Club. He would be taken to an old warehouse outside Tijuana that was owned by the governor. No one would look there.

But the kidnapping was never carried out. As the drug lord's henchmen waited outside, Warden Guzmán's husband choked on a shrimp. He collapsed on the floor, gasping for air and then falling unconscious. His friends tried

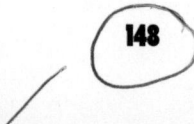

to help him, everyone yelling and giving different instructions at the same time. They pushed down with their fingers and pulled with a fork. After taking turns breaking three of his ribs, they realized that none of them knew how to do the Heimlich maneuver.

The funeral was a success. Everyone was there. Most newspapers published the obituary in bold letters and with a double border. The warden looked better than ever in a sleek black silk suit. She wore the largest and darkest sunglasses she could find to cover her teary eyes, as was customary among new widows.

She said her good-byes to her husband, speaking softly between her teeth so no one at the mortuary could hear her.

"I had hoped you would die a more fitting death, a death more in tune with my career, a scandal, or a murder even. It would have been far more thrilling if you had been kidnapped and killed instead," she said, not knowing that that would have been his end, had he not met the shrimp first. "But this fatal encounter was your destiny, honey, and I couldn't do anything about it. Wait for me up there."

The warden was a very influential figure in her field, and under such tragic circumstances anyone would have done anything to alleviate her pain. So the coroner himself fulfilled her request. He cleared the shrimp stuck in the corpse's throat and gave it to the warden in a baby-food jar filled with formaldehyde. She pasted a strip of masking tape around the jar, inscribing the word *Murderer* on it with a black marker. After the funeral, she had the superintendent open up a hole in the furthermost wall of the prison, place the shrimp inside, and seal it up with a patch of cement.

The news of Warden Guzmán's husband's passing was as unwelcome in the Mexicali Penal Institution for Women as a root canal. Now they had to find another way to coerce the warden to ease up. But as the weeks went by, it became clear to the inmates that his death had worked to their advantage. Libertad was the first one to realize it as soon as the warden came back from her leave. She had screamed at her lawyer for fifteen minutes on the phone right in front of Libertad.

"What do you mean he left everything to her? He can't do that. I'm the wife! I don't care if she was with him for seventeen years, she's still nothing but a mistress!"

Because her husband had left nothing to her, the warden would now be forced to rely on her salary, and whatever money she could make in the prison, to survive.

"Not a word of this," she said to Libertad as she hung up the phone.

"No, ma'am," said Libertad.

And she kept her word. She didn't need to explain to anyone why the warden had suddenly changed her mind about how she ran the economy.

The first thing she did was ask the superintendent to open up the hole in the furthermost wall of the prison. She pulled out the baby-food jar with the shrimp inside and replaced the masking tape. The new strip read: *Hero.* Then she buried the jar in the middle of the beach.

Within weeks, Warden Guzmán had returned all privileges to the members of the White-Collar Clan. The hair salon, the café, the clothing store, all were open for business. Inmates began trading favors and concessions regularly with guards and officials, as they had in the past.

"The warden is not Mother Teresa," said Matriarca. "She just needs money, and we can provide that."

Whatever the reason, Matriarca was so pleased with the warden's new attitude that she came up with a promotion for the beach. She offered free admission on the first day if everyone helped to clean up the weeds and the trash. She was sure that by giving a little taste of her exclusive hangout to inmates who otherwise couldn't have afforded to visit it, she'd increase her regular traffic. Anyone could come up with the nominal entry fee if they were motivated enough.

Of course, the beach was packed on Grand Reopening Day. The Avon lady had placed a huge order for suntan lotion, but it would take two weeks to arrive, so many inmates suffered severe sunburn. Even the following Wednesday at Library Club, Libertad could smell the vinegar that the women had used to soothe their burns. That particular smell became a symbol of their triumph. Even those who had used it sparingly on their salad began smothering the wilted lettuce with it. No more austerity. No more restrictions. Everything was negotiable again.

The warden herself got to work thinking up new ideas to generate extra income, like rummage sales, raffles, Christmas bazaars, and contests. She realized that by punishing the inmates, she had punished herself.

It was around this time of recovery that a cargo boat full of Vietnamese refugees landed on the Ensenada shores. The starving travelers had hoped to make it to California, but they misread the stars, and as soon as they set foot on Mexican territory, the Immigration authorities arrested them.

The men ended up in the Tijuana prison. The women, three of them, were quickly locked up in the Mexicali Penal Institution for Women. Hong, Nga, and Tran, all by the last name of Nguyen. No relation. The only one who could speak a language other than Vietnamese was Nga. She had picked up very limited English the last time she'd made it into the United States, where she completed a six-hundred-hour manicure course at a beauty school in San Gabriel, California, before getting deported back to her country.

Libertad learned all this during the first week of Nga's arrival, as she was one of the few who could understand the woman's broken English.

"Maybe we should help her start a nail salon," Libertad suggested to Warden Guzmán. "There's that little room next to the kitchen where the big freezer used to be."

"You took the words out of my mouth, Libertad," said the warden, excited about the idea.

Within weeks, Nga was doing manicures, pedicures, acrylic tips, and fills. She turned out to be an expert in treating ingrown toenails and even proved successful at curing nasty cases of fungal infection with tea tree oil, putting a stop to the persistent epidemic that had been passed around in the showers for years. The demand for her services was such that inmates and guards had to make appointments at least two weeks in advance. Because she didn't speak any Spanish, she devised a menu-like chart with illustrations of the different nail styles and services for the inmates to choose from.

Tran had been a basket weaver in Vietnam and applied her skills to design intricate hairdos made of hundreds of tiny braids. She immediately joined the other hairdressers at the salon and began training a couple of new girls. Diva just had to have the look that Tran had created, and, being the fashion leader she was, many followed. Hong worked with Nga at the nail salon massaging customers' tired feet and knotty shoulders while they got their nails done. Soon she was doing manicures herself. They named the little room next to the kitchen Nguyen Salon & Spa.

Libertad befriended Nga after she did quite a nice French manicure for her with a little glittery speck right at the center of each nail. Eventually they sat together in the cafeteria every day and smiled at each other, sharing the few English words that Nga could speak. Soon they managed to ignore the cumbersome language barrier and became comfortable just being together in silence.

One Sunday morning, Libertad invited Nga to the beach, and as they lay on their lounge chairs, Nga took Libertad's hand and placed it on her belly. Libertad left it there for a few seconds until she felt a little kick. Then another one. Nga smiled at Libertad and immediately burst into tears.

"My baby, Mexican," she whimpered. "Not American baby."

"Destiny has a sneaky way of shortchanging us," said Libertad, but Nga did not understand.

She had made the journey all the way from Vietnam,

stopping to do hard labor in a sweatshop in the Philippines and then traveling by cargo boat, suffering from hunger, thirst, inhumane sleeping conditions, and, to top it off, morning sickness, so that her baby would be born an American citizen. After all her sacrifice, her baby would be born in another Third World country. For that, she could have stayed home.

I've abandoned the clouds. For now. I know I will come back to them. We are like each other. When free, they roll above it all and travel on, always in search of the most distant sky. When imprisoned in valleys, crowded against sierras, they merge with their cloud friends and become one. Then they cry themselves to death.

All this that envelops me: a permanent stone wall, sizzling cement ground, sky devoid of clouds, a slice of the moon, and women covered in a shield of denial. It is my prison. How many years will it take me to rot?

after the rain stopped, my father and I headed to the nearest truck dealership. I held tightly on to my bag full of bras, afraid that my father would grab it and throw it out the window.

"We can't sleep together anymore," he said.

The yard was huge, with all kinds of tractors neatly parked in rows. We walked around, my sneakers melting on the cracked, scorching pavement, until we spotted a blue Kenworth W900L long-nosed truck with a Studio AeroCab sleeper featuring a customized partition to form two mini-rooms. It was dazzling.

The truck dealer, an obese man wearing a suit and a Stetson hat in unforgiving 108-degree weather could not fit through the truck's door. After struggling for a while, he gave up and let us check it out on our own as he yelled his sales pitch from the middle of the yard.

"It's a super powertrain. Hauls everything. No effort at all! You drive this and you own the landscape."

"What features does it have?" asked my father from inside.

"This here is the granddaddy of all trucks, sir. King of the road! Stainless-steel door kick-panels, chrome bezels for instrumentation, hundred-and-fifty-gallon fuel tanks. Who needs the space shuttle?"

"And the sleeper?"

"Oh, the sleeper, the sleeper! You'll really appreciate the privacy of the customized double sleeper with a partition for you and the little lady. Vista windows, seven-foot-high roofline, snap-on curtains, wall-to-wall carpeting, tuck-away desk, a large-capacity fridge, storage space everywhere, pre-wired outlets for a TV, blender, coffeepot. Just check out the interior. There's nothing else like it on the market."

My father looked out the window. "How soon can you do the lettering on the doors?"

I guess the truck dealer took this question as a yes-we'll-take-it because he began jumping up and down in excitement, like a little child who is promised a trip to the ice cream parlor.

"Two days if you provide the logo." Then he said to himself, but we both heard him, "Bingo!"

After a couple of days, we returned to the dealership to pick up our new truck. I wore a green bra under my shirt. There was a gleaming airbrushed sign on the door: GONZÁLEZ & DAUGHTER TRUCKING CO. It sparkled in the sunlight. I spelled out each letter softly, so no one could hear me. I was the daughter. The one with no name. In those words lay my very identity. Was I anything without my father? No, I was not. Could a company be named Daughter Trucking Co.? No, it could not. Could I live any other life? To answer this last question, I thought about these characters in the books I'd read who lived out exciting lives. I could become any of them if I wanted. I could pick up a book right there and begin reading. But I had work to do.

I walked around the truck checking for dents or dings. I scrutinized the fifth wheel, making sure the kingpin wasn't worn or bent. I climbed on the hood and ran my fingers through the wiper blades, looking for any dead rubber. I inspected the condition of the brake drums and hoses. I checked slack adjusters, torque rod arms, and brushings. I tested every single light and reflector. Everything was clean, operating, and in the proper color. As soon as I'd given the entire truck the once-over, I realized I was becoming a safety freak. A perfectionist. But it didn't bother me at all. In fact, even though I still could not drive, I had to be obsessed with safety. It was survival.

I went in the cab and sat on my bed. This tiny space would be my new house. Like a dog peeing on the shrub outside his master's house, I pulled a black marker from my pocket and wrote the words *Mudflap Girl* in small handwriting right on the headboard. From that day on, that would be my handle, my pron, my name. And so I marked my territory with my new identity, just as my father had marked the rest of the truck with his philosophy. He had ordered an inscription to be painted on the back of our trailer: *Necessity is a better teacher than university.*

Once we approved the lettering and the overall condition of the truck, we went into the office to settle the purchase. My father liked to pay cash, like a drug dealer who doesn't want to leave a paper trail. No one ever asked him any questions. People just took the money. He didn't own a checkbook for fear of being tracked down by the Mexican authorities, so we kept our money in holes that we dug near fences, in caves, or in fields all over the country. Whenever we needed it, we'd just go back and dig it up. He opened up a shopping bag and took out several piles of money, which he placed on the desk. After the truck dealer shook my father's hand, we left the dealership in our brand-new home.

This marked the end of my childhood. I no longer slept curled up by my father, like I had for fourteen years. We both knew we would miss each other's warmth at night, but it was time to have separate beds.

It took me almost a year to get used to sleeping alone, although I knew that my father was just a few inches away on the other side of the partition. In fact, he was so close that I could still hear him and imagine what he was doing.

One night, I was under the sheets trying to read *The Fall of the House of Usher,* but the sleeper was shaking so much that I couldn't focus. I read the same paragraph three times.

> . . . I still retained sufficient presence of mind to avoid exciting, by any observation, the sensitive nervousness of my companion. I was by no means certain that he had noticed the sounds in question . . . the sounds in question . . .

The sounds in question were voices, moaning, and laughter that came from the other side of the thin wall. My father was in his side of the sleeper with a woman by the name of Linda.

"C'mon! C'mon! Give it to me!" I heard him say.

"No. Not yet. I want more," she mumbled.

"Stop! Now, that's enough. It's my turn!"

The truck shook and rocked until I finally fell asleep.

In my dream I was seven years old. I swayed on a faded red swing in the middle of a schoolyard filled with children. They all wore the same uniform, except me. The children stretched their arms to touch me, but missed me every time. Then a boy tried to get me off the swing.

"C'mon! C'mon! Give it to me!" he yelled.

"No. Not yet. I want more."

"Stop! Now, that's enough. It's my turn!"

Then a girl pushed him aside and tried to reach me.

"Let's go to your house," she said.

Another girl stretched her arms to touch me but couldn't reach me.

"I want to see your house. What's your playroom like?"

I couldn't speak. My eyes welled up.

I woke up from my dream with the first rays of sunlight on my face. The truck was still. I looked out the window and saw a big sign by the side of the road, TRUTH OR CONSEQUENCES TRUCK STOP, with a slogan underneath: *That's the Name of the Game.* And right outside the truck, I saw my father kissing Linda.

"With my new hair color, don't you get the feeling you're kissing another woman?" she asked him.

"Yes, but I just grab your ass and I remember where I am," said my father, pinching her behind.

"Am I gonna see you again?"

"Next time I have to pick up equipment in your neck of the woods, I'll look you up. I promise, Linda, I really promise."

"Yeah. You do just that, muffin."

Linda gave my father another kiss, a skeptical one, then got in her car and drove away.

On my wall, behind a body shop calendar featuring a picture of a shiny Porsche with a sexy babe sitting on its hood, I kept count of the women my father had begun sleeping with since we got separate rooms. With a marker, I added one more name and town to the long list: *Linda from Truth or Consequences.*

This habit of my father's had turned into a relentless search for my mother in every woman he met. I was too young then to realize this, but now I understand how much he missed her. Or was it Sonia he missed?

After we left Linda, we headed north. We were on our way to pick up a bulldozer in Wichita Falls. My father drove. I sat in the passenger seat, clearing the dashboard of junk food, candy wrappers, Coke cans, a map, sunglasses. Trash has that habit of multiplying when no one's watching. We were silent for a while. North Central Texas inspires silence sometimes, even more when crossing the Callahan Divide, over by Abilene. Just watching the endless prairie grass, the brushland, and those wooded stream valleys of mesquite, juniper, and cedar put me in a trance-like state. I had seen an armadillo cross the road in front of us on a previous trip. We almost squashed it. I hoped to see one again, so I pressed my face against the window, every so often wiping off the vapor of my breath. I spotted a couple of cottontail rabbits, a raccoon, and a roadrunner.

Everything was in place and the universe throbbed around us in total synchrony, until it occurred to me to ask what I thought was an innocent question.

"Dad?"

"Huh?"

"When am I going to start sleeping with men I meet on the road?"

My father slammed on the brakes. The truck skidded,

the tires screeched, until we came to a sudden halt in the middle of the highway. A car had to make a dangerous maneuver to avoid hitting us.

"What are you? A whore? Have I brought you up wrong? Am I an idiot?" My father was furious.

I thought of all those ladies working the lots. I knew they were sleeping with truckers, my own father being one of them. I'd seen them come out of a black Peterbilt and hop on a gray Freightliner while other trucks lined up behind them. I'd seen them come back into the diners, their hair a mess and their lipstick smeared, and report to their lot daddy.

"Women don't go around sleeping with men they meet on the road. Only men do that!" he yelled.

"So, if only men sleep around, who do they sleep with, cows?"

My question must have left him speechless, because all he thought of was slapping me across the face.

"You better show some respect or I'll ground you!"

I felt the heat of the impact over my entire cheek. But what startled me most was my reaction.

"So, what else is new? I've been grounded in this sleeper all my life."

"Get out!" he said.

I got out of the truck and walked toward a field. The universe had collapsed in two minutes flat.

knew it! He was gonna end up slapping her sooner or later.

I'd say he took too long. Real dads are not like that. I was still in diapers when my dad started educating me.

Well, something must have gone wrong there, with your education, I'm trying to say.

What are you talking about? I know what's right and what's wrong. The fact that I'm locked up here doesn't mean I don't have my own judgment.

You just don't use it sometimes, right?

Well, yeah. You should know about that.

I'm innocent.

Yeah, yeah. That's what we all say.

at the end of each tier in each cellblock was a tiled room with ten showers. Every morning before breakfast the inmates stood in line with their towel and soap and took a three-minute shower, unless they paid extra to the guard on duty. Then they could extend their time for up to six minutes, if they were lucky. In the past, some well-off inmates had been able to negotiate the right to evening showers, but because of the permanent drought conditions in the state, and the hazardous level of pollution in the water from the New River, not even a hefty amount of money could buy that benefit anymore. The water supply was shut down by the Utilities Department at five in the afternoon and turned on again at six in the morning, causing a daily dishwashing backlog in the kitchen and a septic chaos, with overflowing toilets inundating the cells with foul smells all night.

Having used nothing but public restrooms all her life, Libertad didn't complain about the conditions. She knew how to maximize the available resources. She was a savvy Platinum Frequent User of public showers. But there were no points to accumulate. How many gallons of water had she seen go down drains? Still, no one ever rewarded her with a free bath until she became incarcerated.

When she heard about the rampant fungal infections in her first few days at the Mexicali Penal Institution for Women, she knew immediately which precautions to take. So she acquired a pair of cheap rubber flip-flops from the Avon lady in exchange for a month's worth of dessert.

At least in prison she didn't need coins. Water was paid for by the taxpayers, and for that she was thankful.

That day, as Libertad stood in line waiting for her turn and thinking about how lucky they all were for having her Vietnamese friend stop the fungal infections in the showers, a woman known as Cleta started talking to her. This was not common. Normally at that hour of the morning most inmates seemed to have been robbed of their ability to speak. And Cleta belonged to a group who mostly kept to themselves. For that reason it was twice as odd.

"Nice tattoo."

"Thanks," said Libertad.

"What's with Virginia?"

"Nothing."

Libertad wasn't in the mood to talk. She wasn't in the mood to be awake. She had spent two hours writing in her journal, and then Culebra had farted all night, as she always did when they had black-bean soup for dinner, and kept Libertad tossing and turning for hours.

"Is she gone?"

"Yes. Gone forever."

"Can I borrow your soap when you're done?"

"Sure."

Libertad showered in exactly three minutes and gave Cleta her bar of soap.

"You don't have to wait for me. I'll bring it over later. I know where your cell is."

Libertad left, thinking that maybe she was too trusting, too gullible. She figured she'd have to buy another bar of soap, but this time she'd buy a laundry bar. She'd heard it was gentler on hair and scalp.

But her soap was returned that same evening. Before all the cells were locked for the night, Cleta came by and gave Libertad not just her soap, but also a deck of cards. Worn and over-handled, but still a complete set.

"Let's play sometime," said Cleta.

"Maybe on Friday."

You, with your fluff and your whiteness, full of nothing, lonely cloud passing through, all promise, will you deliver some rain today? We're thirsty down here.

My mother is an ice cube in the desert, a fountain pen with dried ink, a blur of dust in a rearview mirror. She is a single pebble of gravel projected into a fender. How can I remember someone I've only known through my father's words? Virginia. She is a name tattooed on my skin. She is history. I am she.

had been crying for a while, leaning against a fence by the side of the road. My father must have regretted his outburst because he walked over to me and sat by my side. He had brought a box of Kleenex and handed me a tissue to dry my tears.

"Let's go."

I got up reluctantly.

A flock of bikers on Harley-Davidsons zoomed by the truck, probably on their way to the annual meetup in Laughlin. I climbed into the cab.

It was during those days after the fight when I began writing poems to my dead mother. Since I never knew her, I made her up. I spent the whole year riding next to my father, scribbling pages with definitions of my mother. Then I'd tear out the pages filled with poems and throw them out the window. Writing was the only way I could leave tracks on the pavement. As the truck sped down the highway, I'd watch the crumpled pieces of paper rolling behind us, pulled along by the vacuum and ending their days on the shoulder, like roadkill. By no means did I consider this to be littering. Tossing these poems was a way to claim the space where they landed as mine. This rite, this secret ceremony I conducted every day, gave me a sense of place. The road was my home and it was eighty feet wide and six-point-four million miles long and had no furniture. To make it livable, I memorized the poems and remembered each and every spot where I threw them, so when we drove by again, I could recite the words by heart.

"Wait till my mother dies," said Maciza to Diva, sitting next to her at the library. "I'm going to write her a poem that will have her digging deeper in her fucking grave."

"Shut up!" Diva sank her elbow in Maciza's ribs.

Libertad stopped her reading, as she did every time someone talked or interrupted.

"If you have something to say to your mother, why don't you say it to her while she's alive?" said Libertad, thinking, all at once, of about one hundred things she would have liked to tell her own mother.

"You're right, so she can resent it forever. I like that better."

Libertad wanted to get up and walk off with Maciza, sit on a lounge chair at the beach and talk at length about her mother. She thought she could help ease Maciza's anger if she listened. But right now she had an audience in front of her and the show had to go on.

My father drove until I was fifteen. Then I took over the steering wheel. But first we had to get me a driver's license. We went to see Cholito in Santa Ana, but he did not feel too comfortable with the order.

"Are you sure you want your girl here driving that big old rig?"

"What's wrong with that?"

"I'm just wondering."

"Well, don't wonder. Just do what you're good at."

We came back the following day and picked up my brand-new California commercial driver's license. And from then on I was officially twenty-one years old.

With my new age in place and all my documentation in order, my father took me to back roads where I could learn to drive our rig. The Mojave Desert had a few of those roads. No four-wheelers. No hills. No cops.

The first time I sat behind the wheel and put the engine in gear, the very first moment when the tires began to turn under my feet at my command, I completely understood why so many people around the country chose to endure icy roads, lousy coffee, highway patrol cruelty, the constant sound of a roaring engine, day-long morning breath, New York City parking, chronic hemorrhoids, Christmas travelers, near-to-the-ground pay, kidney problems, nasty fleet managers, never-ending roadwork, impossible delivery dates, summer tourists, and the middle-of-nowhereness of it all. I also understood why the rest of the world had the romantic idea that trucking was all about travel, adventure, camaraderie, power, and bravado. Both were true. Trucking was all of that. That very day, in the middle of the desert, as my hands gripped the steering wheel and I pulled a sixty-ton load for the first time, I took on a new identity. I wasn't a copilot anymore. I wasn't a passenger in someone else's life. I was in charge. Or so I thought.

 Hey, Speedo Guido. What kind of radio are you on?

Oh, it's an all mouth, no ears, Sweet & Low. I'm driving the anteater today.

Who's got the diesel car?

Say what?

The diesel car!

Ten-four. I couldn't hear you. This is a mud duck of a signal I'm get-ting. My boss man took the diesel car. This piece of shit doesn't even have a bird dog. What's out there?

If you're going eastbound on I-80, check for a bear on the intersec-tion with I-39. He's shooting in the back. Other than that, you got a clear shot all the way to Chicago, copy.

Preeshaydit, Speedo. Hey, by the way, guess who I ran into yester-day at the Flying J? Inocencio González.

The one with the girl?

She's driving now.

Get the fuck out of here! She's a kid!

You haven't seen her lately? I'd trade my better half for her any minute. That girl's got tits, I'm telling ya.

That doesn't mean she can drive.

Hey, she's driving A-OK. She's gonna be a fine long-hauler, if you ask me. She passed me just outside Davenport last night and she was hammered down, man.

I don't care what you say, Sweet & Low, that girl's too young to be driving an eighteen-wheeler.

Forty-two, Speedo, I agree, but you gotta see her to believe it. That girl's got it in her blood.

So, are you gonna jump on her?

Hell, no! I was just kidding. Inocencio won't let you get anywhere near her.

Those tits may be worth the beating.

What do you mean the beating? I can take González anytime.

I didn't mean his beating. I meant your better half's.

friday's card game with Cleta was becoming a ritual. Anything done twice was a tradition and there were many, diverse and honored at the prison. Libertad had learned poker, twenty-one, and other games at truck stops. They'd always come in handy in January and February. She remembered once when she and her father had to go from Fargo to Saint Cloud, and I-94 was closed up. It was below freezing outside, the snowstorm was hitting hard, and they were too tired to chain up. She'd lost her scarf back in Spokane two weeks before and hadn't replaced it. With no books to read, the cards were as welcome as sunshine.

Now they'd made her a new friend. She and Cleta played until lockdown on Fridays, and then on Saturday Cleta would look for Libertad to comment on the previous night. Sometimes she'd find her at odd hours and just sit with her. At breakfast she'd give Libertad her sweet roll.

"I don't like her," said Maciza.

"She's just trying to be nice," said Libertad.

"Too nice."

Libertad dismissed Maciza's comments as a sign of jealousy. But what did either of them know about friendship, anyway? Maybe Cleta just admired Libertad. She spent an hour once discussing what she'd read at Library Club with her, complimenting her on her storytelling ability and her reading skills. Another time she volunteered to help Libertad dust the bookshelves in the library. Or maybe she just wanted something from her. What could it possibly be? A poem?

"Write me a poem," Cleta asked the next Friday.

"You know I charge for those."

"I have money."

"All right. To whom?"

"To me." Cleta took Libertad's hand and said, "Think about me when you write it."

Libertad let go of Cleta's hand and started walking away.

"I can't do that."

"But you said it was over with Virginia."

That's when it all fell into place.

"Virginia was my mother. She's dead. This tattoo is a tribute to her. I'm sorry if I misled you."

Cleta didn't respond. She stood in the hallway of the second tier and watched Libertad leave.

"I'm really sorry," said Libertad as she headed for the stairs. "I'm not your girl. I'm not anyone's girl."

Cleta looked down to the first tier and waited for Libertad to walk right below her so she could send her a fat, gooey, drippy spitball. She aimed it at Libertad's head, but the phlegm fell on her shoulder and slid down her breast.

Libertad looked up.

"Fuck you," said Cleta.

Fridays went by, several of them, and Cleta seemed to have disappeared. Before the whole misunderstanding happened, before the card games, Libertad would bump into her now and then at the beach, or at someone's birthday party. Now she had stopped going to Library Club and didn't eat in the cafeteria. Libertad had no intention of sharing the incident with Maciza, or anyone else, but Maciza had accumulated much more street smarts than Libertad and had figured it out on her own.

"I told you," said Maciza.

"You weren't specific. It's not fair."

"You could have guessed what she was up to that first time, in the showers. Why do you think she hangs out with all those tortillas?"

"It was my fault. I deceived her, but it wasn't on purpose. I guess I'm just too naïve."

"You better believe it."

That night, a moonless night, Libertad put her journal aside and thought about her lack of malice and about Cleta's spit. Then she thought about her mother. She was angry with her for dying. She was angry with her father, too, for failing to teach her the unwritten codes of friendship among women. Had it been a conscious decision? Or had he just not been equipped with that kind of knowledge? Was any man? There were plenty of women on the road, but it seemed to Libertad that she knew the characters in the books she read far better. Women hating one another, conspiring against one another in intricate plots and subplots, betraying those who trusted them the most, loving one another with the ardor of mythical goddesses.

But was it any different with the women on the road? The very real lot lizards loved and hated one another, too.

How many times did Libertad see them in the restrooms applying makeup to cover up scratches and bruises on their faces? She knew those injuries weren't always inflicted by their clients. Lot lizards were known to kill one another for the attention of their pimps and gang up against their competitors at the next truck stop. What about cross-dressers? They abounded, more so among truckers. And the waitresses? Those tired women, bursting out of their uniforms, always a size too small, gave Libertad teary looks of pity, it seemed to her. Some went to the extent of patting her on the head and saying, "Poor kiddo," as if she were standing blindfolded before a firing squad. And then the women truckers. Those came and went, running, on the clock. Some were just voices on the CB radio; others she knew from one route or another. How could she have befriended someone always passing by?

None of these women, none of the tourists and travelers she briefly encountered at rest areas and cafeterias, had ever taught her about friendship, and her father had been no help. It seemed to her that she had watched those women live out their relationships behind a windshield.

She missed Sonia. She wished she could have one of her buñuelos. But she wished even harder that her father had married Sonia instead of leaving her after that catastrophic fight, the one she re-created in her mind whenever she needed to feel miserable, like this night. If Sonia were her mother, she'd visit her at the prison. Or better yet, maybe she wouldn't be in prison at all. She'd be working and living at the Jolly Trucker, and she'd have a jolly family, a jolly home, a jolly life. With Sonia's example and guidance, she would have learned to make friends with lot lizards, waitresses, and women truckers, even some of the more feminine cross-dressers. But instead, she had been thrown into a prison where she had to spend every day and every night surrounded by women. She was learning on her own, and it hurt.

I drove on Highway 160, between Cortez and Durango. My father advised me as we went along.

"You gotta remember at all times that you're hauling a thirty-ton crane."

Another flock of bikers on Harleys passed the truck, each turning their heads to get a glimpse of me as they drove by, perhaps on their way to the annual meetup in Albuquerque.

I slowed down to let them pass me.

"How much longer to Aztec? We could have lunch there."

"We have to go through Durango first. I'd say a couple of hours."

"When are we supposed to drop the load?"

"Thursday."

"Can we go to Carlsbad Caverns? It's right on the way. I want to see the bats again."

"Sorry, we can't. We're not delivering in El Paso this time. I've heard they've set up a military post on the border since the holidays, so the client's gonna be waiting for us in Palomas. I already made the arrangements."

Suddenly my father saw something on the road ahead that sent him into a panic.

"Stop!"

"Of course I stopped," read Libertad to her audience, this time a small one compared with her usual full house. Volleyball finals were being held the following day and the team members, many of whom were Library Club regulars, were frantically practicing out on the court.

By then, I knew the drill. My father got out and climbed into the crane's cab out of my view. He hid on the floor under a tarp he had previously left in anticipation of such an occurrence. I started the engine and continued on. Far ahead on the road I saw a police roadblock. As the line of cars and trucks crept through it, I prepared myself for the act. When I finally got there, I stopped and rolled down the window.

"May I see your driver's license, young lady?" said the Highway Patrol officer.

I gave it to him, looking as confident as I could.

"Brand new."

"Yes, I just got it three months ago."

"Picture's good. Shouldn't you be driving with an adult?"

"I am an adult. I'm twenty-one now, see? Look at the date there."

"I meant to say someone over twenty-one."

"As far as I understand, according to the regulations, no, sir."

The officer gave me my driver's license back and showed me a snapshot of a nice, smiling man with a baseball cap and rosy cheeks, who looked like he could be a dad coaching his kid's team.

"There's a dangerous man in a blue minivan out on the road today. He is believed to have murdered two teenagers over by Lubbock and he might be trying to cross the border into Mexico. If you see him, don't stop for any reason. And call us."

A few miles ahead I pulled over to let my father back in the truck.

"They weren't looking for you, Dad," I said to him as he climbed into his seat. "You've got to stop doing that."

"I'm not taking any chances."

My father looked through one of the rearview mirrors. The sweat from his armpits stained the sides of his shirt down to his waist.

"It's been so long. Do you think anybody remembers?"

"Revenge has no expiration date for those guys. They could still be after me, for all I know. And I have to think of your safety."

"I understand you getting panicked in Mexico, but this is the States. I've never understood your fear of American roadblocks. Since when have the authorities of both countries coordinated any of their efforts? If they can't find five million undocumented workers in plain sight, do you think they'll find you?"

"The difference here is that they don't intend to find the undocumented workers. Me? They want me dead or alive. I just have to keep my eyes open at all times."

"You're overdoing it, Dad. It's getting a little on the sick side, don't you think?"

"You have to understand me. It is safer here, but if I don't want to become shark food, it's better to anticipate every possible chance of being found."

"Can't we get protection from your old university buddies? Aren't all those people big-shot politicians in Mexico now?"

"Precisely. I can't trust them, and I can't trust the others, either."

"But things have changed in Mexico since the sixties, Dad. The government can't get away with murder that easily anymore. You read it in the papers all the time."

"Is there anyone out there who believes what the media says? They're just as corrupt. Besides, what do you know about Mexico? You've never even been there."

He was right. What did I know about a country I'd never been to? All I knew was what I'd heard my father say, what I'd read in books, what I'd seen on television. I so much wished to actually go someday, but with my father's fears, the possibility was as distant as the other side of the world.

"Are you going to change your name again now?"

"Yup."

"How about Macbeth? You haven't used that one. Macbeth González."

"That's a good one. It's for protection, you know that."

"I know, Dad . . . Macbeth . . . whatever. Fake names, counterfeit driver's licenses, false identities. It's as if we're in a witness protection program, only without the witness, the protection, or the program."

We traveled on well into the night without stopping for a rest.

"We were lucky back there," said my father.

Yes, we had been lucky, but luck is known to run out.

ora's poem turned out to be a success. Contrary to the popular belief that poems don't arouse men, both recipients—a mechanic and a pastry baker—were now wildly in love with her. She started arriving late to work from having spent entire nights playing with one man's fender tools, or licking wedding cake frosting off the other man's belly button. She even called in sick four days in a row, and twice later that month she just didn't show up. When she finally did, she drifted around the prison grounds gazing at nothing in particular, whistling some unidentifiable song. She also stopped drinking her customary morning shot of tequila, causing her to fail at locking and opening gates and padlocks. And she definitely looked tired.

"Love is hard work," said Maciza.

That hot and windy evening Maciza was patrolling the cellblock, making sure no one misbehaved in Nora's absence. She had taken it upon herself to ensure good conduct among her fellow inmates. She didn't want to delay her release date by one more day, by getting blamed for any kind of trouble.

Libertad walked along the corridor next to Maciza, pleased by the effect her poetry had on men, even if those men were not hers. Maybe one day she could have one of her own again. Maybe someone she could take care of who would love her back. This time she would figure out how to keep him from straying. The memory of her own experience caused her to feel a sudden pang that became intolerable, and so she exchanged this sad memory for more positive thoughts.

Her new man would buy her a three-bedroom house. It didn't have to be a special house. He could even rent her a small apartment for them to walk around naked in if they wanted. Every morning they'd stretch out on their king-size bed and hear the neighbors chatting outside. Every evening after work, she'd cross her house's doorway and yell out, "Honey, I'm home!" She wanted a yappy little dog called Peterbilt, and that would be as close as she would be to trucking. Then she thought of all those husbands and boyfriends who had forgotten their women the minute they saw them walk into the prison. Did she really need a man to love? Wouldn't she be better off enjoying the home, the bed, the neighbors' gossip, and the yappy dog by herself?

"Remember that pen I gave you when you first got here?" said Maciza, all of a sudden.

"What about it?"

"You never paid me for it."

"I thought it was a welcome present."

"Welcome present, my ass. You know better than that."

"So should I pay you now?"

"With interest."

"What do you need?"

"It's in the warden's office."

ersecutory delusion: A false, rigid, and persistent belief that others are plotting to harm an individual," read Libertad under her breath. The flashlight that Nora had long forgotten she'd lent to Libertad—so in love was she—lit up the page. "Also referred to as paranoia, this disorder can display other characteristics, such as aggression and unjustified fears. Afflicted people don't experience a marked impairment in their daily functioning. Outward behavior is not considered bizarre or out of the ordinary and there lies the danger of overlooking this syndrome."

Libertad closed the book and slipped it under her mattress along with the flashlight. Diva snored. Culebra farted. The moon was nowhere to be seen. Outside, the wind brought the music from a wedding somewhere in town. And intertwined with the melody, the nameless voices of those who were free sent out words like *cake, groom, bouquet, bridesmaids, honeymoon, house*. Someone was moving into a house. She went back to thinking about her father. Whenever he could, he explained to her why they remained homeless, as if justifying his behavior. "If I didn't let you stay with Sonia and enroll in a school, it is because you could be found," he told her once when they had to pull over for three hours in the middle of a blizzard outside Duluth until a snowplow cleared the road. "Right now we are not in any database. We are not listed in any phone book. We don't have credit cards, bank accounts. We pay taxes under someone else's Social Security number. Anyone could have the surname González. We might as well have no last name, it's so common, and that's fine by me. We don't exist."

Delusion. Paranoia. Joaquín González, the professor, the trucker, the specter. He was harmless now. How much Libertad wished she could have saved him from himself. She pulled the book and the flashlight from under the mattress again and read until daybreak.

A hint of winter settled in Mexicali those days. The air was a couple of degrees cooler than normal. Libertad had been trying to find the right moment to talk to Maciza about payment for the pen, so Sunday morning, after breakfast, instead of going to nine o'clock Mass as they usually did, she invited her to the beach. There was hardly anyone there that morning. Three inmates were talking with their friends on the other side of the wall. The inmates had never met these women in person, they only knew their voices. On clear days with mild winds, the activity in the shantytown that had sprawled alongside the prison wall in the past few years could be heard easily. The inmates held entire conversations with the settlers on the other side. But the women were far enough from Libertad and Maciza not to pose any threat, so they sat on a couple of lounge chairs.

Neither of them could afford suntan lotion, but Maciza had managed to steal a small bottle of cooking oil from the kitchen, and as both women applied it on each other, they agreed on the particulars of what Libertad was supposed to do for Maciza in exchange for the pen.

"I need to find someone," said Maciza, careful not to be heard by anyone other than Libertad.

"Is it Pollito?" asked Libertad, straight out.

Maciza spilled the remainder of the cooking oil on her towel.

The noises from the shantytown on the other side of the prison wall were loud: Norteña music coming from cheap radios, turkeys milling around on the dusty patios, women washing clothes in the creek that flowed out of the prison drain, dogs fighting over clean bones, men chopping wood for the stoves. The lives of the free.

"Who told you about my Pollito?"

"Nobody. What do you think I do all day at the warden's office? I organize people's files."

"You go through them, snoop, that's what you do. Have you told anyone about my boy?"

"No."

"See? I have my secrets."

"I respect that. You don't want to talk to us about Pollito and that's fine."

"I do want to talk, but just to you."

"I'm listening."

"I don't want his father to find him first and take him to Colombia. Pollito is in foster care somewhere. If no one knows where he is, no one can tell his dad. He won't know where to look. He's such a prick."

"You want me to help you find Pollito?"

"It's not a favor, it's payment for the pen. I just need you to tell me where he is. As soon as I get out, I'm going straight there to get him back." Maciza settled on her lounge chair, belly up.

"The file is incomplete," said Libertad.

"Incomplete as in missing stuff?"

"It doesn't say where Pollito is. I think there are some misplaced pages. I'll figure it out."

"You'll do it?"

"I'll let you know how it goes."

"Just don't get in trouble for me. It's not worth it."

"Let me decide who's worth getting in trouble for. Haven't you had friends?"

"What for?"

"So you can get in trouble for them. It's the ultimate sign of affection."

It took Maciza a few seconds to recognize Libertad's words as a declaration of friendship. She smiled back, not sure of the proper response.

The morning went by so swiftly that neither of them realized how sunburned they were until Maciza got up to turn over.

"Shit," said Maciza. "Now we have to get vinegar compresses at the spa."

So Libertad and Maciza headed to Nguyen Salon & Spa in their swimming suits to receive one of Tran's famous vinegar and jojoba oil treatments. There was a long line of women waiting outside the shop, so they quickly queued behind the last inmate. Once their spot was secured, they could find out what the line was for and decide if they wanted to wait or not.

"It's the Sunday promotion," the inmate ahead of them told them. "Two for one. Didn't you hear about it?"

Tran had trained three other women to cut hair and this was their first day as professional hairdressers. Libertad and Maciza decided to put up with the pain of their burned skins and use their money to get haircuts instead.

When Libertad's turn came, she sat on the wooden crate that served as a chair and watched the new hairdresser cut away the ends of her short locks. Unlike her last haircut at the warden's office, this time she asked for only a little trim. Maciza sat on another crate next to Libertad and shuffled her bare feet on a thick rug of hair from the forty other inmates who had gotten their hair cut before her. She looked at the wall where Tran had taped magazine clippings with pictures of movie stars as samples of the various dos she and her new trainees were able to replicate.

"I want to look just like that one over there," Maciza said to the rookie hairdresser, pointing at a photo of Madonna.

"Yeah, right, honey. You've got her biceps, now you want the looks, too?"

"You got a problem with that?" Maciza stood up an inch from her. Never mind that the woman was wielding a pair of very sharp scissors.

"It's not going to happen. Just look at yourself. I can't perform miracles."

When Libertad realized what was happening, she pulled Maciza aside.

"I don't think it's smart to get into a fight with your hairdresser *before* she cuts your hair," she whispered into Maciza's ear.

Still frowning, Maciza took her seat on the crate again and let the hairdresser cut away.

By dinner that evening, Maciza had pulled her short hair into a ponytail that looked like it was bitten off by a mule and had forgotten about the experience. But Libertad was concerned about Maciza's behavior. She thought about the many brawls she had witnessed in which her friend had exercised her might against terrified, puny victims.

"How do you have the nerve to beat someone up? Isn't it hard?"

"I could make a living out of that."

"Who taught you?"

"I guess my dad. See this, here?"

Maciza showed Libertad a scar on her thigh. Other women who were eating dinner close by leaned in to take a look.

"That was the belt buckle," she said. "I couldn't learn the pronouns. If I didn't know something, he'd make me get naked before he hit me 'cause he said it wasn't the clothes' fault that I was so stupid. And this one here?"

Maciza showed Libertad another scar, on her lip.

"I forgot my new sweater at my cousin's. I was six or something. He had this big old turquoise ring on his finger. Once he knocked out these two teeth with it."

Maciza showed Libertad the holes where two teeth had been. Now the spaces were half filled with partly chewed tamales.

"I'm telling you, he sure taught me a trick or two."

"Yes. Dads are good teachers, and they don't even know it," said Libertad.

She remembered her father. What kind of scars did she have that were not on her skin? Most were buried beneath, way down in the depths of her memory. He had been a good teacher, too.

 Careful, Piñata, if you're going westbound on I-10 over by Deming, you got a concrete cowboy coming up on your back door.

Thanks, Wonderboy. I can't stand those gear jammers. They're the ones who give us a bad reputation. Are you stopping at the Kactus Kafe?

Yeah, I need to take a shower before I get to Tucson. Plus I'm selling another set of heated mirrors to Macbeth González and I'm meeting him and his girl in San Simon.

You gotta be kidding me! His truck looks like a Christmas tree already! What does he need more mirrors for?

Dunno. Maybe he backs up a lot.

That's freaky, man. I saw his truck last month at the Detroiter over in Woodhaven and I gotta say, there's no room for more. Cat-eye mirrors, side mirrors, wide-angle mirrors, you name it. It's like he's got to know who's over his shoulder at all times.

Just what we need on the roads: a paranoid trucker.

I've seen worse. Hey, listen, I'm beginning to sound like a ratchet jaw. I gotta bug out.

Catch me at the Kactus Kafe? It's a pretty good chew and spews.

Roger wilco.

Now reading from *The Unbearable Lightness of Being,* Libertad addressed her audience as they settled into their seats.

"Where were we?"

"The roadblocks."

"Oh, yeah. I think we're done with that."

Libertad leafed through the book and stopped at page 83.

"Okay, here we go."

In spite of my father's paranoia, our business was better than ever. I drove. He administered our earnings. On that particular occasion, we left Barstow before dawn to deliver a Cat track-type tractor in Yuma before lunch. If you had been an eagle slicing the sky, you would have seen what looked like a very small truck moving along a road below, that bordered saddlebrown, sienna, and chocolate mountains. We were ants carrying leaves along uncertain trails. Sometimes, very seldom, we'd get to talk to someone, as we did that morning.

A stalled vintage pickup truck with wings painted on its sides caught our attention. It was hauling a load too large for the truck's capacity, covered by a tight-fitted tarp.

A beautiful woman in her mid-thirties stood next to the pickup truck cautioning oncoming traffic with a bright-red silk rebozo that floated weightlessly in the desert wind. Her long hair, the color of a magpie, seemed to want to follow her shawl wherever it went, no questions asked. A man dressed as a wrestler with a glittering mask over his face and feathered angel wings on his shoulders pointed at the flat tire.

Perhaps because of the woman's mythical, tantalizing beauty (reason enough for my father to pull over, never mind his fear of a possible ambush by the Mexican authorities), or the buffed-up angel-wrestler flexing his muscles, sweating, and asking to be touched beneath his tight-fitting suit (this, my own reason: I just had to get a closer look), we stopped to help, neither of us suspecting that this was an appointment with fate.

"The lug nuts are too tight," the angel said.

"I've got just the right tool for that," said my father.

He pulled a special wrench out of his toolbox, along with some lubricant to loosen the rusty lug nuts, and got to work. The heat of the morning was cruel.

"You drive this monster?" asked the woman.

"Yes," I said.

"Is it hard?"

"Not really. He's pretty tame, actually. Where are you heading?"

"Los Angeles. And you?"

"My dad and I are dropping this equipment off on the Yuma border. What are you doing in Los Angeles?"

"I'm moving there with my daughter."

"Is he your husband?" I looked in the direction of the angel changing the tire.

"He will be, as soon as we get to Los Angeles."

"And your daughter? Where is she?"

"She's in the back of the truck."

I didn't see anybody, just the oversized load. But at that point in our encounter, I would believe anything.

"Ah," I said.

The men tightened the last lug nut, lowered the jack, and stowed it, cleaning their hands with rags as they walked over to where we were standing.

"We've been stuck here for hours. Thanks, man," said the angel-wrestler to my father.

"Don't mention it."

The woman went to her truck and brought back the figurine of a saint. She put it in my hands.

"Take him. Saint Anthony is miraculous."

"Aren't you going to be needing him?"

"He's already done plenty for me." Then she whispered into my ear, "Keep him upside down. He'll find you a man to love."

As the woman walked past the back of her pickup truck, she caressed the tarp before getting in the cab and driving off with her angel. I stood by the side of the road watching the truck disappear in the distance while my father gathered his tools.

I inspected the statue. It was made out of plaster, and the eyes were shiny marbles surrounded by human-hair eyelashes. The saint was holding a baby Jesus in his arms with such tenderness that I just had to kiss him.

"Will you really find me a man to love?" I asked him out loud, as if expecting an answer.

How could I meet such a man? I was never in the same place twice. Sleeping by the side of the road on coyote nights and indigo dawns. Running from no one, camouflaged by my father's fears. Unrecognizable to everyone. The entire world with its limitless possibilities sprawled outside my windshield, and I was a captive to freedom.

"We can still make it in time for lunch in Yuma. Traffic's light right now," said my father, jumping into the passenger seat of the cab.

"You'll have to work overtime," I said to Saint Anthony before I placed him upside down inside my laundry bag hanging from its designated hook behind my seat.

Later in the week, we stopped at a small truck stop, the independent kind that are still around, with a big blinking sign, MI CASA, then a slogan, *You'll Never Feel So Close to Home,* and on the roof, the buzzing neon cartoon of a giant trucker drinking beer from a mug. We parked next to several other trucks. The eternal hum of the highway seemed to be lulling them to sleep, so still were they.

I made sure that the chains strapping down the landfill compactor we were hauling on the lowboy were tight. I walked around the truck and inspected the fuel tanks. They were properly mounted, not damaged or leaking. The fuel crossover line was secure. My father sat on the cab's step and checked a map on his *Trucker's Guide* with a flashlight and a magnifying glass. It was just another night at the truck stop.

"Let's get some food," my father said. "If we manage to eat dinner in an hour, we'll make it to Chaparral by midnight."

"I doubt it. This place is always packed."

Inside, the atmosphere offered fluorescent lighting, vinyl chairs, Formica tables, and linoleum floors all around. Truckers quickly emptied their super-sized plates overflowing with mashed potatoes, French fries, burgers, macaroni and cheese, tacos, and the specialty, barbecued ribs. Some played dominoes, their eyes bloodshot from lack of sleep. Others watched the TV. It was a basketball game, nothing worth remembering. A few checked out the merchandise at the store. Air fresheners. Spill-proof mugs. Sunglasses. Maps. Chewing gum. A rusty jukebox in the corner blasted Norteña music. Two lot lizards dragged a man into the women's restroom, laughing.

We found a booth and ordered our meals. We were starving. As much as we ate, and we did eat quite a lot, we stayed skinny. I didn't know if this was a blessing or a curse. Among truckers, we were categorized as lanky, and in a way, we had to work harder to earn our respect. My father blamed our physique on our genes, and the final word on the subject was that there was nothing we could do about it. Of course, I quietly believed that spending a substantial amount of time climbing mountains, walking along endless prairies, and rappelling down caves to dig deep holes where we could hide our cash, did qualify as exercise, something other truckers seldom had the time to do. One more proof that genetics and environment are a team.

While we waited, I took a math notebook from my backpack and opened it to a page with a bell curve graph. My father put his finger on the highest point of the crest and said, "So you're saying that the median is right here?"

"That's correct."

My father smiled, proud of me, and checked off the graph with a red pen.

"When are you going to let me give you a B, you smarty pants?"

Suddenly my father noticed a nice young trucker sitting

across from us, looking at me. I could see his eyes sparkle through his thick glasses. At first we ignored him. We continued with my lesson, our food came, we ate, we chatted, but in the middle of dinner, my father got up without saying anything to me and walked over to the trucker's table, leaning so close to the man that I was sure he could smell his onion-ring breath.

"Are you going to stop staring at my daughter or are you going to make me break those glasses of yours?" he asked.

I had to look away. My father returned to his seat. The trucker threw a few dollar bills next to the check on his table and left—not without giving me one last glance.

"You can't be too careful with these losers."

"What did he do?" I asked, knowing the answer.

"Didn't you notice? He was almost licking you with his eyes."

"Through those glasses? He just smiled at me. I thought he was kind of nice, actually."

"No, he wasn't nice. He just looked that way. You have to watch out for those guys. They're usually jerks. And his breath stunk."

I looked in the direction of the window. The trucker climbed into his rig parked outside and pulled away. I wondered if I would ever see him again.

We finished our dinner and drove the long stretch of dark roads all the way to Chaparral. At some point he said, "No man in the world can take care of you as well as I do."

I suspected I could take care of myself. I was slowly acknowledging that I had what I needed to survive on my own, no matter how much my father felt otherwise. For years he had me convinced, but that night I questioned his beliefs for the first time. In the event I ever had a man, I'd keep him around because I wanted to, not because I needed protection.

But a month or so after that incident, I became convinced that something was terribly wrong with my father. Or was it me? We were unloading a wheeled excavator at a yard in San Ysidro. It was a major operation. Our client, a tall man with a thick mustache and dozens of moles on his face, was already there and would take the excavator into Mexico the following morning. His name was Xavier. Two Mexican workers were helping.

"Easy! Easy! Don't bang it! This thing's falling apart already!" yelled my father.

Once the machine was on the ground, my father went into the adjacent makeshift office to fill out the delivery paperwork. We had been paid in advance; we were so trustworthy, so reputable. And we had been paid in cash, of course. One of the Mexican workers, a young man by the name of Jesús, approached me. We were outside, next to the equipment we had just unloaded. He smiled at me, showing me a gold front tooth.

"Are you staying on this side of the border tonight?"

"Yeah. We're off to Yuma tomorrow morning."

"Have you been to Tijuana?"

"A thousand times," I lied. "Who hasn't?"

"You know the Bailongo? It's a dance club."

"No. Never been."

As much as I so longed to set foot on Mexican soil, since

I never, ever had, I knew this wasn't the right time. I wasn't really interested in the man and was about to end the conversation when my father, who was still inside the office, noticed us through the window. Xavier was talking to him, but he had stopped listening and was now watching my every move.

"Me and a bunch of friends are going to the Bailongo tonight. I was wondering if you wanted to come along," he said.

I sensed my father's glare and turned to see him. He was livid.

"No, thanks, I'm busy."

"It's okay. I was just wondering. By the way, I'm Jesús."

Jesús shook my hand, and the moment our hands touched, my father stormed out of the office, ran toward Jesús, grabbed him by his shirt collar, and rattled him like a pair of maracas to the rhythm of a lively tropical song.

"Don't you dare touch my daughter!"

Xavier and his assistant, still in the office, heard the commotion and came running to defend Jesús.

"Stop it, asshole!" yelled Xavier.

The assistant pried Jesús out of my father's grip and our client kicked out hard, hitting my father straight in the chest with the full might of his work boot. He lay still on the ground.

"You killed him!" I screamed to the three men staring down.

But then he seemed to catch his breath and came to. He gasped and inhaled with a loud suctioning noise, got up, and started delivering desperate blows in the air. Two of the men grabbed him from behind so that Jesús could punch him, not without first glancing at me as if he needed my approval. I screamed, "Stop it!" But he ignored me. My father doubled up and almost collapsed, but he managed to get loose and struck Jesús on the nose, causing a trickle of blood to drip down his mustache. Then Xavier hit my father in the crotch and sent him down again, where the three men kicked him viciously in the ribs, in the face, on the back. He writhed on the dusty ground, bleeding, defeated, gasping for air. Jesús wiped his bloody face with his ripped shirtsleeve. The other Mexican dusted himself off. Xavier, panting, kicked some dust on my father's face. He hacked and coughed.

"Take your piece of shit with you and get off my property," Xavier said to me.

I drove. My father sat silently in the passenger seat checking his ribs and cleaning off the blood with a wet towel. Hundreds of cars zipped by, cutting us off in the damnable border traffic, ignoring the gladiator-like size of our truck. Every street corner where I needed to make a turn, I had to maneuver the truck several ways.

"That's no way to treat a client, Dad," I finally said.

"His stupid employee was hitting on you!"

"He asked me out. Guys do that. They ask girls out. Didn't you do that when you were young?"

"Yes, I did. And you know what the only thing on my mind was? It wasn't chatting. It wasn't dancing. It wasn't drinking a cup of coffee. You don't know men at all."

"And it looks like I never will." A car cut us off and I had to stop short.

"Just drive, will you? Forget men. I don't want you getting hurt. Understand?"

I didn't think about my father's prohibition again until a couple of months later, when I met Martin at Las Animas Truck Stop.

libertad sharpened pencils while Warden Guzmán fixed a chipped fingernail with Krazy Glue. It was a quiet morning at the prison. Neither woman paid attention to the desk, a clutter of folders pending review and filing, documents here and there, a stack of phone message slips, a hairbrush, lip gloss, a half-eaten torta, a Minnie Mouse coffee mug, the picture of the warden's late husband and a candle, lit for forgiveness.

"I'll be in San Diego next Wednesday, Libertad, and I'll miss the reading. Can you tell me who Martin is?"

"Sure I can. Next Thursday."

"I meant today."

"I can't reveal that just yet. Sorry."

"Why not? I'm your boss. Don't you trust me?"

"You've taught me not to trust anyone. I don't want any leaks. What if someone's listening?"

"I know a spot where no one can hear us. I've made a lot of very important deals there."

Warden Guzmán dragged Libertad into the supply closet and shut the door. In the darkness of the tight space, Libertad had to give the warden a detailed summary of her next reading, with the warden interrupting whenever she had a question. After a while they opened the door and came out into the hall, where a Health Department inspector waited.

"I was told I'd find you here," he said.

The warden fixed her hair. She seemed to be used to getting caught coming out of a closet accompanied by an inmate, because she proceeded with the conversation as if it was nothing out of the ordinary.

"Didn't anyone escort you?"

"A guard. She brought me here. Did you get the inspection request I sent you last week?"

"You won't find anything new."

"I need to check out the restrooms, the showers, and the kitchen."

"The conditions are still way below par. We don't have the budget to repair anything." Then, making sure the inspector heard, the warden instructed Libertad, "Like I said, get rid of the cockroaches in that closet while I'm gone. You can use my personal can of hairspray. It's in the second drawer of my desk. We can't afford any other form of pest control." She fixed conspiratorial eyes on Libertad's for a long second and left with the inspector on a tour of the facilities.

"This place is a dump, Officer. You'll see what I mean," Libertad heard her say as they disappeared from sight.

Libertad knew that the warden's complaints to the inspector were all about getting a budget increase. She had seen her in action before with other officials. She'd show them the most run-down areas of the prison and take them to the most hazardous corners, always avoiding certain other spots, like the beach.

Warden Guzmán would be out of her office for at least a couple of hours, so Libertad set to work looking for Pollito's documentation.

The third and thickest folder in Maciza's file contained only the first page of a report in English. It explained, in a single sentence, that Maciza had had a son in Calexico,

California. He had been placed in foster care after the baby-sitter caring for him while Maciza was away learned that the mother had been incarcerated south of the border. Libertad searched for the rest of the document in the other two folders but found nothing. She looked for it at the bottom of the file cabinet, but none of the yellowed and crumpled papers that she fished out had anything to do with Maciza. She looked in other inmates' files, the ones next to or near Maciza's. One of them belonged to an inmate who had been released two years before. Another contained the documents of an inmate who had passed away in prison. Some inmates' files were simply lost, perhaps on purpose, like her own. Most of the paperwork in the files was the usual rap sheets, attorneys' correspondence, photographs, declarations, and courtroom transcripts.

Finally, after several weeks searching everywhere— even in Warden Guzmán's personal file cabinet, for which Libertad had made herself a key so she could read the warden's will, out of sheer curiosity—she found what she had been looking for. In one of the several folders that had been pushed to the back of the third drawer of an old credenza that was now used as a table in the hallway, she came across a report in English from the California Department of Social Services, folded in half and tucked in between other pages. It was Pollito's. How it ended up in another inmate's file was not a mystery. As she had learned in the warden's office, chaos was the norm.

The boy's father was Maciza's first husband, a Colombian who had been deported back to his country soon after she gave birth to Pollito. Once deported, anyone could come back into the United States. Easily. Whoever lived south of the Rio Grande knew how futile the border with the United States was. But apparently, he never took advantage of this life-changing opportunity again.

When Maciza killed her second husband with a butcher knife right in the middle of the meat section of a supermarket in Mexicali, the boy, who had been left in California, was taken by Children's Services and placed in a foster home in La Mirada. The report was signed by a child welfare worker by the name of Nancy Bagley.

That night, Libertad imagined Pollito. He'd be about thirteen years old by now. Did he look like Maciza, strong and dark and tall? Had he been told that his mother had killed his stepfather? Did he know she was serving time in a Mexican prison? He would be growing up in someone else's home, being raised by someone else's mother, begging for a little drop of borrowed love. The questions bunched up in her head like housewives around a clearance-sale rack, but she knew she could not get answers unless she contacted Nancy Bagley. And because she had agreed to confidentiality with Warden Guzmán about whatever went on in her office and she always kept her word, she would not be able to discuss what she'd found out with Maciza. She would have to look for Pollito from prison on her own. She rested her head on her pillow and discovered the moon, full and bright and high, peering at her from the edge of the skylight.

I tried to start the truck but the engine just gurgled. My father opened the hood. I gave it one more try. No luck.

"We must have lost the back half of the transmission," I said.

"Hope not. We'd have to get the gear set."

My father dug around the engine for a couple of minutes and finally came back into the truck with a very long face.

"The power divider blew. We're not going anywhere."

I let him throw a tantrum. He kicked the door and slapped one of the mirrors, as if it were the truck's fault it broke down.

"Bad truck," I said.

"Shut up," he said.

I went into Jiffy's, the roadside convenience store where our truck had stalled, and picked up a teen magazine. It was the only one on the half-empty rack, and it had been leafed through enough times to have every page curled at the corners. The article that caught my attention was: "How Celebrities Deal with Their Zits."

"What? I can't sit around for six days," my father yelled into a pay phone by the cash register. "I have a load to deliver. And I don't have a backup tractor. Can't you get the drop-in here any sooner?"

I wished the truck had broken down somewhere else. Pueblo, Colorado Springs, even Lamar would have been a more interesting spot to sit around than Las Animas.

Nothing happened there. I remembered stopping for lunch there a few years back and I figured it would be more fun to spend a weekend inside a casket.

Through Jiffy's window, in between credit-card decals, posters, and neon beer signs, I saw a construction site next to the parking lot. It would become a house, a big house with ample rooms and clean bathrooms, with doors that could stay open all day to let the breeze flow, with a large, functional kitchen and a cozy den where people could cuddle and do whatever families were supposed to do. But the most desirable amenity would be a big mailbox conveniently located next to the driveway where the inhabitants would be happy to get wedding invitations, postcards from vacationing relatives, love letters, bills, bank statements, even junk mail.

I went outside to get a better look. The first floor was almost finished. Workers went in and out of the openings, applying stucco to the drywall. One of them watched me from a window on the second floor, his rowdy blond curls shining in the early-afternoon sun. When he realized I was looking in his direction he waved at me, his arm going back and forth like a windshield wiper. I waved back and quickly turned around to where my father was, concerned that he might have noticed our silent interaction. He hadn't. He was still busy on the phone, negotiating a faster delivery with the parts people. But when I turned back to the construction worker, he was gone.

My father and I sat for a while in the one lunch booth at Jiffy's, sipping a soda, sharing an apple fritter, and considering our options. If we went to Denver, we could get the part and come back in a day or two instead of waiting for it to be shipped to Las Animas. But we had to leave right away before the parts store closed for the evening.

It all sounded like a good plan, but a few minutes later, my life changed. Destiny has subtle ways of detouring people's lives, and I truly didn't see it coming. David and Carmen pulled up into the parking lot, oblivious to the sharp turn of events they were about to cause. An innocent husband-and-wife team, long haulers like us. We had been running into each other here and there for years. This time, their two boys were traveling with them. They didn't know it, but as soon as we saw them, we knew they were our ride to Denver.

"But there's only room for one of you," said David, after my father filled him in.

At the idea of leaving me alone, my father's face turned red, his nostrils flared, and he began scratching his belly. He had to decide quickly.

"All right, honey, you stay here and watch the load while I get the drop-in. I'll be back, hopefully tomorrow night."

Then he asked Benigna, Jiffy's manager, to keep an eye on me. She offered to let me ·sleep at her home a few blocks down the road. She had always wanted a daughter, she said, maybe to ease my father's obvious anxiety.

"I'll be staying at Amalia's in Denver."

I remembered the night my father had invited Amalia to sleep in the truck. She was a moaner, a big one. I'd had to wear earplugs all night.

"She'll be happy to see you. She sure was the last time," I said.

"Maybe, maybe not. I haven't spoken with her in a year. Or has it been longer? Women are so good at keeping track of these things."

My father packed up a change of clothes in a small tote bag, and as he climbed into David and Carmen's truck, he gave me a piece of paper with Amalia's phone number.

"Call me if you need me for anything. And stay in the sleeper during the day."

I watched him leave. For a long while I stood there, in the middle of Jiffy's parking lot, alone for the first time in my life. I suddenly knew, at sixteen, that I could shed my skin like a rattlesnake. I had the potential to emerge from my own shell and become someone other than my father's daughter. I could be a Mudflap Girl at the front of the truck, not way in the back, guarding the tires from mud and debris, away from the action like an afterthought. The carefree wind that enveloped me smelled of diesel and pavement and worn-out tires, but I understood it as prophecy and possibilities.

I thought I heard my father's voice asking me to clean up the cab of our truck. I did. Then I thought I heard him asking me to go into Jiffy's and help Benigna with the customers, and although no one had stopped by all afternoon, I still went inside and helped. But after a while, his voice, those words of his in my head, became weak, like symptoms in the aftermath of a disease. I felt liberated, weightless. So I walked over to the construction site. Two workers were leaving for the day, sweaty and exhausted. They went to the front yard and put their tools in a bin, snapped the lock shut, and hid the key under a nearby rock. I stood by the door of the house and watched them.

They didn't notice me. One of them reached for a hose and washed away the dust of the day. His muscles twitched at the touch of the cool water. I walked past them into the house.

"C'mon! Is she really going to look for that guy?" interrupted Maciza, squirming in her seat, nervous at the potential danger. "I mean, can't she see that all those blondies are like walking cans of worms?"

"Only the blondies?" was Diva's comment. "Stay away from every cute guy unless he's gay. That's Men 101."

"Just listen," said Libertad.

I walked upstairs into a large room. It had an arched window, the same window where I had seen the construction worker wave at me. No one was there. A cheap boom box stained with blotches of paint and stucco sat on the floor. I turned it on. The music in English was gentle, undemanding. I found a piece of blue chalk used by workers to mark measurements on the walls. I picked it up and drew a throw rug on the particleboard floor. I traced a bed where a real one might sit in the future, pillows and all. A dresser by the door. Drapes on the sides of the window. A self-portrait.

The late-afternoon settled in the house, a subtle intruder, like me. I sat on the floor leaning against the drywall and admired my room. I imagined it full of real furniture, wallpaper, and translucent curtains. My real self-portrait would be much better than the one I had drawn. I saw myself sitting by the window, taking in the breeze, wearing a silk flower-print dress like the one I had always wished to own. The construction worker would come back, washed up, shaved, dressed for a night out. He would hold me tight in his well-built and tanned arms. I would let him, our movements slower than the air. The light of the afternoon would play on our skin, like in those music videos I liked to watch on TV at truck stops.

Then my father's voice came back, calling me. "Hey, baby, where are you? We gotta get going." I opened my eyes. He was miles away, but his voice was there, present, vivid. The room was dark and empty. Night had fallen in Las Animas, and I was still alone.

I went back to Jiffy's and ordered a bean-and-cheese burrito and fries to go. Benigna greeted me with a head full of tight curlers and bobby pins sticking out every which way. She had been a waitress before she was born. She gave me a Styrofoam box in a paper bag. I paid.

"I put some salsa in there. It's pico de gallo."

"Thanks."

"Are you sure you don't want to spend the night in my apartment? I've got a trundle bed."

"No. That's okay, Benigna. Like I said, I have to watch the load."

"Is that all right with your dad, staying by yourself in the truck?"

"We do this all the time."

"But he said that you should stay with me."

"I'll be fine."

"Just lock yourself in, sweetie."

"See you tomorrow."

I went to the truck and picked up my book, a flashlight, my pillow, and a blanket, and returned to the room in the construction site, my room. I would spend the night there. I would know firsthand what it was like to live in a house. I would lie on the floor, right where I drew the bed, and I would stretch my legs as far as I could. I'd stare at the ceiling, high up. I would hear the neighbor's dogs barking outside my window. I'd keep it open to let the freshness of the night cuddle my skin.

I sat on the floor, turned on the music so low I could barely hear it, and as I ate my burrito, I read from *The Old Gringo*:

> At the same time, Arroyo thought, looking up to the sky, that everything and everyone had a home, except for him and the clouds.

I stopped reading and thought about the clouds, homeless billows, wandering vapors waiting to dissipate into nonexistence, when the unexpected light of another flashlight hit my face. For a second I was blinded. Then I quickly aimed my own flashlight toward the source of the other beam. It was the construction worker.

"You found my boom box," he said. "See? It says 'Martin' right here. That's me."

"If it were mine, it'd say 'Mudflap Girl,'" I said, still surprised by his abrupt presence.

"Is that your name?"

"One of them."

He sat down next to me, understanding my answer.

"I guess I'll call you Mudflap Girl, then. I'm glad it was

you up here and not someone else. I've already had one of these stolen from another job."

He cranked up the music.

"I was just leaving," I said.

"And I was just picking up my boom box."

But I didn't leave and he didn't pick up his boom box.

"Where is the man you were with this afternoon?"

"My dad?"

"Oh, it's your dad."

"Yes."

"Great. I mean, it's good that you're with your dad."

"He went to Denver to get a part for our truck. It broke down."

"With the pillow and all, I take it you're planning on sleeping here tonight."

"Is that all right?"

"I don't see a sign that says you can't."

Martin scanned the room with the light of his flashlight as if searching for a sign and discovered my drawings.

"Did you do this?"

"It does come off, right?" I was worried that he might get mad at me for such an act of vandalism.

"Why would anyone want this to come off?" Martin smiled, amused. He got up and walked around the room, looking at each of my drawings. He traced my lines with the tip of his fingers. The bed. The pillows.

"You're going to paint over it, right?" I asked, hoping I hadn't caused permanent damage.

"I'll show you how these walls will look when they're finished. Come with me."

Martin pulled me up. His hand cradled mine and didn't

let go. We walked out with our fingers entangled and entered another room, a finished one on the first floor. The walls had been painted white.

"In a couple of days, the room you furnished will look like this. Bland colors. Straight walls. Cold materials. Dead all around."

"Thank God I didn't wreck anything." My hand felt warm in his. I wanted to leave it there, at the mercy of his fingers venturing into the spaces between mine, but then he let go and took a blue chalk out of his pocket.

"I wonder how the rest of the house would look with your furniture."

"But this room is finished already."

Martin looked at me with mischief, broke the chalk in half, and gave me a piece. "Where does the lady want the sofa?"

Lit only by our flashlights, we drew furniture on the walls: a La-Z-Boy, a TV set, picture frames, a coffee table, a flower vase. We pretended to sit on the sofa and fell on the floor. Martin drew a power button on the TV set and a funny face on the screen. We laughed. We sat around. We went back to the room upstairs. We talked. Martin ate cold French fries out of my take-out box.

"Where do you live?" Martin asked me.

"My dad doesn't want to own a place. We live everywhere," I said.

"I live in an earthen house about fifteen minutes from here."

"Earthen?"

"It's made out of earth. I built it myself."

"Must be nice to have an actual place, an address where you can get mail."

Martin held my hand again. "Can I borrow your lips for a minute?" he said.

But he didn't wait for my answer. He kissed me slowly, and I allowed him. His breath found its way to my nose and I inhaled it deep into my lungs. I held it in while I kissed him back.

"Now go, please," I said, fighting all three words. "My father could be back any minute. He'd kill us both." I suspected that Martin wouldn't understand my fear, but I had every reason to be afraid.

"My mailbox is starving. Will you write to me?" he whispered softly, his lips barely touching mine.

"From wherever I go," I said.

He took a pencil from his shirt pocket and scribbled his address on my take-out bag.

He kissed me again, this time a small, soft kiss that seemed to say, *I'll be right back*, or at least I wished that's what it meant. Then he left. From the window, I watched him drive away in his pickup truck.

The night went on, dark and silent. No more flashlight beams or laughter, kisses or entwined fingers. I lay awake in this foreign room. I hugged my pillow and thought about the statue of Saint Anthony resting upside down in my laundry bag back in the truck. I thanked him with a prayer that I made up on the spot, as my father had taught me, for those couple of hours with Martin, even if I never saw him again.

What I felt wasn't love. It couldn't be. We hadn't

overcome any hardships together, we hadn't shared pain or joy, we hadn't satisfied each other's wants and needs. It was simply the first heartbeat of a possible relationship, yet it scared me more than genocide, famine, war, plague, bigotry, betrayal, or politics. I blamed part of my fear on my father. But I also felt ill equipped.

I wanted to stop Martin and run away with him, but what could I offer? I understood the pang deep in my chest as regret for having asked him to leave. I held on to the image of his eyes, blue and deep, his hair, curly and untamed, his lips, his breath. And his words, every one of them. Even in the innocence of an inexperienced sixteen-year-old, I knew that kissing Martin had been the most dangerous thing I had ever done. That's when I noticed the boom box.

he's too good to be true. She better not write one word to the guy. The bastard's gonna fuck her over one way or another."

Maciza sat next to Libertad at the beach. It was a Sunday and everyone was there. This time, the two friends had dragged their lounge chairs under the shade of an umbrella. Protected from the sun, they could talk longer and not sweat as much. The drought was worse than ever and they were allowed to shower only once a week. Maciza embroidered the initials *S&M* with red thread on a heart-shaped pillow.

"You'll see. I just know men," she kept going. "'Where does the lady want the sofa?'" she mocked Martin in a deep voice. "Yeah, right, like I buy that."

Libertad felt uncomfortable with the conversation. She wanted to tell Maciza all about Martin. But she didn't even try. She knew it wouldn't come out right. She'd have to wait until the following Wednesday. She noticed the initials on the pillow.

"Who's S&M?"

"Son of a bitch and Maciza."

"But you hate embroidery."

"Yeah, and needlepoint, too, but don't tell me it's no fun embroidering these fucking initials," she chuckled. And as she said this, she accidentally pricked her finger with the needle and a little drop of blood stained the crooked letter *S*.

"Oh, well," she sighed. "Nothing is perfect."

Libertad took Maciza's hand and applied pressure on the pinprick with the edge of her shirt.

"You'll be all right," Libertad said. "All wounds heal."

"Don't we know?"

The morning slipped by. The two women gossiped, they took a nap, and they each had a large glass of horchata with ice, compliments of Matriarca, who was still trying to lure Libertad back to her old housekeeping job. But the uneventful day ended abruptly when Rarotonga came looking for Libertad in a panic.

"It's Nga, she's asking for you."

Many children had been born in the prison infirmary, as rundown as it was. Most births were easy. These were women who did not shy away from pain, even the deepest one of all, the one men could never understand or feel, no matter how much they tried to emulate by practicing sports like hockey. Every inmate had been able to go back to nurse her baby in her cell within a few hours of the delivery. Cellmates claimed the right to be the baby's aunts. Some even argued over who would be the godmother. Births at the prison were a much-needed reason to rejoice. But Nga, who had given birth unexpectedly, four weeks before her due date, could not stop bleeding.

Libertad gripped her hand and spoke soothing words to her in English. She held the baby girl close to Nga's face so she could kiss her little head.

"Your baby is beautiful," whispered Libertad in her ear.

The warden had rushed to a nearby hospital to get a doctor, a real one. Tran and Hong whimpered in a corner of the room, helpless and scared, and said words no one understood. Nga shivered. Rarotonga prayed to the Virgin of Guadalupe, her plaster image on a wooden stand hanging from the wall above the bed, surrounded by votive candles and dusty plastic roses. The nurse had run out of clean towels an hour ago and was now wiping the blood with her own apron.

Warden Guzmán came back with the doctor, a young intern from the Municipal Hospital's maternity ward, who hastily got to work trying to stop the hemorrhage.

Nga asked the warden to come to her side and said, "My baby, Mexican girl. You keep, Mrs. Warden." She held the warden's hand tight and turned to Libertad to make sure she had heard her last wish.

The day after Nga was taken away in a casket to be buried in a common grave at the local cemetery, Warden Guzmán took the baby to Saint Jude's Catholic Church and baptized her. "I named her Bienvenida," she said. "But you can call her Nida. Nida Guzmán." And that same day, she phoned her contacts at the Civil Registry and pulled a few favors to get a counterfeit birth certificate naming her Nida's birth mother.

"What if someone asks why the girl looks Asian?" asked the clerk.

"I've never needed to explain myself, not even to my parents," she snapped back, and that was the end of it.

She also offered Tran and Hong their freedom. Legally, she didn't have the authority to release inmates on her own, but she had done it before and no one had seemed to care. She told them that they could go back to Vietnam. They could stay in Mexico. They could even attempt to cross over to the United States. In other words, they were free to do whatever they wanted. Without Nga as their translator, it was very difficult for Libertad to get the message across in English, but the women finally understood. They exchanged a few words and, between the little Spanish they had picked up and their hand gestures, they asked the warden if they could stay in the prison. The warden was not surprised.

"You can stay only if you learn Spanish and you teach Nida to speak Vietnamese," she said.

From that day on, Hong was in charge of Nguyen Salon & Spa, and Tran became Nida's devoted nanny.

I combed my wet hair in front of a mirror. My long black locks stretched and then bounced back in rebellion against the comb that tugged and pulled and wanted to punish. I had just taken a shower at a small truck stop three blocks south of Jiffy's after a sleepless night at the construction site. I had kept thinking about Martin's kisses. A couple of other women truckers brushed their teeth and talked with their mouths full of toothpaste.

"No long hauls, 401(k) retirement, no-touch freight, stop-off/layover, and get this: no loads to New York City!"

"Golly! I'm switching! Do they take husband-and-wife teams?"

"You betcha. Sandie and Julio Pérez just joined. I'm telling ya, this is the deal for any owner-operator."

"I gotta talk to Elias. We're so fed up with Norton. We haven't been back to the house in three weeks. And you know what the fleet manager said? 'Who's waiting for you anyway? Your stupid cat?'"

"Jerks abound, I'm telling ya."

I listened. The women noticed me.

"How often do you get home?" one of them asked me.

"I'm home every day. I live in the sleeper."

The women seemed to know who I was.

"Oh, yeah. You're González's daughter. The heavy-haulers. Benigna told us about you. I'm Nina, sweetie. I drive the cabover Freightliner that's hauling the reefer parked right outside. You ever heard of Mammarama?"

"No."

"Well, that's me. Mammarama."

"She owns the panorama," grumbled the other trucker as she spat out the toothpaste in the sink. "You better get that name in your head, kiddo. She's got thirty-two years' worth of road experience under her belt. I'm Rita."

"The toughest señorita," said Nina. "And she ain't kiddin'."

I introduced myself, "I'm Mudflap Girl. Nice to meet you."

Nina put a dab of shaving cream on her eyebrows and shaved them off as she spoke.

"Listen, hon, if you need anything, just holler. I'll be around until noon."

I couldn't help but stare at Nina. Her eyes seemed to pop out now that she had no eyebrows.

"Thanks. My dad's coming back soon."

Nina pulled out an eyeliner pencil from a pouch and drew a very dramatic, thick arch above her left eye.

Rita offered me a cigarette. I declined with a polite gesture.

"You got no ma, right? That's what I've heard."

"Right."

"She gone?"

"She's dead."

"Hey, sweetie, I know how that is. My own ma passed on when I was nine. Maybe that's why I'm on the road all the time."

"I can relate, really." I picked up my towel and clothes. "Bye now. Hope you get home soon."

"Don't I wish! I still have to go to the yard and get my ducks in line for the scale house next week."

I walked back to Jiffy's. It was still too early to be thinking about breakfast, but any distraction from the hurt of having said good-bye to Martin was welcome. I ruffled my curls just a bit so as not to cause them to frizz, and as I approached my truck, I saw Martin sitting on the hood, leaning against the windshield, taking in the early-morning sun, the boom box in his hand. He jumped down from the hood right in front of me.

"I was hoping you'd still be around," he said. "Come with me, to my house. If you don't have other plans, that is."

I didn't give the invitation a second thought. My father was still gone. I would be back before he was. He'd never know, I convinced myself.

"No plans."

The audience at Library Club seemed to have doubled. Somehow the word had gotten out. "It's going to get steamy," was the gossip passed from cell to cell during the days before Wednesday. Warden Guzmán sat in the front row, feeding Nida her bottle of formula.

Libertad read, well aware of the inmates' expectations, looking up from the page now and then to gauge their level of attention.

I climbed into the sleeper, hung my towel from a hook, stashed a roll of twenty-dollar bills and a sweater in my backpack, and carefully placed Saint Anthony upside down in the big compartment, not before giving him a grateful kiss. I jumped into Martin's pickup truck and we left without giving Benigna any explanation.

"I took the day off work to do some stuff in my house. You can help me finish building a shed for Salpicón, my horse," he said. "It's almost done."

"I've never built anything."

"It's a piece of cake. Have you ever made mud pies?"

"Sure. When I was little."

"Same thing."

We drove through an oasis-like verdant ribbon. Then the highway took us to a semiarid region of sage and juniper. It was a prairie with scrubby grasses, but the sandy places made it seem like it wanted to be a desert. The distant horizon changed from plains to mountains.

"Those are the Spanish Peaks," said Martin, as proud of their beauty as if he owned them.

For the first time I traveled with a man who was not my father. I couldn't help but judge his driving skills, jerky and awkward. He wasn't paying attention to the road, but then again, I could not keep my eyes off him and that was his distraction. I wanted Martin to kiss me again, to run his hands up my thighs. I had an urge to touch his skin, to entangle my fingers in his hair. I wanted to marry him every day and sleep by his side from that day forward. Yet my feelings and my thoughts were butting against each other. I kept hearing my father: *Women don't sleep with the men they meet on the road.* Then again, I hadn't met Martin on the road. A house, by definition, is the opposite of a road.

We traveled on a bumpy dirt trail into a canyon, and after turning a curve, we arrived at a green plain blanketed with grasses and willow trees. Stone walls with layers of colors—so rare I had no names for them—surrounded us.

And snuggled in this lush mirage, on top of a slope with a creek running at its base, was a circular house shaded by a family of ponderosas. The plants growing on its roof made it look like a human head with a plentiful hairpiece, its windows, startled eyes.

Martin parked in the driveway. A chocolate-colored horse splattered with white spots kept cool under the shade of a willow tree next to the house.

"That's Salpicón. A pure Appaloosa," said Martin. "And that's his hut." It was halfway built. It stood near the main house and was also circular.

Then he opened the front door and invited me in.

"Ta-da!" he said, proud of his creation.

We walked inside. The house was round and warm and pleasant as a womb. Unmilled beams held the wooden roof. The walls were seamless and the color of earthenware, and their sandy texture reminded me of the New Mexico adobe homes I admired so much. The floor was made out of tongue-and-groove boards. The furniture was easy, inviting, and there were pillows everywhere, rugs underfoot. A cozy, unmade bed covered with a thick blanket sat on a loft, reachable by a ladder. Every window carefully framed a dazzling landscape and the glass made the view shimmer. I walked around, taking in the environment, mesmerized.

"You really built it yourself?"

"You bet. My grandpa left me this land when he passed on. A few acres, way more than enough for me. My mom visits sometimes. She lives in Colorado Springs with my grandma. They're city girls."

Martin plugged the boom box into the wall and cranked up the volume.

"Do you notice anything weird? Strange? Unusual?" he asked me as if he was quizzing me.

"You mean, aside from everything?"

"The music. Why is the boom box plugged to the wall if the power lines don't come all the way out here? Where is the electricity coming from?"

I looked around for an answer but drew a blank. I stared back at Martin, puzzled. Then he took me to a window and I saw metallic panels of some sort in the backyard.

"I harvest sunshine," he said. "The whole place runs on solar energy."

Then he ran to the kitchen sink, which was full of dirty dishes. He turned the faucet on and a generous splash of water flooded the tile basin.

"And how do you explain this?" he asked.

I shrugged.

"It's the water from the creek. I collect it. I've got more than I'll ever need."

Noticing the pile of dirty dishes, I just had to say, "I can see why."

We both laughed. If Saint Peter were giving me the grand tour of heaven, I would be enjoying it almost as much, minus the urgent need to touch his lips with mine.

"Ready to play with mud?" he asked.

The music from the boom box invaded the house, snuck out through the open windows into the yard, and bounced off the canyon walls, creating an echo. It was still early in the morning. We could probably work for a couple of hours before the autumn sun forced us into the shade.

I helped Martin prepare a mix of soil, sand, water, and straw. Then we each grasped two corners of a tarp, filled it with the mix, and rocked back and forth slowly, rolling it from side to side.

"It's an ancient building technique. I learned it back in Oregon," he said.

Regardless of where he had learned what, I just wanted to drop the tarp and run to his arms. I wished I could lick the sweat off his neck. He noticed me staring at him with God knows what kind of look, and when he added water to the mix, he looked back at me with a dreamy grin on his face, held it for a long second, and we kept going. I didn't need to wonder what he really wanted to be doing.

"Now the dance," Martin said.

He put the tarp on the ground, took off his shoes, and had me do the same.

"It's the mud pie jig."

We began dancing barefoot, smearing the mix to break up the bigger lumps. Then we added straw, holding bunches in our fists and releasing them slowly. As they fell, they sifted down onto the mix. Martin showed me how to do it, embracing me from behind. I couldn't resist and pushed back against him. I felt the bulk inside his jeans. He leaned. I pressed. We kneeled next to the tarp, our mix flat, and made mud pies the size of footballs, as if we were kneading bread dough. Martin held my arms and guided me through the motions. His skin smelled of dry earth barely wet with drizzle.

"I told you this would be fun," he said, and his smile made me shiver.

Once we were done making oval mud pies—cobs, as he

called them at one point with an air of authority—Martin climbed to the top of the hut's wall. I passed the cobs, which seemed to harden as soon as we'd shaped them, to him and he stacked one on top of another in a spine-and-rib pattern, like laying bricks, all around the edge. As the morning turned into midday, the wall got taller. We stopped a couple of times to drink water from a thermos before we finally finished.

"Now all it needs is the roof and the door. But that will wait until next weekend."

We stood in the middle of the yard, covered in mud, and admired our work. He put his arm around me, gave me a long and thankful kiss, and took me inside the house.

"**I knew she'd** fall for that. What an idiot!" Maciza was mad as hell. "Now, this is one goddamn son of a bitch you're reading about, Libertad."

"Shut up! You're just bitter," said Rata.

"Bitter? Wait and see. Those goody-goody guys are the worst. Can't you see he's just using her as a slave to build his stupid little hut?"

"I'm stopping the reading right now if you don't shut up," said Warden Guzmán. "You want double needlepoint hours?"

The inmates had forgotten that the warden was in the audience. They all stopped immediately. Libertad resumed, disturbed at the thought of Maciza, her dear friend, not liking Martin.

"All right, so we left off when they went inside the house, right?" She opened the book again.

224

Martin and I went inside the house. I was exhausted. My body ached. I was hungry. But I cherished every minute of that morning. I had built something that would stay where it was. I had turned earth into a dwelling and in the process had been charged with a new feeling of desire. I realized that I wanted Martin more than anything and I didn't know how to have him. I wished my mother had stayed around at least until she could tell me the secret.

I looked around me. This was his house, Martin's house. His handprints were everywhere, in each cob on the walls. Its roundness welcomed me. Its warmth caressed me. I had always thought that a house should be square, its roof, gabled. But I was quickly unlearning.

"You must have read Tolkien," I said.

"Who?"

"Do you feel like a hobbit sometimes, living in this house?"

"A what?"

Of course, I thought. Some people don't have to read books to imagine things.

Martin walked me to the bathroom, a small nook like a cocoon, with a skylight above the shower and a door—the only one in the round house—and turned on the water.

"Can I borrow you for a little while?" he said.

Martin took me into the shower and gave me a kiss on my forehead. Then on my cheek. And finally on my lips. I kissed him back. He pulled up my T-shirt, covered with mud, and as we undressed, everything else except us became irrelevant. We let the water wash the mud off our skin as we touched each other. A medal of the Sacred Heart hung from his neck. I washed it.

"Today I'm doing things I've never done before," I said. He put his finger softly on my lips. "I know," he whispered.

We made love drenched under the generous splash of the shower. He washed me, I rinsed him. He played with my hair. We toweled each other.

I put on a pair of Martin's shorts and an extra-large, clean T-shirt. We sprawled on the sofa, shared a pitcher of iced tea, and didn't say much. I listened to his breath, the air coming and going, still pushed out by the excitement of our lovemaking. I wanted his breathing never to stop. I wished I could listen to it for years on end. And again, as it did whenever I thought about my mother, the vulnerability of life crashed into my chest like a blue jay into a window. I wanted this man to live forever, with me by his side. But we'd die someday, one before the other, and there would be pain, a lot of it. Martin rubbed my feet.

"Whoa! I got a blister on my toe."

Martin went to the bathroom and came back with a small Band-Aid that he carefully placed on my blister.

"I forgot to mention that cob mixing can be rough on tender feet. But you did dance the merengue like a pro. You just have to walk barefoot around the house more often to toughen your feet."

"I don't have a house."

"How about truck stops?" he said playfully. "Their floors must be awfully clean."

"**How about prison** floors?" said Culebra.

Some of the inmates giggled. They needed to. A joke was imperative to let the emotions spill out. The shower scene had been too intense for some love-starved women. Although overnight spouse visits were allowed and even encouraged by the warden, and a few of the cells in a remote section of the facility had been specially equipped for that purpose with queen-size beds, most inmates had been quickly forgotten by their men and replaced. The only women who managed to get visitors were the prostitutes, having made prior arrangements with the warden, who usually knew their clientele, mostly politicians.

"What's wrong with the prison floors?" asked the warden, who didn't take criticism well at all.

Culebra sank in her seat, expecting some sort of punishment, then blurted out, "I guess we'll just have to double our efforts sweeping and mopping, right?"

A few inmates sitting close to Culebra gave her a nasty look.

"Resume, please, Libertad," said the warden.

Martin packed a lunch and a water canteen and we hopped on Salpicón. We rode on a narrow trail around the canyon, our bodies moving back and forth on the saddle to the pace of the horse. I wanted so badly to make love with Martin again. I wished my body were larger so I could feel more.

When we arrived at the end of the trail, we tied Salpicón to a cottonwood and began climbing the big ancestral rocks of the canyon. Finally we reached a small cave hidden from plain view. We went in. Martin took his flashlight out of his backpack and lit up the cave's walls as he had done in the half-built room at the construction site. But instead of my rough drawings, these walls of rocks were filled with ancient petroglyphs of mountain sheep, elk, deer with long, branched antlers, and human figures.

"Nobody knows about this. And I plan to keep it that way."

I looked at the drawings with respect, breathing slowly so as not to disturb them. Martin held my hand and we walked out of the cave, blinded by so much daylight, and stood at the edge of the rocks. The horizon was everlasting, just the way I liked it. I could see Martin's house right below us.

"How did you find this place?"

"I was looking for a spot to build my house."

"Why didn't you build it here? This place is perfect."

"That's precisely why. This is a site that cannot be improved. Why would I want to wreck it by building a house here? I'd rather build a house on a so-so lot and make it better by bringing water to it and planting a garden. Places like this one should be left undisturbed. They're sacred."

"Are there more sacred places on your land?"

"There's one more."

We rode on Salpicón down the slope, back past the house, until we arrived at a small cornfield.

"This is my first cornfield, ever."

"It's turning out really nice. Do you water it at all?"

"I've got a channel to get the water from the creek over here. Feel the soil." Martin kneeled down, grabbed a piece of soil, and crumbled it in his hand. "See how it's a little moist?"

I sat on the ground and touched the dirt in Martin's hand, leaving it there a bit longer than needed. I couldn't help it. We kissed until we found ourselves making love again, this time nestled in between the cornfield's rows. I felt his gold medal of the Sacred Heart hitting my chin, quietly and rhythmically, alternating with drops of sweat falling from his forehead over my face. His skin was warm, smooth, and tan. Mine was tinted light brown like the soil beneath, a soil so soft it molded to the shape of our bodies. The corn leaves, beginning to dry, announced that the crop would soon be ready for harvest.

He whispered, "Stay with me."

We lay side by side at the edge of the cornfield, propped up by the water channel's border. We ate our lunch as the sun set, orange clouds, scratches across the sky of the grasslands.

"I was conceived in a cornfield," I said.

"So we might be continuing a family tradition?"

I looked at Martin, not really knowing if I should be scared of the thought or not.

It was early evening when we arrived back at his place. When I jumped off Salpicón I felt the blister on my foot. Martin noticed my pain and quickly picked me up and carried me inside the house.

The next morning I woke up on the bed in the loft. Martin was sleeping beside me. I still wore his T-shirt. I went down the ladder and looked around the entire circular house. Martin peered down from the loft.

"You look so good, so early," he said.

I thanked him, and then I just had to ask, "Where do you keep your books?"

Martin came down the ladder. He was wearing nothing but boxer shorts.

"My books? Over here." He shuffled a few pillows

around the sofa and pulled out a book from underneath: *How to Build Your Own Earthen Home*. He wiped off the dry dirt clods stuck to the mangled cover and handed it to me.

"Is this it?"

"Yes," he said, a bit embarrassed. "It's got lots of pictures, though."

"Well, you've got more books than I do, that's for sure."

"I go into bookstores and look around, but I never know what to get."

"How about schoolbooks? Didn't you save any?"

"No. I dropped out in sixth grade. I did have some from elementary school, but my dad took everything when he left."

"He left you forever?"

"One day my mom and I came back from Thanksgiving at my grandma's in Colorado Springs, and the house was empty. No books, no furniture, no dad."

I thought about my own father, looked at the clock in the kitchen, and felt a sharp pain between my ribs.

"But it's okay," said Martin. "He wasn't home all that much anyway. And I couldn't really read the books well. I'm a slow reader. I skip letters, even whole lines, the words just dance around on the page. I get headaches if I try too hard."

"If I see you again, we'll go to a bookstore. I'll help you pick a book and I'll read it to you. I'm really good at that."

"What do you mean *if* you see me again?" he asked, aghast. "You're staying with me, aren't you?"

I couldn't answer. Anyone would lose the ability to speak before such a bold statement. He embraced me and said, "I don't want to make you do things you don't want to. I just know I could live with you forever."

"It's my dad," I said, almost in a whisper. "I have to get back and explain to him what's going on with us. But I have to go right away, before he returns to Las Animas. I don't have permission to be here."

On the way to Jiffy's, I pulled the figurine of Saint Anthony out of my backpack and gave it to Martin. "He's supposed to be very good at getting lovers together. Keep him. Maybe we'll see each other soon." And although there was much to say, we didn't speak at all. As we pulled into the parking lot, I saw my father standing next to our truck.

Dear Miss Bagley,

This is the third letter I've written to you, without getting a response. I hope this one finally makes it into your hands.

I am writing to inquire about a boy who was placed in foster care in La Mirada, California (please see the attached copy of the document that states so and the report that explains why the boy was placed in foster care). His name is Juan Martínez. His mother's name is María. She is serving a sentence in the Mexicali Penal Institution for Women and is soon to be paroled. Since I can write in English and I am her best friend, she has asked me to contact you and find out the whereabouts of her boy and to possibly arrange for her to start the necessary procedures to get the boy permanently reunited with her once she is released from prison. I thank you for your kind interest in this very important matter.

Yours truly,
Filomena Hernández

Libertad signed the letter to Nancy Bagley using her driver's license name and managed to put it in the outgoing-mail pile just as Warden Guzmán came into the office with Nida in her stroller and Tran behind them carrying a hefty diaper bag.

After the warden adopted Nida, she had gone to San Diego and bought all kinds of beautiful baby clothes at the fanciest shopping centers, and picked out a stroller that could have been designed by a NASA engineer, two easy-to-clean high chairs, one for home, one for the office, and a car seat that only needed an air bag and wheels to qualify as a luxury vehicle in itself. She had the crib linens custom-made in Tijuana by a lady from Barcelona who also made wedding gowns for the most affluent brides.

The warden dabbed some sunscreen on Nida, put a cute hat on her little head, and sent her with Tran to the beach to get some sun. The children from the day-care center were playing outside with a few of the mothers, and Nida could enjoy their company.

"Come back in half an hour," she instructed Tran as she showed her the hands on her watch. Tran nodded and left with the baby.

"Do you think we should get new toys for the day-care center?" asked the warden.

Since Nida came along, the warden had begun paying more attention to the children living in the prison. The day-care center had been in operation even before the warden's time. But lately she had focused her energy on improving this facility by changing the flooring, adding some furniture, and now, suggesting they get new toys.

"Educational toys," said Libertad.

"Right."

"Have you ever wondered why Nga decided to leave Nida in your care?" asked Libertad, who had learned that the best way to approach the warden was to be direct.

"I never had to wonder. I knew why right away. Of all the women who surrounded Nga in the prison, I am the most powerful and rich. I have no children of my own. And I am free. She had to think fast. She was dying. But she made the best choice."

Who could argue with that? Libertad thought about her own mother, who did not have time to make a choice about the fate of her own baby. Had she not been spared such a difficult task, would she have wanted her to live with her father?

"Are you coming to Library Club this afternoon?"

"Do you think I'd miss it?"

artin and I parked next to the truck. My father walked over. I rolled down the window.

"Get out," he said to me.

I picked up my backpack and my sweater.

" 'Get out,' I said."

I got out of the pickup truck. My father was as angry as I had ever seen him, and this became immediately clear to Martin, so he got out of his truck, too.

"Good morning, sir. It's my fault."

"You leave my daughter alone!" my father yelled at Martin, and he pushed him away with all the force he could muster.

Martin stumbled but did not fall. My father pushed him again. How could Martin defend himself respectfully and at the same time stop my father's aggression? But he didn't have much time to think. My father punched him in the stomach and began beating him. Martin, who weighed a third more than my father, all muscle, stopped the blows, grabbed him by the arms, threw him to the ground, and pinned him with his knees.

"Calm down, sir. I'm not going to hurt you. Just calm down."

My father could not move under Martin's weight. He made an effort to relax, and after Martin made sure he was quiet, he let him loose. My father got up, dusting himself off.

"Say good-bye to your friend," he said, spitting some dirt. "The truck's fixed."

My father dragged me away. I couldn't keep up with his pace and almost tripped. Martin followed us.

"She didn't do anything wrong. Don't hurt her, please!"

"You stay out of my family!"

"Write to me, Mudflap Girl!" I heard Martin yell.

My father shoved me into the truck. He did not say a word. He started the engine and we pulled out of the parking lot and onto the road. He bit his lip so hard that a drop of blood rolled down the edge of his mouth. I wondered if by the end of his life he'd have no lip left to bite.

We drove away from Las Animas, traveling long hours before he said anything.

"You gave it to him!" He spat out those words as if they were drops of cyanide on his tongue.

I didn't know what he was talking about. My address? My phone number? We didn't have any of that. How could I give it to him?

"You gave the goddamn fucker your virginity!" My father couldn't keep his eyes on the road. "Answer me! Did you?"

I had. I had wanted to. Should I feel any guilt? How could something so magnificent be so horrendous?

"Are you going to lie to me?"

Now, this offended me.

"I have never lied to you and you know it," I said. And then, in a lower voice, I said, "I did make love with him. Three times."

My father slammed his fist on the steering wheel and said, "What do you think your mother would have thought of you?"

"The same she thought of herself when she fell in love with you."

"It's not the same. Your mother was ten years older than you are when she and I met. And don't even think you're in love. You know nothing about that. This guy just wants you for sex. Don't you understand?"

Was this man my father? The liberal, the activist who wanted to look like John Lennon, participated in student revolts, lived out of wedlock with my mother before marrying her, and now had a different woman in every town? His attitude didn't make sense, but nothing did those days. I pulled out of my pocket the paper bag Martin had written his address on and ironed it out with my hand.

"I'm going to stay in touch with Martin. I'll write to him every week and I will marry him someday and live in his house. He has a house, a real one."

But my father snatched the paper bag from my hand and quickly threw it out the window.

"Make it easy on yourself. Forget the bastard."

Defeated, I opened the window and saw the paper bag fly away and disappear. I glanced at the brake pedal as an impossible alternative. My father's foot stepped on the accelerator as if he were killing a tarantula. I touched the surface of one of my many rearview mirrors with the tips of my fingers, trying to feel Martin's image, a texture on the glass to hold on to. I hadn't memorized the address. I felt the sharp pain of a pulled muscle. Only the muscle was my heart. After a while, all I could see through my tears was a tiny point where the parallel lines of the highway finally met, becoming insignificant.

veryone in the prison knew not to bother Maciza when she was exercising. She had her routine. And it was sacred. Running up and down the stairs for an hour before daybreak (she had earned special permission from the warden to leave her cell before everyone else), doing odd jobs here and there during the day, like stacking crates of supplies in the warehouse, or washing the Administrative Office windows, dangling from a rickety scaffold three stories high, and in the afternoon, sparring with Rarotonga—who had replaced Chapopota after her release—instead of watching the soap operas.

When Libertad found Maciza, she was lifting the cafeteria benches and setting them on the tables so she could mop the floor. She did this every night after dinner, all by herself. It was a monumental task that should have been done by a crew of four janitors, but if she didn't exert herself to the point of exhaustion, she would not be able to sleep.

"I know where Pollito is," Libertad said to her across the empty hall.

Maciza put down the bench she had just lifted and sat on it. Libertad sat next to her and handed her Nancy Bagley's letter addressed to Filomena Hernández.

"You have no idea what I've done to get this information," said Libertad. "I could be a detective."

Maciza took the letter and stared at it without saying a word.

"As soon as you get out, cross over to La Mirada," said Libertad. "Here is the address. Ask for this social worker. Nancy Bagley. She will take you to Pollito and start the process so you can get him back. It's not going to be easy, but she says it looks really good."

Maciza had learned rudimentary English while she worked in the United States, but at that moment, every word typed on the page seemed to her an incomprehensible hieroglyph. She ran the tip of her thumb across the Department of Social Services logo and began to cry.

Libertad hugged her tight, and in the embrace Maciza felt all those beasts with sharp claws and bogeyman smirks, the sprites created by her own fears, the demons she'd fought off in her nightmares since she was separated from Pollito, suddenly become inoffensive creatures that dissipated into nothingness with their tails snug between their hind legs. Pollito was alive. He was still her son. Someone was looking after him, and it wasn't Pollito's estranged father.

"Of course, the Colombian asshole, the scum bucket, the sleazebag, would never find my Pollito in foster care," she said, gritting her teeth, relieved. How long before she was released? She wished she could start a mental countdown, but she didn't know what the final date was.

So elated were the two friends that neither of them noticed Cleta until it was too late. Libertad took the first blow.

"You fucking liar!" yelled Cleta. "You said you were nobody's girl!"

Maciza sprang up and in one swift move yanked Cleta's shirt, turning her around and slamming her fist on her jaw.

Libertad tried to pull Cleta away from Maciza, but by then, both women were punching, scratching, biting, and slapping each other. Maciza stopped Cleta's fists easily and managed to immobilize her with a lock she'd learned from the wrestling matches she liked to watch on TV.

"It's not what you think, you douche bag," said Maciza.

Cleta tried to wiggle out of Maciza's grip, but Maciza was too strong for her.

"I could kill you if I wanted," she whispered in her ear. "You leave us alone, you hear me?"

Maciza let go slowly. Cleta straightened her shirt, wiped a drop of blood off her nostril, and left the cafeteria without saying a word.

"Don't you ever come near us again," shouted Maciza toward the door, which was already shut.

The two friends' breath came out hard and fast after the unexpected attack. Libertad looked at Maciza, scratched and bitten, and felt a sudden uneasiness.

"Promise me you won't get into any more fights, Maciza. You can't afford to stay here one more day than you have to," said Libertad.

"I promise."

Maciza checked the severity of Cleta's bite on her arm, Libertad fixed her ponytail, and both women laughed loud.

I sat on a curb, leaning against one of the truck's tires. I felt protected under the stars. Coyotes howled in the mountain behind me. I welcomed their song. Headlights came and went, slashing the darkness of the highway. The rest area was quiet except for a caravan of RVs filled with loud bingo-playing retirees parked a good hundred feet away from my rig. I wrote in my journal.

It is possible to let the roads impose their distance between us, and still feel the warmth of your words caressing my skin . . .

I erased and corrected.

. . . my sin.

I looked up into the night and continued to write.

This parting, as forced as it is, is nothing but a pause, a silence between two notes in a long song. Until I can again be contained by your soul . . .

I erased and corrected again.

. . . your soil, I will be sick with my desire for you.

The following morning we traveled on a deserted road. I stopped at a crossroads. My father checked a Colorado map on his worn-out *Trucker's Guide.*

"I knew it. This road does not go to I-70. Where did you get that idea? It takes us straight into Highway 50."

Frustrated, I made a right onto the other road.

"I hope you're not trying to pull one on me. Do you think I still suck my thumb?" asked my father.

I spent months trying to return to Las Animas, needing to smell Martin's hair. I invented detours that led to the road to his house. My father would always guess my intentions and avoid passing through the area. By then, he had assumed that Martin lived in or around Las Animas, so he even turned down trucking jobs if they happened to go anywhere near it.

Libertad had to stop reading. Nida had been born a colicky baby and was having an episode in the warden's arms, right in the front row.

"Put a plastic bag with warm water on her belly," said Maciza.

"Give her little pats on her back, she's got gas," said Venadita.

"It must be the diaper. It's too tight," said Rarotonga.

"She's just tired, put her to bed," said Rata.

"Nonsense," said the warden.

She got up, followed by Tran, and left the room. At the door, she said to Libertad, "Let me know what goes on with this girl of yours."

"You, too," said Libertad.

As happens with most people who are obsessed, I did stupid things. I daydreamed at the wheel, I became daring as an Aztec Eagle knight, one minute I was under anesthesia, and the next I was an explosion. Everywhere I looked, I saw Martin's blue eyes. Everything I heard sounded like his voice, even the wind that whistled when it slid through the edge of my shut window, more so when I was going past sixty.

I had to see him again and explain why I hadn't written, why I hadn't visited. That was my sole mission. The closest we had been to Las Animas in a year was Raton, New Mexico. We had just picked up a soil compactor and were fueling up at a quaint and pleasant truck stop on I-25 run by Betty Ann, a sweet widow in her late seventies who knew all the latest lot lizard gossip and blurted it out at every opportunity. I checked fluids and bumped tires. My father went to the restroom. He took a magazine, so I knew he'd be a while. I waited for him to close the door before I opened the truck's hood. I quickly jiggled some wires and pulled out a hose. Then I shut the hood, threw the hose into a nearby field, like a Frisbee, and continued fueling until my father returned. I said nothing. We got in, I put the key in the ignition and started the truck, but we didn't go anywhere.

"What now?" I asked. I could be a good fake.

"Oh, my God."

My father got out and looked in the engine for the problem. I joined him.

"What is it?"

"I don't know. Everything seems to be in place. Wait. We're missing a hose."

My father wiped his hands with a rag. "Remember that parts center we passed over in Maxwell? I'm sure they've got this hose."

"Am I going to have to wait here?"

"Hell, no. You're coming with me, young lady."

My father went into the store to find a ride. In the meantime, I opened my can of peanuts, took out several twenty-dollar bills, and put them in my pocket. Soon he came out of the store with Oscar, another trucker. He was an old, heavyset man with a protruding belly, wearing a John Deere cap, flannel shirt, worn-out jeans, and tennis shoes—not for running, regular exercise being out of the question for truckers, but for stepping on the pedal. His eyes were sunken and drained, resigned. He smoked non-stop and held a spill-proof mug in his hand. He sipped coffee from it every few seconds. We walked to his rig: an older Mack model. Nice paint job, though. He hauled a reefer. Oscar noticed me.

"She coming, too?" he asked my father.

"Is that okay?"

"Lord have mercy. I gotta warn you. Ladies don't like my truck."

"It's all right. I've seen all kinds of trucks," I said.

"Oh, yeah? How long've you been on the road?"

"Since before I was born."

"Well, you ain't seen my truck. That'll add to your experience."

We climbed in and drove off. The three of us sat in the front. I sat by the window, my father in the middle. The sleeper was small and messy. It was the crawl-into type. Oscar's truck had an orange shag carpet all over the floors, walls, and ceiling, like those customized vans from the early eighties. It even had a broken eight-track tape player. He had photos of nude girls in provocative poses posted throughout the entire cab. Oscar pointed at the photos and said, "I betcha they've all got pictures of truckers taped to their dressers' mirrors. We're sexy, too, you know." He pinched his belly and burped. Three air fresheners in the shapes of Christmas trees and one in the shape of a strawberry hung from the CB knobs. Oscar grabbed the mike and offered it to my father.

"You want to call ahead and check if they've got the part?"

"No, that's okay. It's a pretty typical part. A hose."

"Damn hoses."

"Yes, they think they're snakes and fall out on the road to catch some heat from the pavement," I said.

Oscar stared at me, intrigued and amused at my comment. I knew we could be friends.

An ashtray the size of a salad platter for a family of six sat by the side of the driver's seat. It had no room for one more cigarette butt. My father struggled not to sit on it.

"You mind reminding me to throw this out at the parts place? I forgot to clean it this morning," said Oscar.

Suddenly, a yellow jacket appeared out of nowhere and tried to escape through the shut window. Oscar produced a fly swatter and killed it off with one assertive whack, the insect ended up smeared on the windshield in front of him. It was hard to tell which one it was, with all the other splattered bugs on the outside of the windshield. It was summer, by the way.

"This is war. You gotta have the right weapons."

Oscar pulled out a squirt bottle, sprayed a liquid on the yellow jacket's remains, and cleaned them off with a rag.

"See? Where's the evidence? No casualties. You can have all those animal-rights activists come in and check out the place. They won't find nothing. One more MIA."

Oscar lit up another cigarette with the butt of his previous smoke before finding a spot for it on the ashtray. Then he pulled out a stuffed bunny with floppy ears from under his seat and snuggled it between his legs.

I wondered.

A flock of bikers passed us, probably on their way to their annual meetup in Las Cruces.

At the parts store, my father went inside to get the hose. Oscar stayed in the truck to finish his smoke. I took the ashtray and emptied it in a trash can by the door. I could see my father from the window, picking out the hose, talking to the salesperson.

I returned to the truck to give the ashtray back to Oscar, climbed into the passenger seat, and shut the door in a hurry. My father was already paying. This was my one chance and I couldn't let it go.

"Quick, Oscar! Let's get out of here! Just head north. I'll explain on the way," I said.

Oscar reacted instinctively and sped off. I looked back through the rearview mirror and there was my father, running out of the parking lot with the hose in his hand, trying to catch up with Oscar's truck.

"Oh, lordy, lordy! What the hell am I doing?" asked Oscar.

"Please, Oscar, go faster!" I pleaded.

Oscar drove his Mack like a race car, passing four-wheelers as fast as he could, returning obscene gestures involving fists and middle fingers, and breaking every rule of roadside behavior. He was hungry for excitement.

"I just knew you'd do something like this. I saw it in your eyes. Is he your boyfriend?"

"He was."

"That man could be your father."

"He thinks he is."

"I know. Don't tell me. He beats you up. Am I right?"

I nodded.

"Fucking bastard. What is it with you women? My daughter got involved with one of those, too. A no-good son of a bitch. Good thing his liver gave out and he dropped dead on the kitchen floor before he had a chance to kill her."

"Is she okay?"

"Oh, sure. She's with a police officer now. At least he takes it out on other people."

I looked in the rearview mirror, still a bit nervous, although we had traveled for quite a while.

"So, where to?"

"It's north of Trinidad, over by the Comanche grasslands. Just drop me off on Highway 109. I'll tell you where."

Libertad put the book down to blow her nose. She had a cold. Almost everyone did at the prison those days. They all shared the germs, but never the precious Kleenex. Her audience stared at her as if urging her to continue, so she took her time making sure her nose was clean, folding her Kleenex in a nice little square, and sliding it inside her bra before she picked up the book again. When it was that quiet, it was possible to hear the tortilla machine groaning painfully in the kitchen, as if it suffered from menstrual cramps.

I recognized the dirt road that led to Martin's house and asked Oscar to pull over.

"Thanks, Oscar."

"Are you sure you want to stay here?"

"Yes. My friend's house is just around that little canyon."

"Careful with those hoses on the road," Oscar chuckled. But then he got awfully serious and gave me his final advice in a fatherly tone. "Now you go find yourself a guy your own age. And don't take no shit from anybody."

Why isn't this man my father? I thought. I handed him a twenty-dollar bill, but he didn't take it.

"What's this?"

"Please."

"Forget about it."

"Thanks, Oscar."

I gave him a kiss on his sweaty cheek. Then he pulled the stuffed bunny from between his legs and put it up to my face.

"She gets a kiss, too. On her whiskers."

I kissed the bunny and got out. His truck disappeared, leaving behind a reckless dust devil, and I began to walk along the dirt road.

"I just ran away," I said to myself, out loud, hoping that by doing so I'd begin to believe it. I had become not just a fugitive from the Mexican authorities, but from my own father. The difference was that, as opposed to the military or whoever he believed was after him, my captor knew exactly where to find me. There was no point in running. I couldn't hide. And I didn't want to. Not anymore. So I figured that my best option would be to confront him. Martin would protect me. All we had to do was wait for my father to show up at Martin's house. I had to hurry up and warn him.

When I finally arrived at the round earthen house with grass growing on its roof, my face was sticky with sweat. I imagined myself taking a cool shower with Martin in his refuge, his hands lathering my weary body. I gathered the last reserve of stamina I had and ran into the front yard. His pickup truck was gone. The house was locked. I peeked through the kitchen window and saw that the sink was perfectly clean and the washed dishes were neatly stacked up on the countertop. I went around the yard and looked inside through several windows. The pillows on the sofa were nicely in place, his one book sat on the coffee table, and there were no clothes lying around. Then I made the worst discovery of all: a pair of women's shoes, high-heeled shoes, on the floor by the door.

I collapsed to the ground.

Libertad put *A Brief History of Time* down and dried a tear off her cheek. The inmates stared at one another, some of them feeling deep pity for her.

"Sorry," said Libertad, her nose all stuffed up and red. It wasn't just the cold. It was all that accumulated sadness trying to flee.

Maciza ripped a wrinkled Kleenex in two, gave one half

to Libertad, and took the other for herself. She was also on the verge of weeping.

"I'm glad that didn't really happen to you, that it's just a book," said Rata. "Fucking Martin."

"I told you. I know a bad man when I see a good one," said Maciza. "And you know the worst thing of all?"

"No," said Libertad.

"Always, and I mean always, the other woman is skinnier."

"And prettier," added Rarotonga.

"And better in bed," said Venadita.

"I don't think we need to squeeze lemon juice on our cuts," said Libertad between sobs.

After a couple of minutes, she composed herself and continued with the story.

I hitched another ride after spending two days hiding in the cave with the ancient drawings, still crying and wondering what Martin had meant by "I could live with you forever." The first ride, a Swift truck, took me from Timpas to Trinidad uneventfully. Nice man. Listened to *The Valley of the Dolls* on tape, unabridged version. Didn't say a word. Dropped me off near an off-ramp by the Trinidad Lake campground. A few cars zoomed by. Four-wheelers had stopped giving rides way before my time.

I wondered if I should be less trusting, like them, when a big Freightliner long nose stopped. It was hauling a flatbed full of sheet metal. I ran toward it and hopped in. An older couple with a tiny Yorkie welcomed me to the back of the cab. The dog's name was Bandit and licked

my arm. Pictures of several children decorated the burgundy vinyl padding on the walls. The grandkids, I assumed. Maybe they'll get to see them at Christmas, I
thought, if they're lucky. A collection of videocassettes
was neatly labeled and stored on a shelf. Porno movies,
every one of them. A bag of melting Kisses sat on the
dashboard.

"Are you going all the way down I-25, sir?"

"Yup. All the way to El Paso."

"I can get off in Las Cruces."

It was a clean shot down I-25 from Trinidad. I was heading straight to the Jolly Trucker, and what drew me there
was Sonia. As I left Martin's house, dragging my soul
down the dirt road, her buñuelos came into my mind. I
saw myself holding one in my hand, crispy and warm,
sprinkled with sugar and dipped in syrup, its smell of cin-
namon overflowing my nostrils. At first the memory of
Sonia's crunchy fried sweet bread felt intrusive. But it was
what it was, a mirage of the heart.

I walked into the Jolly Trucker feeling guilty and excited. How long had it been since I last saw Sonia? Four
years. I was thirteen when my father had made a fool of
himself and we darted out of her truck stop.

I went past the gift shop and into the cafeteria. A couple
of drivers drank coffee loaded with cheap rum and played
dominoes. Most people were in a hurry. At two bits a
mile—or if they were owner-operators, a dollar a mile—
they had to be. Sonia was in the back, cleaning the
jukebox.

"Jesus of Veracruz!"

I didn't think she'd recognize me. I threw myself in her arms as if I had seen her the day before and broke down.

"I left my dad, Sonia."

"I know. He's been looking for you everywhere. Even under the linoleum floors of every truck stop, for Christ's sake!"

"He called you?" Now, that was unexpected.

"He's called everyone. Your picture's not up on the board with all the other missing kids because you know how paranoid your dad is about these things, afraid of being in the spotlight and such."

"Please, don't call him. Not yet."

We went into the Four-Wheeler Wreckage Museum and sat on one of the benches in front of a charred, crunched pile of scrap that had once been a Pinto. She hugged me, rocking me back and forth like a tired ocean. She let me cry all I wanted. I told her about my father's sickening paranoia, the fistfights with the men. Martin. And then, how I had escaped.

"I knew something like this would happen between you two."

"I just need some time before I talk to him."

She took me to her house down the street from the museum, settled me in the guest room, the room that once had been mine, with the stuffed bear still on the pillow, said she'd be back in a little while, and went to the Jolly Trucker. I got into bed and turned off the light. I could hear the eternal hum of trucks passing by on the freeway, hauling produce, furniture, livestock, automobiles, construction materials. Everything anyone could possibly need. I closed my eyes and tried to see my future, but it was blank. I felt as if I had just finished a book that was missing the last chapter.

"I lost Martin," I said to Sonia, who walked in with a glass of milk and a giant buñuelo at two in the morning.

"If he's got a woman, there's not much you can do."

"But I just know she's the wrong woman for him."

"Well, truth is, you don't know her."

"I saw what she did to his place. It's spotless. He must hate that. You should see the way he usually keeps that kitchen. Now, the way it's been cleaned up, I'm sure there are more germs in an operating room."

"Maybe he's with somebody now, but that doesn't mean he'll be busy forever. Hang up and try again later."

Sonia pretended to hang up an imaginary phone.

"What about your dad?" she said. "You can't keep on hiding from him."

"Can you talk to him?"

"I will."

 Don't bug out yet, Meteor. Have you heard about Mudflap Girl?

She's gone missing, right?

Man, the word sure gets out.

I heard about it in the shower rooms at Love's over by Oklahoma City. How did you find out, Spitfire?

González is going crazy. Haven't you heard him? He's been asking everyone on the CB radio, day and night. When he's not taking over channel 19, he's on channel 5. Looks like everyone's looking for the girl now.

I bet she ran away with some guy. That's what Myrta, my niece, did. When the birds learn to fly, that's all they want to do.

I hear ya.

And I don't blame the girl. Who would want to stick around Atticus?

Who's Atticus?

That's González's new handle.

I thought it was Holden.

That's an old one.

Whatever. The guy's nuts. I hope he finds her, though.

I hope not. Let her move on, for Christ sake.

You say that like it's easy. What's Atticus going to do without her? She's like his lung.

Speaking of which, how's the emphysema doing?

I miss my smokes.

Yeah. We all miss something or someone that might not be necessarily good for us. Listen, I'm bugging out. I need to get some shuteye.

Roger wilco.

You've got to keep in touch, Maciza."

Libertad worked up foam out of a bar of laundry soap and lathered her hair. The brownish water, as it spurted out of the showerhead, was a blessing, but not even such luxury consoled her. Maciza had just been notified of her release.

"Sure will."

Maciza showered in the next stall. They had to be quick. The line of inmates was still long and the city would be cutting off the water at the prison in twenty minutes.

"So, what now?"

"My sister wants me to go help her watch her kids. She's got more than she can handle and none of the three ex-husbands help at all. But I'm going straight to find a coyote who will cross me over to the States. I've already got some names."

"Let me know when you find Pollito."

"Yup."

"What about my little favor? Are you going to look for Chapopota?"

"Of course. Are you kidding? We're on a mission."

A mission it was. Libertad got closer to Maciza and lowered her voice.

"Will you really do it? Will you take care of this guy for me?"

Maciza wasn't sure who "this guy" was, and Libertad was releasing the information on a need-to-know basis.

She couldn't allow her secret to leak. It would spread around the prison like the West Nile virus.

Maciza had to admit that this secretive, CIA-quality mission excited her, more so the part about not really knowing the whole plan just yet.

"Of course we'll take care of him for you. Whoever the guy is, I'm sure he fucking deserves it. Besides, we owe you one."

Libertad swallowed some water and looked Maciza straight in the eye, as if in warning.

"Just don't kill him."

"Like I've told you, we'll make sure he lives through it, if that's what you want. You gotta trust Chapopota. She knows how far she can go."

Libertad smeared some soap on her face. For a moment she thought about backing out of the scheme she had so carefully conceived, but it was impossible. Warden Guzmán was involved now. Libertad had decided to ask for her help and she had enthusiastically agreed to participate, not only volunteering ideas, but also providing some of the gear Maciza needed to execute the mission. There was no turning back.

Libertad's time was up and she hadn't rinsed well, but she got out of the shower quickly, still with soap behind her ears, before the women standing in line started a riot. She didn't even wipe the wall dry with her towel as she always had.

It was past three in the morning. Someone's radio was blasting in the town outside. Libertad could hear it in her cell. She wondered if the neighbors cared to complain, but this was not the United States. Here in Mexico no one complained because everyone was a transgressor. Ever since she arrived she had seen people overstepping their limits, and to her surprise, those affected never protested. She had figured out quickly that lawsuits and other ways of making people understand that their freedom ended where another's began were useless.

The music became distant and the thought of Maciza leaving overwhelmed her. She raised her head and looked around. Maciza was sound asleep. She could make out her silhouette in the darkness. She could hear her snoring. Who would take her cot? She had the best mattress, even a better one than Rata's. There was already speculation about it. If the administration didn't raffle it off soon, there would be a nasty fight. It didn't matter to Libertad who would take Maciza's bed. Her friend was leaving a bigger space at Library Club, where she had defended her seat, snapping at anyone who dared to take it. Who was Libertad going to invite to the beach? And who would protect her from an aggressor? She knew no one messed with her because she was Maciza's friend. She felt vulnerable and lost.

"Libertad?"

"You're awake, too?"

"Listen, I know your stories are true. I've known all along."

"Have you, now?"

"Well, almost. I did figure it out early on, but I didn't want to blow your cover. And I'm not telling anyone, so don't worry about that."

Libertad stared at a spiderweb on the ceiling, next to a brownish stain from an old leak.

"Yes, you're right. I am Mudflap Girl."

Her confession sounded like when superheroes, in the most climactic moment of the comic book, reveal their secret identities to their sweethearts.

"I told you you'd blab your guts out one way or another."

"I had to get it out somehow and I did."

"Feel better now?"

Libertad turned to look in the direction of Maciza's bed and smiled in the darkness.

"Thank you, Maciza."

My father's lip bled. He had been biting it throughout his conversation with Sonia.

"You deserve it. What makes you think you can keep a girl from growing up? She's seventeen!" She sounded angry, but I could tell she was worried sick.

I sat in the next booth at the Jolly Trucker cafeteria, scared and keeping quiet. It was midnight. People at nearby tables listened to the argument.

My father turned to them, defiant. "What?"

The truckers went back to their plates, but their ears stayed on the fight. Free entertainment was hard to come by and this was better than anything on daytime television. My father got up, grabbed me by the arm, and headed to the door. I dragged my feet, not out of rebellion, but simply because they did not respond. Pleading for help with my eyes, I turned to Sonia.

"We're leaving," said my father.

As we walked to the door, a fly buzzed around the counter for an entire minute before it landed on the apple pie. Everyone in the room heard it. The fly.

For two weeks my father didn't say a word to me. I followed him around the country, somber, expectant. I tried to start a conversation a few times, but he ignored me. He dug up all our savings, going to every single site where we'd buried our money over the years. San Bernardino, Escondido, Fresno, Santa Barbara, Amarillo, El Paso, Fargo, Aurora. There didn't seem to be a route, a pattern. He missed a couple of spots in Nevada, one by the Santa

Rosa Range, the other near the Lava Beds, perhaps $180,000 worth, I figured. Maybe he forgot about those, I wondered. I didn't remind him. I helped him hide the money in the truck. Every compartment was stuffed with dollar bills.

He called Cholito from a motel room and asked him to produce the necessary counterfeit documents to get our truck south of the border and to FedEx everything to him ASAP. Permits. License plates. Birth certificates. Passports. Visas.

"What do you want the girl's name to be this time?"

"Filomena Hernández," my father said.

I hated every single name he'd picked for me over the years. Fermina Martínez. Plutarca Gómez. Gervasia Pérez. I just went by Mudflap Girl.

"What about her age?"

"Make it twenty-one."

My father shaved his head before we left the motel on our way to the border. I didn't dare ask him what was on his mind. I was too worried about his behavior, too afraid of the consequences of having escaped from him, and too excited about finally going to Mexico. That's the way feelings are, I thought. They come in packages, like socks.

The border was still hundreds of miles away. Much could still happen. A police barricade could send my father into a panic and we could turn around and hightail it all the way to Canada. Or maybe, just to frustrate me, he'd decide to stay in the United States. I wanted to keep going south, far from Martin, into Mexico. I wanted to see the land that my father loved so much but had not had the courage to go back to. And because I only had a romantic idea of what Mexico was like, I resorted to the portion of my brain that would have developed corny and clichéd travel brochures if I'd worked in advertising, and imagined colonial cities unspoiled by time, legacies of two very different cultures living as one, nestled between mountains and waterfalls. I pictured tiled-roof church domes reaching for the heavens in divine fervor, meandering cobblestone streets leading to moonlit patios where sleepy trios played old boleros, balconies hugging one another, porches greeting the rains, and hidden gardens waiting for couples to fall in love. I also imagined the city where my father grew up. A population of how many million and counting? He said he had been born there, but jokingly he promised he'd never do it again. Not in Mexico City, where so many people live but few can claim to be local. Cabdrivers have a death wish, cops are muggers, two million people live in makeshift shacks on rooftops, and cars run over forty pedestrians every day. I had to go there. I had to see and taste and smell everything that so many Mexicans in the United States missed so much they ached.

But why was my father crossing over to Mexico? Why was he taking such a risk?

Los Algodones was a small border bridge, deserted, forsaken, its customs office a prefabricated building with no clear definition of which country's land it stood on. Tumbleweeds rolled around in the wind, ending up entangled in the chain-link fence. The line dividing the United States and Mexico was indistinct and fragile and uncertain.

The Mexican customs officer, a middle-aged man, took the documentation folder from my father's hands and opened it. The first piece of paper, the one on top of all the others, was a hundred-dollar bill. The officer took it and put it in his pocket. Then he walked around the truck to inspect the load, an old, oversized crane, and finally stamped a piece of paper in the folder, giving us clearance to go through.

Once on Mexican soil, my father said his first words to me in two weeks. "I didn't go to college for nothing."

After we traveled for quite a while on a narrow road between sand dunes and wastelands as desolate as a bald man's head, my father said, "We're dropping this crane in Ensenada and then we're heading south to Isla Ángel de la Guarda."

"Where is this island?"

"It's in the Sea of Cortez," he said with a new calm in his voice. "I've heard it's spectacular, and no one goes there."

"Are we going on vacation?"

"We're moving there."

I said nothing. Did it matter? He was in charge, and making all the decisions for the two of us, as always. I was driving the truck because he wanted me to. I was on a Mexican road because that was his wish. I was moving to some deserted island I'd never heard of and it wasn't my choice. But I had to admit that being in Mexico astonished me. This was the enchanted country where anything was possible. A Mexico I only knew through my father's memories was now thrumming under my truck's tires, and every bump and pothole held a welcoming jolt that banged my seat and went up my spine.

"Why there? Why Isla Ángel de la Guarda?"

"Any place with the words *guardian angel* in its name has got to be safe."

One thing was for sure; I'd be far from Martin. It suddenly became clear to me what my father had meant when he said men would only hurt me.

I drove west on Highway Mexico 2 on our way to Ensenada, and as I got closer to Mexicali, I noticed that the same route number had been assigned to six different roadways. My father noticed my confusion.

"Don't mind the signs. Down here they mean nothing," he said, without taking his eyes off the road.

This was my first taste of what it was like to drive on Mexican roads. My father knew them well. He remembered. As I drove, he gave me a few instructions now and then, like "Watch the curve," or "This is a school zone, slow down." But he said nothing more. I hoped he'd bring up the subject of my escape, of everything that had happened, make an attempt to talk it out and put it behind us, way behind, where it belonged. But instead we arrived in Mexicali in silence.

Driving across town, through a maze of streets in residential, industrial, commercial, and vacant areas, was an ordeal I did not ever want to repeat. Were there any traffic rules in Mexico? Was it all about survival of the fittest? Then we should be kings. But in truth we were nothing but a helpless sixty-ton monster trying to maneuver around unpredictable four-wheelers. My father remained quiet, almost as if he enjoyed my suffering, watching me defend myself from the cars that zipped by us, surely teasing us on purpose, all the way to the outskirts of the city.

An unwieldy and painful silence accumulated in the truck's cab. We ascended the La Rumorosa Grade, negotiating its many suicidal curves and impossible doglegs, watching for falling rocks and passing vast expanses of badlands and ravines where nothing would ever grow. Once in a while, I'd see the carcass of a car, rusty and looted, dumped by the side of the road, or tossed way down a precipice. Who had been driving those cars when they crashed? What were they thinking? Was it an older couple in that crumpled Oldsmobile, moving south to open up a bed-and-breakfast? Or maybe a young man in that mangled VW bus, running away from the draft back in the seventies? Why hadn't these wrecks been picked up? Perhaps there was no law forcing insurance companies to retrieve totaled vehicles. Hiring a tow truck would cost more than what they could get for the car from a junkyard. I thought about Sonia. She'd certainly find a use for them at the museum.

When we reached the summit, the land changed, became more generous, allowing for patches of grass here and there. Color and life seemed to return to the landscape. As the road turned, a flock of sheep crossed it unhurriedly right next to a sign that read TECATE 20 KM. I stopped and waited for them to get to the other side. Once they'd done their thing, I sped up again, wondering if they were on their way to some annual meetup.

"I'm sorry for everything I've done, Dad," I said, finding it impossible to bear one more minute of silence, hoping to start a conversation that would lead to reconciliation. But instead my apology served to unleash my father's rage. The fury he had been containing for two weeks rushed out of him.

"Sorry, my ass! You went looking for the bastard. What are you? A bitch in heat?"

"Don't call me that!"

"What are you, then?"

"I'm your daughter. And all I've done is learn from you. Didn't you run away, too?"

Then my father did what I considered a stupid act, given the fact that I was behind the wheel. He whacked me across the face. Was he crazy? Or did he want us killed? He should have realized how dangerous it was to hit the driver of a truck while speeding down a winding road and hauling an oversized crane. My cheek burned, my lip split and began to bleed, and that just set him off. I tried to defend myself, but my arms weren't protection enough against his blows. With the corner of my eye I glanced at the ravine to our left. I tried to hold on to the wheel. He would not stop, so I stepped on the brakes. The tires screeched on the scorching pavement. I jumped out, ran toward the slope, and began hiking downhill. I held on to rickety bushes and weeds to avoid slipping further down into the void. I heard him cursing right behind me. As he got closer, I wondered how this fight would end. Would he kill me? I was sure he had lost his mind.

Then he fell. Somehow he tripped and rolled right past me, toward the bottom of the ravine, until he managed to grab a root that stopped his fall right at the edge of a much steeper incline.

I ran back into the truck and drove away quickly, leaving him behind, screaming for me to return and help him. I knew he'd be all right. He would climb out, check his scratches and bruises, and hitch a ride. He'd find me again. He had practice.

A few minutes later, as I took a soft curve, a passenger bus approached me from the other direction. I waved at the driver, as was customary. He waved back, and right then, as he passed, I felt a hard jolt and heard what seemed like thunder.

"Whoa! What the heck?" I said aloud, not understanding what had happened.

The truck skidded and I quickly maneuvered it back under control until I managed to stop.

I looked in one of my rearview mirrors and saw that the passenger bus had lost its roof. It had been shaved off like the top of a can of anchovies. The bus was still going but idly losing speed, until it stopped in the middle of the road. When I noticed that the old crane I was hauling had its boom twisted and hanging off the left side of the lowboy, I knew what I'd done. I jumped out of the truck, unharmed, but shaking.

"That's impossible!" said Maciza.

"Oh, yes, it's quite possible," explained Libertad. "As it turned out, the crane's boom unlatched and swung out to the other side of the road just as the passenger bus approached in the opposite lane. With the impact twenty-six passengers lost their heads, including the driver."

Diva gasped. Pinche Bruja opened her mouth, but no sound came out. Vedette held Venadita's hand tight. Maciza said, "Oh, shit!"

Libertad closed the book, put it on the shelf behind her, and continued telling her story, looking straight into the eyes of each inmate in the audience.

I walked over to the bus. Someone pushed the crumpled door from the inside and nine children of different ages came out onto the road, still stunned but uninjured, followed by a man zipping up his pants and a woman fastening her bra under her shirt, and finally, a midget who screamed and spun aimlessly on the road like a top. Because of their height, or the position they were in at the time of the impact, these were the only passengers who survived.

Among the many travelers who rubbernecked as they passed the wreck, I saw my father sitting in the passenger seat of a pickup truck. When he saw me, he made the driver stop, then he got out and ran to me.

"Let's get out of here! I've got a ride, quick!"

I couldn't speak. I just stared in the direction of the bus, shaking.

"C'mon! This man's taking us to Tijuana!"

He tried to push me into the man's pickup truck, but I got away and quickly grabbed the midget, holding him like one would hold on to a palm tree during a hurricane. My father tried to pry me away, but I wouldn't let go.

"Don't let him take us!" the midget screamed in my ear, still in shock from the accident.

As my father dragged us both across the pavement, I

heard sirens in the distance. An ambulance, perhaps. A police car. Maybe more. My father heard them, too, and glanced at me with eyes of terror and despair before he got into the pickup truck.

That was the last time I saw him.

It could not be proven that the security lock on the crane's boom was defective. It might just have been un-latched. The Mexican authorities took a long time to determine if the crash was caused by accident and mis-fortune, was negligent homicide, or even if I had criminal intentions. I was finally convicted of involuntary man-slaughter and several other felonies as a result of the sus-picious circumstances in which I was found at the time of the accident. It took the investigators months to sort out all my counterfeit documentation. As for the hun-dreds of thousands of dollars stashed away in every com-partment of the truck, they finally concluded that they were legitimately mine, but by the time they made that decision, most of the cash had disappeared. The authori-ties had been quick to retrieve it before it could be prop-erly accounted for. The rest of the money, whatever was left, was used to pay for the material damages. The truck was impounded and I never saw it again. But, as you all know, since in Mexico one is guilty until proven innocent, I was immediately incarcerated at the Mexicali Penal In-stitution for Women. And it was here, in this prison, where I finally learned what it is to live in a home with no wheels.

For a good two minutes, Library Club was silent. No one made a comment, no one moved from her seat. The inmates stared at one another, wondering what was happening, edgy and uneasy, like farm animals a few moments before a major earthquake.

"This is the end. The last book. I have no more stories to tell you," said Libertad.

ow what?

It's over, Rata. The warden said we're going to wrap lollipops for the candy factory in Tecate. All export merchandise. That's what we're going to do instead of Library Club.

What about Libertad? What's she going to do?

Wrap lollipops, what else?

Listen, Diva, I haven't talked about this to anyone, but I've been thinking, you remember how Libertad ended the story?

Yeah, what about it?

I don't know, I'm just wondering if everything she read to us was stuff that really happened to her. It all sounded so real.

Maybe.

So she did kill all those people?

By the way she said it, I'm pretty sure.

Jeez! Must be hard to carry all that guilt around.

Yeah. More so if you didn't do it on purpose.

Maybe it didn't really happen. Or maybe it did, but instead of twenty-six passengers, she only killed four.

You mean she might have exaggerated?

Could be, for the sake of making the story more dramatic. You know the stories around here. They're hard to compete with.

We'll never really know.

She's not gonna tell.

And I'm not going to ask her. It's better not to know for sure.

I guess so.

They never seem to be the same. The clouds. I wish they'd bring the sweet breeze from the roads up north with their smell of burnt rubber, exhaust fumes, and diesel. But they're white and predictable and bring nothing but shade.

I am alive and that is my punishment. I have been spared death to feel remorse. It happens every day. I wake up, I remember, I feel the weight of their absence. I'd trade myself for any of them but it's not possible. Bringing back to life all the people I killed is the one wish at the top of my list.

aciza's farewell party included a piñata stuffed with cigarettes and tampons and candy dipped in chili powder. Libertad presented her with a care package that the Library Club regulars had put together. It contained two pairs of jeans and a pair of sneakers that would fit a young teenage boy, and a prepaid phone card to call Children's Services once she crossed over into the United States.

Libertad could not stand to see her friend go, but watching her leave was a delightful sight. Maciza walked toward the West Gate accompanied by the counselor in charge of parolees as if she were the baton girl heading a parade. When she approached Libertad, standing among the crowd that had gathered to say good-bye, she stopped to give her one last hug and then kept on going.

Libertad made a quick account of how long the two women had shared their tiny cell. How many conversations had they had, deep into the night? How many hours a day had they seen each other's faces? Was there anything left unsaid?

"Wait, I forgot to tell you something," said Maciza, running back to where Libertad stood and whispering in her ear. "Look me up in the phone book in Calexico when you get out. My name will be Marcela Martínez."

Maciza cleared the gate, shook the guards' hands, and walked out onto the street. She'd head straight to find a coyote who would cross her over, take care of Libertad's secret plan, now that she knew who "this guy" was, and had all the necessary information and precise instructions to carry it out, and then she would find her Pollito.

Chapopota knew why Maciza was at her door that morning. They'd already been in touch. As they packed up, Maciza gave Chapopota the details of the best gossip from prison, anything she knew Chapopota would hate having missed. Chapopota relished every bit of news and wished there could be some sort of yearly reunion where all the girls who'd left the prison could get together. Maybe she'd call Warden Guzmán someday and propose the idea to her.

After she was released, Chapopota had gotten a job in San Ysidro at a money-exchange place and hadn't stolen one penny. In fact, she had once called Warden Guzmán collect to tell her about her accomplishments. Within a month she received a letter from the warden on official prison paper complimenting her. After a coworker read the letter to her, she ironed its wrinkles and folds and pinned it on a wall in her apartment as if it were a diploma.

She had bought an old VW bus with her first few paychecks. It was in good shape, considering its twenty-two years of prior service, so she and Maciza traveled in it to the Jolly Trucker, eating junk food and sleeping at rest areas, just like Libertad had told them she'd done in her truck years way back. According to Libertad's instructions, Sonia would know where to find Joaquín.

They parked the VW bus between two rigs and waited until nightfall, and walked to the cafeteria window to check out the situation inside. It was a slow night. A thin woman dressed in black and using a cane limped around the tables talking to the few customers still around.

"That must be Sonia," said Maciza.

Suddenly they saw a man approach her and put his arm around her waist.

"Is that Libertad's dad?" asked Chapopota.

"I think it is. He kind of looks like her, don't you think?"

"How can we know for sure? He doesn't have green eyes like her."

"Let's go inside."

They dressed in authentic Mexican military uniforms provided by the warden purposely for this particular mission. They also wore black ski masks to conceal their identities. According to Warden Guzmán's instructions, it was imperative that no one knew they were women.

Then they slipped in unnoticed, and for a while, they hid in the storage room, where they could see everything that went on in the cafeteria. Customers slowly trickled out into the night. There was hardly anyone left, except for a drunken trucker who was playing the same Norteña song over and over on the jukebox. Sonia took his keys away without experiencing much resistance. She must be an expert at that, Maciza thought. But when the man who seemed to be Joaquín tried to walk the trucker to the lounge to sleep, the trucker vomited two six-packs of beer plus his dinner right on his shirt.

"Why don't you take a shower and we'll put him in his truck later?" said Sonia.

She gave the man who seemed to be Joaquín a fresh

towel that she pulled from a closet behind the counter and a Four-Wheeler Wreckage Museum T-shirt with a photo of a car wreck and a new slogan, *Better Late than Never.*

"I'm going to lock the museum and I'll be right back," she said as she grabbed a cluster of keys from a hook on the wall.

Maciza and Chapopota waited for Sonia to leave and quickly sneaked into the showers in the back of the cafeteria. They heard the water running in one of the stalls and opened the door. The man was unbuttoning his shirt, and to their good luck, they immediately noticed the unmistakable tattoo on his chest: *Birginia.* Without further proof of identity, they began beating him with all their might, using clubs provided by the warden.

"This one's for the captain you killed, fucking bastard!" yelled Maciza, trying to fake a man's voice.

"And this one's for the captain you killed, fucking bastard!" repeated Chapopota, not knowing what else to say.

"Stop! Please!" cried Joaquín.

"And this one's for giving your students bad advice," said Maciza.

"Yeah! Bad advice!" repeated Chapopota.

Then she took out a combat knife, slashed Joaquín's belt, and pulled down his pants.

"Should we cut his balls off?"

"No. I just had dinner and I'm full. I could use an Alka-Seltzer, though." Maciza burped, just for effect, and pushed Joaquín back to the floor, where he curled into a ball.

After watching him writhe, moaning and whimpering like a run-over dog, Maciza got close to his face, pulled him up by his shirt collar, and whispered, "We're even now."

Joaquín spat out a tooth when he uttered, still in shock, "You mean, this is it?"

"Yeah. We don't throw fuckers into the Gulf anymore. It's already too polluted."

Maciza straightened her uniform shirt and Chapopota put her combat knife away.

"Let's go back to Mexico. We have to report this retribution to the Military Camp and close the Joaquín González case."

The women turned off the shower to avoid wasting water and left the Jolly Trucker as Joaquín fainted dead away on the blood-smeared white-tile floor.

Further down the road to Calexico, now on their next mission, a peaceful one to reclaim Pollito, Maciza and Chapopota yelled and screamed in excitement, their adrenaline robbing them of their usual civil behavior. They high-fived once and again, like two adolescents.

"Man! You're good!" said Maciza.

"No, *you're* good!"

Suddenly, Chapopota slowed down the VW bus and looked at Maciza as if the greatest idea of the millennium had come into her head.

"Let's start a business."

Maciza considered the proposal for a second. "Oh, yeah!"

"Man Beaters, Inc." Chapopota imagined the sign on the glass of their business door, in bright, shiny letters.

"We'll beat the shit out of the man of your choice," added Maciza, as a slogan.

They high-fived again.

he visitors' hall at the Mexicali Penal Institution for Women had no booths with bulletproof windows. It had no security cameras monitoring inmate activity. No wiretaps, peep holes, or other high- or low-tech spying devices. Guards stayed by the door and checked on the visitors now and then. That was as far as surveillance went. A few vinyl-covered couches and chairs served as a visiting area. It was a simple space, but its warmth promoted quiet conversations and a good environment for family togetherness, compliments of the warden.

Libertad walked in with a counselor and saw Joaquín sitting on a burgundy sofa. He had a couple of scabs on his chin and his cheek. His nose was badly swollen. He was missing a front tooth. He had aged.

They hugged. Joaquín could not hold back his tears. Libertad offered the sleeve of her shirt to dry his face. After a few minutes of awkward silence, interrupted only by Joaquín's sobs, they sat next to each other.

"I'm sorry, Libertad. I'm so sorry. I feel so ashamed for hitting you, for not staying with you at the accident. I just went straight back into the States. It was all my fault. For all I know, I forgot to latch down the boom."

Libertad wished she had a few tears for the occasion. Her father's confession certainly deserved them.

"We'll never know how it all happened exactly, Dad, but it's not important anymore."

Joaquín looked around. Two guards standing by the door were splitting a piece of gum. One tossed the wrapper on the floor. Joaquín took Libertad's hand and squeezed it against his chest.

"And I scared Martin off, even though I knew how much you wanted him. What was I thinking?"

"It's all right. He's with someone else now, anyway."

"I want to make it right for you, Libertad."

"There's no way. Just forget it."

Joaquín blew his nose and picked a scab, causing a little drop of blood to trickle down his lip. Libertad dried it with her sleeve.

"Why did it take you so long to come down and visit? I'm easy to find."

"I was so goddamn afraid. I couldn't cross the border to Mexico. I was paralyzed."

"Yes, that's what fear tends to do to people."

"I've spent all this time hiding at Sonia's. She and I are back together now. I don't even have a truck anymore."

"So, did she send you? I don't hear from you in years and then you show up as if you'd seen me yesterday, just like you did with all your women."

"It's different now. I don't have to hide anymore."

"Is that so?"

"They found me. The soldiers. It's over. All they did was beat me up. These injuries are from the beating I took. See them?"

"How could I miss them?"

She checked them up close, impressed with Maciza and Chapopota's job. Then she thought of the asteroids up in the sky, how they rotate around the sun until another object hits them and they change their trajectory.

"So they're not going to cut your balls off?"

"No."

"They're not going to throw you into the Gulf of Mexico for the sharks to eat you up?"

"No. They're done with me."

Libertad took a deep breath and smiled the smile of triumph, and a sudden whiff of Sonia's buñuelos invaded her mind.

"Well, that's great news, Dad. What are you going to do now?"

"I'm going to get you out of here. We're going back into business together, you'll see."

"I don't know about that. You worked so hard to keep me out of trouble, and getting me in trouble ended up being a good thing. Now I know there are other things besides trucking."

"Please think about it. We'll do it on your terms, I swear. We'll do whatever you want. I just want you to forgive me."

"I've had plenty of time to do that, believe me."

"Is there anything I can do for you? Just ask, Libertad."

"I'll think of something."

"I'll think of something myself."

Joaquín kissed Libertad and walked to the door accompanied by the guard. Before he left, he turned back to look at his daughter once more.

"I'm running out of books," she said across the visitors' hall.

he box of used books came a month after Joaquín visited Libertad. She unpacked it slowly, caressing every cover. Some were her favorite novels, the ones she'd read on the road. Others were new to her. Now that she no longer held her Library Club, she could read at leisure. As she unpacked, she sorted the books into piles to be placed on the shelf later. At the bottom of the box, she found one last book, a mangled one that she recognized at once. It was *How to Build Your Own Earthen Home.*

She pulled off a little blob of dry clay stuck on the cover and opened it. It was Martin's copy. On the first page, in nearly incomprehensible handwriting, there was a note for her: "My dearest Mudflap Girl, Study this book well, because when you get out, we'll add a new room to our house. I've been loving you all this time, Martin."

"I need to see the warden right now," she said all of a sudden. Nora, who was standing next to Libertad checking out the new shipment of books, offered to escort her to the Administrative Office.

Libertad walked so fast that Nora could barely catch up with her. They rushed across the prison, all the way to Warden Guzmán's office, where she was getting ready to leave for the day. It was Friday afternoon and her social life waited for her outside.

"She wants to see you," said Nora, huffing from the run.

"Can this wait until Monday?"

"Is it possible to find my file?"

The warden stared at Libertad as if something was wrong with her or the way she ran the prison.

"I would like to check my release date. You know I've been very happy here, but I think I'm ready to go now."

"Let's talk on Monday. I'm taking Nida to Sea World this weekend and I have to cross the bridge over to San Diego before it gets too crowded."

Without Maciza, the days seemed dull, Sundays most of all. One could be dead and not notice it. Libertad dreaded this particular weekend. Now, all of a sudden, she felt the full force of the anticipation she'd managed to suppress so successfully during her incarceration weighing in on her, a crushing pressure on her chest.

She was able to convince Nora to let her bring her new books into her cell and read them between Friday night and Sunday afternoon. She hoped this would keep her mind occupied. But it was impossible. As the weekend wore on, she played in her mind hundreds of different scenarios of her future encounter with Martin. As soon as she got out she'd head straight to Las Animas. She'd show up as if she'd left the day before. There was no grudge to hold. How could there be? After all, technically she had been the one who left him, the one who never wrote or returned, disappearing without an explanation.

On Sunday night, in her cot, she pressed Martin's book against her chest. Was his house a mess again? Did he really miss her? Was the woman gone? She thought about the high-heeled shoes she'd discovered the last time she went to his house. She imagined the woman, beautiful and perfect to the tiniest bone, wearing the shoes and making futile attempts at keeping up with Martin as they hiked up to the cave with the petroglyphs. Libertad smiled at the image. Of course, anyone who owned those shoes could not have stayed with Martin for long.

Monday came.

"It says here in your documentation that your release date was last year, right around this time. You are free to go," said Warden Guzmán with a raspy voice that Libertad had only heard when the warden said things she did not want to say.

"Please don't take it the wrong way. I've been very happy here."

"I understand, Libertad," said Warden Guzmán. "It's not about me."

"Not at all. You've been the best warden I've ever come across."

"I'll miss you."

"I'll come back to visit."

"I know you will."

The warden gave her a hug and pushed her away gently.

few days later, Libertad's farewell party took place in the library. Tamales and hot chocolate were served. Almost eighty of her Library Club regulars attended. Many of them had written her good-bye poems, even Nora, who had discovered a hidden talent, a way with words, and was now selling love poems herself. Rarotonga gave her a pack of chewing gum. Diva gave her a plastic bracelet. Matriarca, twenty dollars, an unheard-of amount for a farewell gift. After the event, Libertad walked alone to every corner of the prison, memorizing the details, remembering shared confessions, accusations, secrets, laments, grievances, and words of encouragement and hope. At the beach she felt a void in her stomach. No cruise ship would ever give her as many memories as that strip of sand.

She went back to her cell. There wasn't much to pack. She put her rolls of toilet paper filled with words, her three notebooks, the old pen that Maciza had given her when she was first incarcerated, its ink long ago depleted, a couple of shirts, three pairs of pants, her flip-flops, the gifts she had just received, and what few toiletries she owned into a cardboard box. The books, except for *How to Build Your Own Earthen Home*, she'd donate to the prison.

Before she was discharged, the warden called Libertad into her office and gave her two things: Maciza and Pollito's phone number and an envelope with enough money that, if well managed, would enable her to survive for at least a month.

"It's an honorarium for your services."

God provides, Libertad thought. He always does.

"Thank you."

Right at noon, Libertad walked out into the deserted street carrying the box with her belongings. Her friends watched her from the gate. Diva and Rata, who were standing in the front row, were able to witness the entire scene. Parked across the street was a brand-new, gleaming red Kenworth T800 truck with a studio sleeper. On its door, the glittery silver lettering surrounded by a purple border sparkled in the harsh sun. It read GONZÁLEZ & FATHER TRUCKING CO.

Trash rolled around the truck in a nasty dust devil just as Joaquín stepped out.

"I suppose you remembered the money we left buried in Nevada," said Libertad, glancing at the truck as she handed him her cardboard box.

"You should always set some savings aside for emergencies," he said.

Then, as Diva and Rata later described the moment to the inmates who were not present, a younger man got out of the truck holding a plaster statue of Saint Anthony, head down.

"That can't be Martin," said Rata.

Libertad walked straight toward him. She reached for the statue, turned it around (thus putting an end to the saint's torture), and kissed the man in the middle of the dust devil with the passion that Diva and Rata had only seen in Venezuelan soap operas.

"My Mudflap Girl!" he said.

"I go by Libertad now."

They kissed again.

"It *is* Martin!" said Diva from behind the gate.

"It can't be. That guy is as ugly as a mug shot. Martin's supposed to be a handsome stud."

"You're right. This one's way too scrawny to be him."

"And where are the blond curls shining in the afternoon sun?"

"She did say her stories were all made up."

"Fucking liar."

efore they crossed over on their way to Las Animas, Libertad, Martin, and Joaquín went to the accident site, as Libertad had requested right after they left the prison. Joaquín drove.

"That's the spot."

How could she forget?

Joaquín pulled over and parked. Both men waited in the truck. Libertad got out with her cardboard box and walked on the tall grass by the side of the road to where twenty-six white wooden crosses marked the tragedy. Some of them had vases with wilted flowers. Others had wreaths, or ribbons, their colors fading in the cruel desert sun. One had a passport photo nailed right at the center, a smiling young woman. Part of the bus's windshield was still lying there after all those years. She read aloud every one of the names inscribed on the wood with the familiarity of someone naming close relatives on a Christmas list. She opened her box and pulled out her rolls of toilet paper. Then, carefully, she knelt in front of every single cross, kissed each one, and wrapped them all with the rolls of paper where she had written long letters of apology.

Cars passed by, oblivious to the meaning of Libertad's ritual of redemption. A few drivers turned their heads. Others just moved along. Libertad jumped back in her brand-new truck where Joaquín and Martin waited, sat in the driver's seat, started the engine, and headed north, to the border, leaving behind each of the crosses tenderly enveloped in long strands of thin white paper that undulated gently in the wind, as if waving good-bye.

trucker lingo
a glossary

All mouth, no ears   Cheap, bad quality CB radio

Alley cat   Less than sophisticated pretty lady

Alligator   A piece of blown-out and shredded tire lying on the road

Anteater   Cab-over truck

Back door   The rear of a tractor unit, or truck

Back out   Driver has finished talking on the CB radio

Bambi Deer on or close to the highway

Barber   Low overpass

Bear   Police

Bear bait   Truck creating a speed tempo

Bear cave   Police station

Bear in the air   Police chopper with radar

Bear report   A trucker informing another trucker about the presence or absence of the highway patrol on the road

Better half   Spouse

Big road   Interstate Highway

Big truck   Tractor power unit

Bird dog   Radar detector

Boss man   Boss

Break 5   Requesting access on channel 5 on the CB radio, or to cut in on a conversation

Break 19   Requesting access to Channel 19 on the CB radio, or to cut in on a conversation

Breaker   Driver requesting access to CB channel

Breaking up   To lose the CB signal. Hearing static

Bugging out   Saying good-bye

Bulldog   Mack brand truck

Bull City   Durham, NC

Camera   Police photo radar unit

Can I get a break one-oh?   Request access to CB channel

Can you read me there?   Do you hear me?

Cat   Caterpillar construction equipment

Catch you on the flip-flop   I'll see you on the return trip

Checking ground pressure   Inspectors checking legal weight on a truck

Chew and spews   Trucker joint, restaurant

Chicken coop   Inspection station, weigh station, scale house

Chicken ranch   Brothel, house of pleasure

Clean shot   Highway clear of highway patrol units

Comic book   Trucker's logbook

Concrete cowboy   Reckless trucker

Container   Enclosed, box-like trailer

Copy   I heard. Now you can speak

Crotch rocket   Motorcycle

Diesel car   Nice, big rig

Dirty Town   New York City

Driving deadhead   Driving non-stop

Dropping a load   Delivering a cargo

Drybox   Plain freight trailer (non refrigerated)

Eighteen-wheeler   Truck or tractor with attached trailer adding eighteen tires altogether

Eighty-five-ton Triple Twelve trailer   A special flatbed designed to haul heavy, oversized loads

Fifth wheel   A round, rotating, structure in the back of a tractor, or cabin where the driver sits, used to attach the trailer, or the unit where the cargo goes

Flatbed   A flat trailer to haul machinery

Fleet   Two or more trucks owned by the same person or company

Flip-flop   Return trip

Foglifter   A funny, entertaining, CB talker

Forty-two   I agree

Four-wheelers   Cars

Freightliner   Truck brand

Gatlin' Jim   Savvy trucker

Gear jammer   Reckless trucker

Go ahead, breaker   Access to a specific CB channel accepted. You may speak, cut in

Go horizontal   Sleep

Gouge on it   Speed, accelerate past the speed limit

Gratin' Jane   Rookie female trucker, grinds the gears

Hammer lane   Fast lane on a freeway

Hammered down   Speeding past the speed limit

Handle   Driver's CB nickname. Also: Pron

Harvey Wallbangers   Rude, reckless, disrespectful drivers

Heavy-hauler   Truck driver specialized in hauling oversized loads

Hire on   To drive someone else's trucks

Home twenty   Home

Kenworth Seminole   Truck brand and model

Load   Cargo

Load of garbage   Load of produce

Long haul   Cross-country trip

Long-hauler   Trucker specialized in cross-country trips

Long-nosed truck   A tractor that has a large, protruding front for the engine

Lot   Truck stop

Lot lizard   Prostitute working the truck stops

Lowboy   A kind of flatbed

Meat wagon   Ambulance

Motor City   Detroit, MI

Mud duck signal   Bad CB reception

No-touch freight   Trucker doesn't have to load or unload the cargo

On a mission   Delivering a cargo

Over your shoulder   What's the road like behind you?

Owner-operator   A trucker who owns his own truck. Also known as "OO"

Peterbilt   Truck brand

Picture taker   Police car with radar

Plain wrapper   Police car without insignia

Put her up to 5   Tune in to Channel 5

Pron   Driver's CB nickname. Also: handle

Radio   CB radio

Ratchet jaw   A CB user who talks too much, taking over the airwaves

Reefer   Refrigerated trailer

Rig   Truck

Roger   Agree

Roger wilco   Good-bye, leaving the CB channel

Rolling parking lot   Two-story trailer designed to haul cars

Run the double nickel   Go 55 miles per hour

Running a fat load   Hauling a load exceeding the legal weight limit

Seat covers   Women

Shaky-Town   Los Angeles, CA

Shooting in the back   Police checking trucks' speed with radar

Shut-eye (get some)   Catch some sleep

Sin City   Reno, NV

Sixty-ton Expando low-bed trailer   A type of flatbed to haul heavy-duty construction equipment

Skateboard   Flatbed

Sleeper   A small area behind the truck's cabin where truckers have a bed and storage space. It can be as complete and sophisticated as the interior of a boat or a camper

Ten-four   I can hear you. I understand. Yes

The house   Trucker's home

Tractor   The front part of a truck, includes the engine, the front tires, the fifth wheel (where the trailer is attached), and the cabin where the trucker sits

Wiggle wagon   Double or triple trailer truck

Yard   The place where trucks are kept when not in use. The headquarters

Yardstick   Mile marker

You got a copy on me?   Can you hear me?

You got your ears on?   Is your CB radio turned on?

Reading Group Guide

About the Book

In the Mexicali Penal Institution for Women, the inmates may not know when or how they'll eventually reenter society, but the rules of the prison are understood by all: money buys privileges; no favor is free; and every inmate's crime is known by all. Every inmate, that is, except Libertad, who can't bring herself to admit to her fellow prisoners—even her best friend Maciza—the reason for her incarceration. But Maciza insists that the story will come out with time, and in a way that is not quite understood by all in the prison, it does. Behind the guise of fiction, Libertad's story is slowly revealed in the Library Club she creates for her illiterate prison-mates, as Libertad flips through book after book pretending to read a serial work of fiction that is all too true. As her story unfolds, we learn of a fugitive professor, a passionate marriage, small miracles and mystical deeds, and a girl who learns everything on the road. Meanwhile, the real world of the prison goes on, as the women buy and sell small luxuries and negotiate prison politics until, slowly, they are rehabilitated and become free to go—though not necessarily according to their sentences. In truth, it is the warden who decides when the women may go, though the prisoners' own motivation plays a significant role. For Libertad, it takes the telling of her story to be ready for her own release, and week after week she unveils pieces of it to her eager audience as she marks her days with a journal of the clouds, and echoes of her life on the road rumble on as if to confirm her tale. Against the backdrop of imprisonment, the story traces the path toward tragedy, and the beginning of new friendship and forgiveness.

Questions for discussion

1. Warden Guzmán takes advantage of her position for her own gain and is sometimes motivated by her desire for money rather than her strict responsibilities as a warden, but she also displays an understanding of her prisoners that leads her to recognize Chapopota's rehabilitation and at times, also kindness. How much do you think the warden cares about the women under her watch? Is her system, such as it is, effective in promoting the inmates' welfare?

2. When Libertad is greeted at the prison gates by her father and Martin, the inmates remark that Martin is not handsome enough to be the man in the story—revealing that Libertad's account of her past in Library Club is perhaps not the strictest truth. Are there any other parts of her story you would doubt? Is there anything you suspect she's left out?

3. What portion of the Library Club do you think believes that Libertad's story is a work of fiction? Are those that believe she is truly reading from books written by others gullible to believe this, or is this a willful delusion?

4. The book begins with Libertad's wish that she could bring back all the people she killed. What was your initial

impression of her crime? How did our suspicions evolve over the course of the book?

5. Was Libertad's arranging to have her father beaten an act of kindness, or was there some malice involved? Do you think she forgave him for his mistakes?

6. Many of the women in the prison seem to have invented names to use in prison. What does this say about the culture in the prison? What do the inmates' names—Matriarca, Maciza, Diva, Libertad—say about the women themselves?

7. How do you envision Libertad's life after her release? Will her relationship with Martin be happy? Will she continue on the road? How do you think her relationship with her father will change?

8. Do you think Maciza will be a good mother to her son, Pollito? Why or why not?

9. When the Vietnamese prisoners ask to stay in prison rather than go free, the warden is unsurprised. In fact, this is not the first time in the course of the book that a woman has made such a request. Why would they want to remain incarcerated? What do they—and what do you—find appealing about the prison?

10. When Libertad saw high heels in Martin's tidied-up house, what do you think the real story was? Was there another woman? Is that, as Libertad explains it, only natural

given her own long absence and silence, or is there a more innocuous explanation?

11. After Libertad's departure, it is announced that the time slot once held by Library Club will now feature sessions of wrapping lollipops for a candy factory. How do you think this change will affect the prisoners? Do you think the prisoners will find other group activities to fill the same creative or therapeutic needs that Library Club addressed? Do you think they'll need to?

12. What makes Libertad's story so compelling for her audience?

about the author

Photo by Jorge Alcaide

María Amparo Escandón, a Mexican born and raised writer, had her American debut with her best-selling first novel, *Esperanza's Box of Saints,* and its Spanish version, *Santitos,* in 1999. Now, *González & Daughter Trucking Co.,* her second novel, establishes her in a special place in fiction as a cleverly humorous, quirky, and compassionate writer with an eye for the magical reality of everyday life. Escandón's work has been translated into 17 languages and is currently read in more than 85 countries. She teaches Creative Writing at UCLA Extension and is an advisor at the Sundance Screenwriters Labs in Mexico and Brazil and at the Fundación Contenidos de Creación Fiction Workshops in Barcelona. She lives in Los Angeles with her family.